MURDER
IN
MINIATURE

ALSO AVAILABLE BY KATIE TIETJEN

Death in the Details

The Maple Bishop Mysteries

Murder in Miniature

A Maple Bishop Mystery

Katie Tietjen

NEW YORK

Books should be disposed of and recycled according to local requirements. All paper materials used are FSC compliant.

This is a work of fiction. All of the names, characters, organizations, places, and events portrayed in this novel are either products of the author's imagination or are used fictitiously. Any resemblance to real or actual events, locales, or persons, living or dead, is entirely coincidental.

Copyright © 2025 by Katie Tietjen

All rights reserved.

Published in the United States by Crooked Lane Books, an imprint of The Quick Brown Fox & Company LLC.

Crooked Lane Books and its logo are trademarks of The Quick Brown Fox & Company LLC.

Library of Congress Catalog-in-Publication data available upon request.

ISBN (hardcover): 979-8-89242-181-2
ISBN (paperback): 979-8-89242-284-0
ISBN (ebook): 979-8-89242-182-9

Cover design by Amanda Shaffer

Printed in the United States.

www.crookedlanebooks.com

Crooked Lane Books
34 West 27th St., 10th Floor
New York, NY 10001

First Edition: September 2025

The authorized representative in the EU for product safety and compliance is eucomply OÜ Pärnu mnt 139b-14, 11317 Tallinn, Estonia, hello@eucompliancepartner.com, +33757690241

10 9 8 7 6 5 4 3 2 1

To Mom and Dad

PART I

Chapter 1

January 6, 1947

When the knock came at her door, Maple Bishop was in her living room staring at a tiny family.

The four of them—a mother, a father, a daughter, and a son—were seated around a kitchen table. In their little world, everything was just so. A cheerful red teapot was perched on the stove. The pale blue bows in the little girl's braids matched her pinafore perfectly. The father's briefcase, made of real leather, sat in the hallway next to the son's soccer ball. A knitting project rested on the side table, ready for the mother to resume when she moved into the living room.

Maple picked up the little girl and examined her dress. She used a pair of sewing scissors to clip a miniscule stray thread. This dollhouse was exactly what the customer had asked for, down to the hair color of the children and the wallpaper in each room.

It was tidy. It was detailed. It was . . . boring.

Her visitor escalated from knocking to ringing the doorbell.

Maple sighed and put down the scissors. She knew she should feel content, even grateful, and she did—after all, her custom dollhouse business was booming. Her financial situation was looking up; she had come a long way from being a penniless war widow to an entrepreneur in mere months, using her imagination, her attention to detail, and her own two hands.

And yet . . .

She walked to the door and opened it. Ben Crenshaw was standing on her steps. He smiled, and his dachshund, Frank, wagged an excited tail. Maple opened her mouth to greet them, but before she could say anything, she heard a hiss from behind her. Frank dove behind Ben's leg with a whimper as Mack, Maple's orange cat, streaked out from the house, swiping for the dog's nose.

"Oh!" Ben adjusted the position of his cane and stepped back, shielding Frank as Maple scrambled to catch her unruly cat. Mack evaded her and took off across the yard. Ben nearly lost his balance, and Maple grabbed his arm to steady him.

"I'm sorry," she said, watching as he regained his footing. Having survived a bout of polio, Ben relied on his cane to get around, and Maple felt guilty that Mack had almost knocked him over. Then, she felt awkward about feeling guilty; Ben surely didn't want her feeling bad for him.

As far as Maple was concerned, this was far too many feelings.

To cover this onslaught of uncomfortable emotions, she dropped Ben's arm, crouched, and held out her hand to Frank, who sniffed it and gave his tail a tentative wag. She looked up at Ben. He smiled down at her, but there was some tension around his eyes. Mack had also tried to attack Frank the last time Ben had brought the dog over.

"I'm sorry," she repeated. "He's just . . ."

She gestured vaguely, not sure how to complete the sentence. Uncertainty was not an emotion to which Maple was accustomed.

"It's all right."

They stood awkwardly on the stoop, and prickles of nervous heat broke out across Maple's back. Having both lost their beloved spouses, she and Ben understood each other's grief. They got along well and enjoyed each other's company. When Maple had experienced a financial disaster in the fall after her husband's death overseas, her relationship with Ben had progressed to something resembling colleagues; Ben had invited Maple to sell her custom dollhouses out of his hardware store downtown, which had helped kickstart her new career. Now they were . . . well, Maple wasn't certain how to classify exactly what they were, and that—she suspected—was the source of the prickles.

She said the first thing that came to mind. "No snow."

Ben nodded. "Odd for this time of year, isn't it?"

They'd resorted to talking about the weather. Even Maple could tell this wasn't going well.

The church bell across town chimed six times.

"Six o'clock," Ben said. "I can't believe we're going to be able to watch President Truman right in your living room. The first televised State of the Union address, and we're going to see it live!"

They'd moved on from weather to politics. Maple wasn't sure that was better.

"Well, come on in." Maple winced at her overly hearty tone.

She turned away from Ben, leading him and Frank into the living room.

"The new house is beautiful," Ben said, admiring the dollhouse Maple had been brooding over when he arrived.

She thanked him. Then, she turned her attention to the new television set in the corner, about which she had mixed feelings. She had purchased it the week before—not on a whim, exactly, but also not with a great amount of planning, which was unlike her.

"Wow, look at that!" Ben's voice was tinged with wonder.

She frowned even as she turned it on, wondering why she'd felt the compulsion to own one of these machines. She wasn't one to splurge, and while her dollhouse business was doing well, she still had to be careful with her money. The screen was tiny, especially compared to the large one in the theater two towns over, and the cabinet that held it was bulky. Maple thought the machine looked a bit like a troll hunkered down in her living room. So far, every time she had tried to watch anything on it, she'd grown restless within minutes. Whenever she listened to the radio, she was always doing something else at the same time—chopping vegetables, sweeping the floor, working on a dollhouse. The radio felt like a companion. Conversely, this new box wanted to hypnotize her—to distract her from the world around her—and so she regarded it with suspicion.

Then again, perhaps the allure of distraction was exactly the reason she'd bought it. She glanced at the tiny, tidy family in their tiny, tidy house and just barely stopped herself from sighing.

She switched on the television and, a moment later, she and Ben watched the president stride into the House chamber to the tinny applause of the lawmakers gathered there.

"Wow," Ben breathed again, and Maple felt a flicker of annoyance. She sat next to Ben on the sofa. Frank curled up at their feet, happy as a clam now that Mack wasn't attacking him. They watched as the president urged Congress to work together with him for the good of the country, but Maple's restlessness overcame her before Truman was into the second paragraph of his speech.

Did other people just . . . sit and watch? Maple couldn't imagine how.

"Would you like something to drink?" she asked, standing abruptly.

Ben looked away from the television and at her, startled. "Uh, no, thanks."

"*Fourteen million World War II servicemen have returned to civil life*," Truman said gravely as Ben's eyes returned to the screen.

Maple, turning to go into the kitchen, felt a dull pang of sadness. She looked over at her mantle, on which rested a framed American flag—a visual reminder that her husband, Bill, had been among the nearly 300,000 who hadn't returned home.

The president continued, "*The great majority have found their places as citizens of their communities and their Nation.*"

Kenny Quirk, the young officer who had become Maple's friend after the case they solved together, had a father who returned from war with some unwanted companions: nightmares, tremors, and frayed nerves. Maple had hired Ken Sr. to help when her custom dollhouse business really took off a few months ago. He was doing a great job using his carpentry skills to help keep up with the demand for dollhouse orders, and she supposed he fit Truman's description, but—having had a front-row seat on his struggles to assimilate—she wondered whether perhaps the president was oversimplifying servicemen's reentry into American society.

The jangle of the telephone interrupted her ruminations. She grabbed the receiver off its cradle.

"Hello?"

"There's been a fire. We've got a body. Can you come to the scene?" said Sheriff Sam Scott.

Maple couldn't deny the thrill that shot down her spine at his words.

"Yes," she said, pleased with how neutral and calm her voice sounded.

"I'll pick you up in five minutes."

Never one for small talk even when there wasn't a death to investigate, the sheriff hung up.

When Maple had first met the sheriff just over two months earlier, after she discovered a local farmer's dead body, their relationship had gotten off to a rocky start. Troubled by the direction of his investigation, Maple had recreated the death scene in miniature to highlight inconsistencies. Though he brushed off her help initially, decrying what he dubbed her "death dollhouse" as an abomination, he eventually been forced to concede she was right. Along with Kenny, the sheriff's deputy, they finally solved the case.

Then, Sheriff Scott had hired her as an independent consultant. The arrangement, which was on an as-needed basis, meant that, from day to day, Maple was free to continue working on her new and booming business making and selling custom dollhouses—the ones that showcased domestic bliss rather than sudden death. When the sheriff needed her keen eyes and photographic memory, he would call on her. At first she was pleased—flattered, even. He wanted her help. He saw her as a valuable resource.

It had occurred to Maple, though, that this particular arrangement also kept her out of the sheriff's hair. He had been furious at what he had viewed as her interference in the Elijah Wallace case, at least at first. Part of her wondered whether he'd created this position just to mollify her; after all, he was the one with all the power in the relationship. He could call her in—or not—according to his whim.

Tonight was the first time he'd done so, but maybe she was overthinking things. After all, Elderberry was a sleepy little town most of the time; she wasn't aware of any situations that would've necessitated her services since their last case together.

"Is something wrong?" Ben asked from the living room.

"No. Well—yes. Someone's died in a fire. I'm afraid I have to go."

She tried to arrange her expression into a regretful one even as her heart pumped with anticipation. She strode across the living room and clicked off the television.

"Oh, no." After a moment, Ben got to his feet, picked up his cane, and began making his way to the front door.

Maple wasn't sure whether Ben's disappointment stemmed from the news of an unexpected death, their evening together being cut short, or the fact that he wouldn't get to finish watching the president's address on television.

"Well," she said, "sorry about this."

She opened the door for him, and Frank waddled out behind him. As Ben turned to say goodbye, Maple was craning her neck over his shoulder, straining to see whether the sheriff was pulling onto her street yet. Ben lurched toward her. Maple, assuming he had lost his footing again, put out a hand to steady him. His forehead crinkled in confusion, which caused her confusion, too.

Ben sighed. "Goodnight, Maple."

As soon as Ben was gone, Maple opened her hall closet. As was her custom, the first thing she did was run her hand along the sleeve of the pale blue peacoat that had once belonged to her brother, Jamie, sobering at the sight of the dried bloodstains. Then, she donned her own burgundy coat.

In the hallway, she stopped to check her reflection and adjusted her matching hat, noting that her face looked flushed and her eyes bright. As she heard the car turn into her driveway, she patted her pockets to make sure her gloves were there if she needed them, took a deep breath, and opened the front door.

It was the most excited she'd felt in months.

Chapter 2

Sheriff Scott was hunkered down in the driver's seat. Maple cut across the path of the headlights and opened the passenger door.

"Thanks for coming," he said.

Nonplussed, she slid into the passenger seat. She had fully expected him to greet her by grousing about the fact that someone had been inconsiderate enough to die on a cold winter evening; after all, he had spent much of the last investigation complaining about how much paperwork the death of Elijah Wallace, a local farmer, had generated for him. Instead, the sheriff sounded subdued and looked pained.

"What can you tell me?" she asked as he pulled the car out of the driveway.

The sheriff flicked his eyes toward her and then back onto the road.

"Fire was reported just before I called you. It's a cabin on the outskirts of town. One dead body."

A long pause hung in the air.

"All right. What are you *not* telling me?"

The sheriff sighed. "The dead man appears to be Daniel Perkins. He lived in the cabin with his uncle, Phillip. Dan was one of Kenny's best friends growing up."

"Oh, my."

Kenny—who was idealistic, eager, and loyal—had proven himself to be an excellent friend and an officer devoted to truth and justice. Maple's heart squeezed for his loss.

"Did you know him, too, then?" she asked.

"Sure did," the sheriff said heavily.

"I'm sorry." The words seemed entirely inadequate, but she said them anyway.

"Daniel was a firefighter," the sheriff continued. "Another firefighter—Peter Johannsen—drove out to pick him up for his shift and found the cabin ablaze. He was able to extinguish it, but not soon enough to save his colleague."

Maple contemplated the irony of the situation.

"Then he drove to Kenny's house to alert him."

"Why?" Maple thought it would've made much more sense to summon the sheriff by phone or at the office.

"No phone at the cabin and no neighbors. It's very remote out there. And Peter—the one who found the body—was the third musketeer. He was Kenny's other best friend."

"Oh, no."

A pause hung in the air. Maple could tell the sheriff had something else to add but didn't want to say it.

"There's more, isn't there?"

The sheriff made a point of keeping his eyes on the road. "Well, the new doc's on his way, too. Name's Strong. Got here from Minnesota via Boston earlier today."

Maple's stomach dropped a little, but she was determined not to let the sheriff know. "That makes sense. After all, he's the coroner, too, now."

Before his death overseas, Maple's husband, Bill, had been the town doctor, a role that had traditionally been combined with that of county coroner. Their mentor, Dr. Patrick Murphy—whose seminars on legal medicine she and Bill had attended together in Boston when he was a medical student and she was in law school—had been Bill's predecessor and had briefly stepped back into the role to cover after Bill died.

The sheriff shot her a quick sideways glance, and she read the concern in his eyes.

"I'm fine, Sam. It'll be nice to meet him—and, besides, we've all got something much bigger than my feelings to worry about."

Maple hoped that addressing the sheriff by his first name, which she rarely did, would signal to him that she really and truly was fine.

Or maybe she was hoping to send that message to herself.

"He's in agreement with you about the whole medical examiner thing."

The sheriff was referring to Maple's insistence, which stemmed from her training in legal medicine and had strengthened after her first death investigation, that the coroner system should be abolished and replaced with medical examiners in each state.

"I should hope so," she said. "I'm glad he has enough sense to think that the person officially designated to investigate and rule on causes of death should be someone with actual medical training and not just some cousin of the governor who's owed a favor."

Although Vermont still used the coroner system, Maple was grateful that at least their state had a history of appointing medical professionals to fill the roles.

"OK, OK, spare me the lecture." The sheriff held up a hand. "You're preaching to the choir, you know. I'm already on your side."

She watched his expression sink into one of resigned despair. Maple searched for the right words, but before she found them, she smelled the fire.

It seeped into the car, burning her nostrils and making her eyes water. The car jolted over a pothole, causing her head to smack against the roof, but she barely noticed. She was too busy thinking about the smoke. She inhaled the acrid smell, held it in her nostrils for a count of three, then let it out.

They rounded a corner, headlights bouncing off rocks and twigs. The farther they drove out toward the outskirts of Elderberry, Vermont, the rougher the road got. Though the night was cold, Maple rolled the passenger-side window down. The air stung her eyes and made them water. She breathed in again, this time pulling the smoke and the chill together all the way into her lungs. She imagined them mingled there incongruously—the fire and the ice—until the burn became too much. She let it go with one good exhale but felt oddly empty.

"It's freezing. Do you mind?"

Maple glanced over at Sheriff Scott. She took in his raised eyebrows and frowning chin. A few months ago, he would've barked an order at her. Now, he was asking huffy rhetorical questions.

Progress. Despite the circumstances, she smiled a little to herself as she rolled the window back up.

"I can smell it," she said. "The fire."

"Yeah, me, too," he grunted. "But it doesn't mean we need to choke on the smoke *and* freeze to death before we're even on the scene. We've got the whole night for that."

We.

She gazed out the window. They were in an area of town she had never been to before, and now smoke whispered across the windshield like ghosts. The road was becoming more of an overgrown path. Maple pointed at snapped branches on either side of them that had clearly been the victims of a large vehicle plowing through in a hurry.

"Fire truck?" she asked.

"Must've been," the sheriff agreed.

The driveway veered suddenly to the left, the sheriff swerved to stay on it, and Maple got her first glimpse of the cabin. It was nestled in a valley beneath the small local mountain, which Maple was familiar with from her frequent hikes. In fact, she realized with a jolt, she had seen this property before from the vantage point atop her favorite trail. She remembered thinking how nice it looked from way up there—an acre or so of forest had been cleared away to make room for the cabin, a small fenced-in garden, a tiny shed, and a chicken coop. It was its own little cozy microcosm, self-sufficient and away from the bustle—and nosy neighbors—of downtown. An image of Ginger Comstock, the town gossip, flashed across her mind; Maple felt a pang of envy for the people who lived here away from all of that nonsense, but it was almost immediately replaced with dread as her eyes swept across the damage. The half dozen chickens clucked softly as they paced inside their coop; they were not immune to the grim atmosphere.

Maple could tell that, before the fire, it had been a cheerful little house, made of logs and with window boxes and a brick chimney. Now, wisps of smoke drifted up from the third of the house the fire had chewed up before the firefighters tamed it. The segment of wall facing her reminded Maple of a grotesque jack-o'-lantern; burned sections had collapsed inward in the approximate shape of two mismatched eyes and a black slash of mouth.

Her gaze followed a trail of footprints in the ash-laden grass up to where Kenny and two firefighters stood in the beam of light coming from the truck. As she watched, one of the firefighters removed his hat and let it fall to the ground before rubbing his eyes. Kenny turned to Maple and the sheriff but didn't wave. His eyebrows knitted and shoulders slumped, he instead turned back to the hatless firefighter; he and the other firefighter placed hands on the third man's shoulders. A cold rock formed in her stomach.

"That's Peter Johannsen," the sheriff said. "The one without the hat."

The third musketeer, Maple thought.

Sam's voice was steady, but Maple detected an undercurrent of dread.

The sheriff parked next to the fire truck, and he and Maple climbed out and walked over to the other three together. Maple could see two other vehicles parked on the other side of the fire truck—a rusted black pickup with at least two flat tires and a dark green pickup that seemed to have skidded to a halt and parked hastily next to it. She also noted that the hatless firefighter was a good deal younger than his colleague, who wore a badge that said "Chief." The sheriff limped to a stop beside her, wincing a little; the bullet wound he had suffered in his leg during their last investigation still hadn't entirely healed.

"Chief Curt Orson," the sheriff said with a nod, shaking hands with the firefighter. "This is my colleague, Maple Bishop."

The firefighter turned tired gray eyes to Maple.

"I'm a consultant," Maple explained as they shook hands.

Despite the circumstances, she felt a small thrill; it was the first time she had used her new title to introduce herself and the first time the sheriff had called her a colleague.

In his left hand, Maple noticed he was clutching what looked like a mask. He must've seen her looking, because he held it up. It had bugged-out eyes and an odd-looking hose protruding from the center.

"Respirator mask," he explained. "We use them sometimes if the smoke's really bad, but by the time I got here, I didn't need it anymore."

He walked to his truck and tossed it in the cab, his shoulders slumped in dejection.

Kenny scuffed the toe of his boot on the ground. Maple moved next to her friend and patted him on the back. He shot her a sad, grateful look.

Orson, returning to where they stood, sighed. "Daniel was one of my trainees, along with Peter here. He . . ." the man trailed off. The sheriff clapped a hand on his shoulder.

Kenny cleared his throat. "Daniel grew up down the street from me. The three of us—" he gestured toward Peter—"played together all the time as kids, but then Dan's family moved to Boston when we were in eighth grade."

Orson recovered enough to speak again. "Daniel wasn't terribly close with his parents. Told me he never took to the big city." He jerked a thumb at the cabin. "Said his uncle was more like a father to him than his own father was."

"He'd come back every summer to visit for a few weeks," Kenny said.

"He'd only just moved back here and started training with us a few months ago," concluded Orson, "after he got back from overseas."

So, he'd been in the war, Maple thought, and now the young firefighter was dead in a fire. Maple looked again at the cabin, where the sizzle of water on ash could still be heard.

"I'm so sorry," Maple said. The words, as she knew from personal experience, were entirely inadequate.

"Where's Philip?" asked the sheriff. "He wasn't home when it started?"

Chief Orson cleared his throat. "He's gone on one of his runs." He turned to Maple and explained, "Daniel's uncle is a long-haul trucker. Sometimes he's away for weeks at a time."

Peter's dull voice chimed in, "Mr. Perkins left two days ago." The young firefighter's face trembled. "This shouldn't have happened. Dan was a firefighter, for God's sake. How could this—"

He put his hands over his face and sobbed. Kenny put his arm around his friend's shoulders.

"Any idea how the fire started?" the sheriff asked.

"Hard to say," Orson replied, "but I can tell you the point of origin was near the head of Daniel's bed, which is where we found him."

Maple frowned. "A candle, maybe? But would a firefighter be so careless as to leave a candle burning when he fell asleep?"

Orson sighed again. "I'd hope not, but you can't rule it out. Some of these young guys, they get cocky right off the bat. Think they're invincible."

"What else can you tell us, Curt?" the sheriff asked.

Orson nodded once, and Maple could see him gearing up, tapping into his decades of experience to do the job that needed to be done, regardless of his personal attachment to the victim.

"Five rooms." Orson nodded with his chin toward the cabin. "Kitchen, bathroom, and other bedroom are still intact. Living room's got some damage."

Wiping his eyes, Peter joined the conversation. "I came to pick up Daniel for his shift." He gestured to the black truck. "He was still working on that truck. It's not drivable yet. When I got here, the fire had already started. I was able to get it under control quickly. It's lucky I was in the official vehicle and not my pickup today."

Maple shot a glance at the sheriff. "If Daniel had been scheduled to work that night and expecting his friend to come pick him up, why was he lying in bed?"

Orson shrugged. "It's a little unusual, but then again we work strange hours sometimes. You get used to catching a nap whenever you can."

"Had Daniel been working strange hours recently?"

Orson scratched his chin. "Well, no. It's been pretty quiet on the fire front. Winter, you know. Nothing big or structural until now."

The sheriff spoke next. "Peter, did you see or hear anything unusual when you arrived? Aside from the fire, of course."

"No, I can't think of anything—but then again, I was focused on the fire."

"No other cars coming or going?"

"I didn't see any. Can I . . . be excused? I'm sorry. This has been—"

The young man's face crumpled, and the sheriff nodded. Kenny took his friend by the shoulder and steered him to a spot a little way away. Maple watched him settle Peter on the ground and place a hand on his shoulder before coming back to join the others.

"Kenny," the sheriff said, not unkindly, "why don't you sit this one out?"

"With all due respect, Sheriff," Kenny said, straightening up to his full height, "absolutely not."

"Son—" the sheriff began.

Kenny held up a hand to stop him. "Don't."

There was a steeliness in Kenny's manner that Maple had never seen in the young man before. Sheriff Scott opened his mouth to respond, then seemed to think better of it. Maple followed his gaze to Peter, who now sat on the ground with his head down, back to Kenny. Several seconds went by, during which Maple knew the sheriff was weighing whether or not to pull rank and insist that Kenny sit out the investigation of his childhood friend's death. Maple, who had witnessed the sheriff make split-second choices with great decisiveness in the past, was surprised by his delay. Finally, the sheriff shook his head and put his hands up in a gesture of surrender. Then, he looked at Maple.

It took her a beat to realize he was waiting for her to make the next move.

"Okay," she said briskly, hoping her voice didn't give away her surprise at this turn of events. "Well, what I'd like to do first is walk slowly all the way around the outside. That will enable us to get a full picture and study the whole scene before disturbing any possible evidence."

"I agree," said the sheriff simply.

Inclining her head toward the cabin, Maple said, "Shall we?"

The four of them walked toward the wreckage, leaving Peter Johannsen alone with his grief.

Chapter 3

Starting at the close edge of the burned section, Maple began to walk counterclockwise, slowly, around the perimeter of the cabin, so that she examined the intact portion first. She wondered why her instinct had led her in this direction. Was it because it made sense to get a feel for the house as it had been before the devastating fire took a man's life? Or was she subconsciously postponing the inevitable moment when she would encounter the body?

Her eyes swept the ground as she walked toward the lone window on the cabin's south-facing side. Flecks of ash covered the grass like a thin carpet, her feet stirring gray puffs into the air.

A new smell, mixed with the smoke, assaulted Maple as they got closer to the cabin. It reminded her of the church picnic she and Bill had attended when they first moved to Elderberry. Ginger Comstock's husband had been roasting meat over a fire pit and left it on too long while he was chatting with other men from town. With a sickening start, Maple realized that she was now smelling Daniel Perkins.

She veered to her right, away from the cabin, and doubled over. Her stomach heaved once, twice, three times, but nothing came up. Dimly, she realized she had skipped lunch that day. A strong hand rested on her shoulder. She looked up and saw the sheriff offering her a handkerchief with his other hand, a grim and sympathetic expression on his face.

"Hold this over the lower part of your face and try to breathe through your mouth."

She took it, her hand trembling a little, and did as he said. A few steps away, Kenny, too, looked queasy; both the sheriff and Chief Orson wore looks of resignation. Maple was sure they'd smelled this before. After a few shallow breaths, she felt steadier.

"Do you get used to it?" she asked.

"No," the sheriff replied, dropping his hand from her shoulder. "It's more like you just . . . learn to expect it."

Maple wasn't sure how to feel about that, but there was a job to be done. She squared her shoulders and stood up, fighting to tamp down the nausea that rose stubbornly in her. Pressing the handkerchief to her mouth and nose, she put one foot in front of the other, steering the small, solemn group back toward the death scene.

If it were possible to ignore the smell and the ash that still drifted through the air like gray snow, then—facing in this direction, at least—there was barely any indication there had even been a fire. That observation chilled her. Odd, she reflected, that looking at the *un*damaged portion of the building troubled her so much.

Maple moved her face as close to the window as she could without actually touching it and tried to peer through the glass, but from this close she realized she could barely see anything. The soot and water had frozen into a nearly impenetrable layer of grime. Her exhale sent a little cloud into the night air.

The sheriff used the side of one gloved hand to rub a circle in the window. Maple peered in again and this time could see into the tiny kitchen. The counters were wiped clean. The wall was lined with open shelves, on which sat cans and jars stacked in neat rows. The rectangular table, beautifully hand-crafted, took up nearly half the space. It hadn't been cleared after dinner. One chair had tipped over and lay on its side in the middle of the floor. A plate and cup still sat in front of the other chair, which was askew; it looked as though its former occupant had pushed back from the table in a hurry. Maple saw a knife next to the plate. She adjusted her angle and peered down at the floor, where she spotted a fork under the table.

The neat orderliness of the shelves and counters clashed with the chaotic state of the rest of the kitchen. Maple's gut feeling was that the shelves revealed the true nature of this home: simple, sparse, and well-organized.

"What've you got so far?"

Maple turned to the sheriff standing behind her. Keeping her voice low, she filled him in on her observations about the kitchen.

"Given the state of the rest of the room," she concluded, "the mess at the table is surprising. I'd have expected him to clean up after dinner and before going to bed."

The sheriff pulled a toothpick from his pocket. "Unless the uncle's the neat one and the nephew's a slob while he's away."

Maple nodded, conceding the possibility. "Kenny? Any insight about that?"

Kenny shrugged. "I wouldn't say Daniel is—was—particularly neat or messy. Just kind of . . . regular."

"I wonder why the chair got knocked over. Was there some sort of tussle with an intruder, perhaps? Or was he in a hurry? But, then, why would he have been in bed?"

No one had an answer. Maple led the men around the house to peek in a second window, where Sheriff Scott again rubbed away grime so they could take turns peeking in. This one turned out to be the living room, which had the same overall feel as the kitchen: sparsely but neatly furnished. There was a threadbare loveseat with a folded blanket resting on the back, a wooden rocking chair, and a small coffee table perched atop a new-looking oval-shaped braided rug. The only item on the coffee table was a newspaper. Small, faded curtains hung in the windows, but they were in the open position, so Maple had no trouble seeing inside.

Maple's eyes swept toward the hall, where she spotted the bathroom; it had no exterior windows, so examination of it would have to wait until they entered the house.

"Ready?" the sheriff asked.

She nodded, and they continued around the house in a counterclockwise direction. The cabin was so small that it only took them about ten steps before they were around the corner and peering in the window of what must have been Phillip Perkins's bedroom. Maple's eyes swept the room, noting the neatly made bed and tidy dresser. There was nothing remarkable or seemingly out of place about the room.

Her eyes swept the ground as they turned to walk the last few feet to where the body lay. Frantic footsteps had left chaotic imprints on the frosty grass and the layer of ash and soot that coated it. Did they belong solely to Peter, or had someone else been responsible for some of them—maybe someone who'd come here to do Daniel harm? Maple peered at the ground for a long minute before deciding there was really no way of telling. If a killer had left a trace of himself behind here, that evidence was lost.

The only room left was Daniel's. The sheriff stepped in front of her to lead the way this time; Maple wondered if he sensed her trepidation and was trying to make it easier for both her and Kenny, who inhaled sharply as they prepared to view his friend's body; it almost felt as if the sheriff was their shield, protecting them from what was to come.

There was no need to inch up close to the window as she'd done on the other side. There was, in fact, no window left anymore—just a jagged, gaping maw where the fire had chewed up the house and spit it back out.

And the body.

Even though she knew he was there—was *expecting* him to be there, for goodness' sake—the sight of Daniel Perkins lying in bed jolted her. She tightened her grip on the handkerchief over her mouth, willing herself not to start dry heaving again. From her vantage point, she was looking down from behind the head of the bed. The entire top part of his body was black and melted, nearly unrecognizable as a human, and the wall behind the bed was the one that had sustained the brunt of the fire's damage. The fire had left the lower portion of Perkins's body largely alone; the blue and green crosshatch pattern of the quilt peeked out from beneath soot and grime. Daniel had been lying on his back when the fire consumed him, and the outline of his legs from the knees down was clearly visible underneath the quilt.

She glanced at Kenny, who stood next to his uncle; the sheriff had one hand resting on his nephew's back as they both solemnly took in the sight of the body. Then, she forced herself to observe the rest of the room.

The chair next to the bed had been upholstered in a cornflower blue that matched the quilt. A small wooden bureau was nestled on the other side of the bed. A mirror was affixed to the top of it, but soot had coated the surface; it would be impossible to see a reflection in it anymore. The only item on top of the bureau was an alarm clock. The state of the room—or, at least, what remained of it—told Maple that Daniel had been as tidy as his uncle, making the state of the kitchen even more curious.

The sound of tires on gravel broke her focus, and she frowned, looking toward the driveway. She watched a black car park next to Sheriff Scott's vehicle. A tall man unfolded himself out of the driver's side. He clutched a black medical bag identical to the one Maple's husband had carried.

Her stomach lurched. She began to turn back to the scene in front of her, but a flash from the car caught her eye. The passenger side door was opening. A girl who couldn't have been more than thirteen stepped out.

Maple whipped around to face the sheriff. "Is that his *daughter*?"

Surprise flitted across the sheriff's face. "I . . . think so?"

They watched as Dr. Strong leaned over the roof of the car and spoke to the girl, who crossed her arms over her chest in a sullen way and said something back to him. They were too far away to hear the exchange, but the girl made a big show of hurling herself back into the seat and then slamming the door closed. Dr. Strong stayed still for a moment, seeming to take a deep breath before turning to the cabin and making his way toward Maple and the three men. He was lanky and graceful, moving with confidence down the frosted grass; Maple supposed the Midwesterner was no stranger to winter.

"Is it customary in Minnesota for coroners to bring children to death scenes?" Maple's tone was colder than the January air.

"Shhh, he'll hear you." The sheriff arched an eyebrow at her, his message clear: *be nice*.

Maple knew that her negative gut reaction to the appearance of the new doctor—well, even just to the idea of him, really—was unfair, unreasonable, and unprofessional. Maple tried hard to arrange her face into a look of polite neutrality as the new doctor arrived at where they were standing.

"Dr. Strong," said the sheriff, shaking his hand. "Thanks for coming."

He then introduced Kenny, Curt, and Maple. The doctor, who had a thin face with pronounced frown lines, shook everyone's hand in turn, but he looked distracted and kept glancing at the burned cabin. Orson gave him a quick rundown of the facts, and he nodded.

"Thank you. Nice to meet you all," he said as he snapped on a pair of gloves.

Maple noted that Dr. Strong seemed eager to dispense with pleasantries and carry on with the important work at hand. In Maple's book, that was one point in his favor; she found herself wondering whether Dr. Strong might turn out to be a professional kindred spirit.

She watched as he approached the body with no trepidation whatsoever. Maple felt suddenly amateurish for her own reluctance. As the doctor put down his bag and began to examine the body, Maple, Kenny, the sheriff, and Orson stayed where they were and watched him.

"I wonder . . ." Maple started, but trailed off, hesitant to say what was on her mind.

"What?" Kenny whipped around to look at her with a fierce expression.

Maple glanced at the sheriff, trying to ask with her eyes whether she should be completely forthcoming, given that the deceased was Kenny's friend. Seeming to catch her drift, he nodded somberly.

"What?" Kenny demanded again.

"Why didn't the fire wake him up? It's a little surprising that it just consumed him as he lay asleep. You'd think at the first touch, he'd have jumped out of bed and tried to put it out. Unless . . ."

Kenny closed his eyes. "Unless he was incapacitated."

"It's a valid question," Strong said. He kept his eyes on Daniel's body even as he contributed to the discussion happening twenty feet away. "Drugs, alcohol . . . I'll see if I can get us some answers there after a full autopsy."

Maple kept her gaze on Kenny, who suddenly looked even more glum.

"Daniel got himself in with a bad crowd in Boston," Kenny said, anguish in his eyes. "Drinking, drugs. Other stuff." Kenny must not have liked what he saw in his uncle's and Maple's expressions, because he hastily added, "But he quit all that when he left the city. He moved back here after the war for a clean break. He made a fresh start."

Maple wondered what Kenny meant by *other stuff*, but before she could ask, Strong spoke up again.

"I also want to know whether there's smoke in his lungs."

Maple nodded, seeing his point. "If there's no smoke, it would mean he never breathed it in."

". . . which would mean he was dead before the fire started," Strong concluded.

". . . which *could* mean someone killed him and then set the fire to cover it up," the sheriff said grimly.

Dr. Strong put up his hands in a slow-down gesture. "We won't know enough to speculate about all of that until after the autopsy."

Kenny nodded his agreement, but seemed unable to abandon speculation entirely.. "Who would want to kill Dan?" he asked.

"He was a nice kid. A hard worker. Everyone liked him," Orson said in a strangled voice.

Maple thought about Elijah Wallace, the farmer she had discovered dead in his barn, who had been widely despised. There had been no shortage of people who might've wanted him dead, and even more people who were happy to never have to see him again.

Daniel was different.

The sheriff turned to the fire chief. "Curt, how long do you suppose the fire was burning?"

Orson eyed the cabin and then looked at the sheriff. "I'd say about ten minutes."

Maple looked at the sheriff and then at Kenny. "It'd be an awfully tight timeline if it was murder." She held up one finger at a time as she ticked off her points. "Kill Daniel, set the fire, and then race out of here before Peter arrives to pick Daniel up?"

The sheriff nodded. "Peter extinguished this fire pretty quickly, based on how much of the rest of the cabin is still intact; it would seem unlikely he wouldn't have encountered the killer fleeing the scene. After all, there's only one road in and out of here."

Maple looked at Kenny. "Did Peter and Daniel get along OK?"

Kenny stared at her blankly for a moment, and then the realization of what she was implying caused his expression to harden. "Yes. More than OK. Peter didn't kill Dan."

He glared at her, and Maple put her hands up in a gesture of surrender.

Kenny opened his mouth to reply, but the sheriff put a hand on his shoulder and said quietly, "You know it had to be asked, son. No stone unturned."

Dr. Strong rejoined the group and held out his hand. A small metallic cross rested in his palm. "I found this on the body."

Orson picked it up gently. "It's Dan's lapel pin. I pinned it on him myself after his training. The Maltese cross. It symbolizes a firefighter's willingness to lay down his life in the protection of others."

The chief's face crumpled, and the doctor looked away, giving the other man space.

"Well, I've gotten what I need for now. If there's nothing else from your end, I'll go get the gurney."

Maple started. "You're going to transport a dead body in the same car with a little girl?"

"Maple," muttered the sheriff in a warning tone.

Strong's expression went stony. "My parenting decisions are none of your business. I'll do my job, and I'll do it well. That's all you need to know."

Maple opened her mouth to reply, but the sheriff cut her off by clearing his throat a little louder than necessary. "Let me help you, John."

"But he—"

The sheriff caught Maple's eye and then looked meaningfully over at Kenny and back to Maple; he didn't want his nephew to have to watch while they moved his friend's body. Her annoyance evaporated. She nodded once in understanding and agreement.

The sheriff and Chief Orson accompanied the doctor up the hill toward the coroner's car. Kenny started to follow, but Maple grabbed his arm.

"Kenny, don't," she said softly.

Kenny turned to face her and pressed his lips together as tears pooled in his eyes. Maple paused, unsure what she should do. She wished the sheriff had stayed here with Kenny. He might know what his nephew needed right now. The idea of helping a hostile doctor transport a dead body to a car where a girl sat waiting was potentially preferable to coping with all these emotions. Finally, she pulled him into a hug. He stiffened at first, but then she felt him sag against her. He buried his face in her shoulder. This, she felt sure now, had been the right thing to do.

Over his head, Maple watched the three men at the top of the hill open the back of the coroner's car and pull out a gurney. She caught the sheriff's eye and shook her head once, indicating that she needed another minute to get Kenny squared away. He leaned over and said something to Orson and Strong. The three men stood next to the car, waiting to collect a dead man, while Dr. Strong's daughter sat in the passenger seat with her arms still crossed tightly over her chest. The animosity radiating off the girl was almost palpable from where Maple stood, and she felt a clenching in her gut. There was something very wrong with this tableau.

Kenny picked his head up and wiped his eyes on his own sleeve. "I'm sorry."

"There's nothing to be sorry about," Maple told him, pulling her attention away from the scene at the car.

He swallowed hard, avoiding eye contact. "Right."

"After they take him away, we still have work to do," Maple said. "We'll have to go into the house and examine everything more carefully up close. If you're up to it, we could use your help. You knew him, so you might be able to spot something amiss that your uncle and I wouldn't."

Kenny nodded. "I'll be up to it. I just . . ."

Maple moved to Kenny's side and placed her hands gently on his shoulders. She turned him to face the hill where Peter Johannsen still sat alone. Maple knew Kenny was torn between professional duty and personal grief. She also knew the way to get him over that hill was to remind him of another duty—to his surviving friend.

"Peter needs you," she said gently.

Kenny shot an anguished look at Daniel's body.

"No," Maple told him, not unkindly. "The others will tend to Daniel now."

Kenny's eyes lingered on Daniel for a long moment. Then, he took a deep, shuddering breath and nodded. He set off toward the young firefighter, and Maple watched him lean down and speak to his friend. Then, the two of them turned so that they faced away from the cabin, looking instead at the side of the mountain, where stars shone in the sky above—and where, not too long from now, the sun would rise on a new day.

Chapter 4

Maple, Sheriff Scott, and Kenny were the last ones remaining at the scene an hour later.

"Well," said the sheriff, his voice a mix of awe and exhaustion. "Let's go get some rest, and then we'll get back to it."

"Wait." Maple squinted and pointed up the mountain. "What's that?"

Above the tree line was an outcropping on the side of a hill where some of the thick pines that plastered the rest of the mountainside had been cleared away. She could see a light and smoke curling up over the tree line. She walked several hundred yards to the right in order to get a better view. From her new angle, she could just make out the corner of a house, including the chimney.

"Does someone live up there?"

The two men squinted at where she was pointing.

"Huh, that's interesting." The sheriff furrowed his brow. "That's Old Man Patterson's house, but he died back in the summer." He shot a glance at Maple. "Don't get excited, now. It was old age, plain and simple."

Maple made a face at him, but her brain was busy generating questions. Who was in the house? What was the view like from that outcropping? Had they seen the fire?

"We need to interview them," Kenny said. "Find out if they saw anything last night."

Maple murmured her agreement. She was fascinated by this house built into the side of a mountain. Who lived there, so far away from the bustle of downtown Elderberry? Maple had spent many hours hiking in this area, and she had never come across a house before. She wasn't even sure how they would go about finding their way up to this house when the time came to conduct their interview.

"We'll meet at the station at noon, but first . . ." The sheriff took Maple and Kenny each by one shoulder and turned them to face the cars. "Sleep. That's an order."

Something about the sheriff's manner as he drove Maple home made her think he was on the verge of saying something but was holding himself back. She wondered if it was about her interaction with the new doctor and decided to get out ahead of his criticism.

"Look, I'm sorry, all right?" she said brusquely. "I shouldn't have started off by criticizing Dr. Strong. But, honestly, who brings—"

"OK," the sheriff said, holding up a hand to stop her. "First off, that's about the worst apology I've ever heard. You say you're sorry for criticizing the man, and in the very same breath you criticize him?"

Maple sat back and crossed her arms over her chest. It occurred to her that she was adopting the same pose as the petulant-looking daughter in the coroner's car. She uncrossed her arms and clenched her fists together in her lap instead.

"Secondly, yes, that was a bad call on your part. It's his daughter and his business, and we don't know the story there. The girl's mother doesn't seem to be in the picture. Besides, it's not as though he had her down at the scene examining the body and traipsing all over the evidence."

In her peripheral vision, she saw him glance sideways at her.

"Fine," she said coolly. "I see your point. I'll apologize to the good doctor next time I see him."

The sheriff sighed. "All right, but there's something I'm more concerned about at the moment, and that's Kenny."

At this, Maple looked directly at him. On his face, she saw worry, uncertainty, and an undercurrent of steely determination. He turned into her driveway, pulled to a stop, and looked at her.

"He's too close to this case. Do I pull him off it?"

Maple was struck by how old he looked all of a sudden. How vulnerable. Her prickliness about Dr. Strong faded, and she rested a hand on the sheriff's arm.

"I can't answer that for you, Sam."

He shook his head. "I know."

"I'll see you at the station at noon."

Maple tried to sleep, with minimal success. By the time 5:30 AM rolled around and she was still tossing and turning, she gave up and got dressed. She decided to go to the diner her best

Maple made a face at him, but her brain was busy generating questions. Who was in the house? What was the view like from that outcropping? Had they seen the fire?

"We need to interview them," Kenny said. "Find out if they saw anything last night."

Maple murmured her agreement. She was fascinated by this house built into the side of a mountain. Who lived there, so far away from the bustle of downtown Elderberry? Maple had spent many hours hiking in this area, and she had never come across a house before. She wasn't even sure how they would go about finding their way up to this house when the time came to conduct their interview.

"We'll meet at the station at noon, but first . . ." The sheriff took Maple and Kenny each by one shoulder and turned them to face the cars. "Sleep. That's an order."

Something about the sheriff's manner as he drove Maple home made her think he was on the verge of saying something but was holding himself back. She wondered if it was about her interaction with the new doctor and decided to get out ahead of his criticism.

"Look, I'm sorry, all right?" she said brusquely. "I shouldn't have started off by criticizing Dr. Strong. But, honestly, who brings—"

"OK," the sheriff said, holding up a hand to stop her. "First off, that's about the worst apology I've ever heard. You say you're sorry for criticizing the man, and in the very same breath you criticize him?"

Maple sat back and crossed her arms over her chest. It occurred to her that she was adopting the same pose as the petulant-looking daughter in the coroner's car. She uncrossed her arms and clenched her fists together in her lap instead.

"Secondly, yes, that was a bad call on your part. It's his daughter and his business, and we don't know the story there. The girl's mother doesn't seem to be in the picture. Besides, it's not as though he had her down at the scene examining the body and traipsing all over the evidence."

In her peripheral vision, she saw him glance sideways at her.

"Fine," she said coolly. "I see your point. I'll apologize to the good doctor next time I see him."

The sheriff sighed. "All right, but there's something I'm more concerned about at the moment, and that's Kenny."

At this, Maple looked directly at him. On his face, she saw worry, uncertainty, and an undercurrent of steely determination. He turned into her driveway, pulled to a stop, and looked at her.

"He's too close to this case. Do I pull him off it?"

Maple was struck by how old he looked all of a sudden. How vulnerable. Her prickliness about Dr. Strong faded, and she rested a hand on the sheriff's arm.

"I can't answer that for you, Sam."

He shook his head. "I know."

"I'll see you at the station at noon."

Maple tried to sleep, with minimal success. By the time 5:30 AM rolled around and she was still tossing and turning, she gave up and got dressed. She decided to go to the diner her best friend, Charlotte, ran with her husband. Maple needed some friendly faces right now just as much as she needed a hot meal. By the time she walked to the diner, the sun had just begun to peek out from the horizon. The diner wouldn't open to the public for another hour, but Maple had her own key.

 Charlotte had given her this key ages ago, and Maple had given her one to her own house; they had an understanding, initiated by Charlotte while their husbands were overseas, that they were always welcome at each other's homes. Charlotte used her key regularly, and—Maple begrudgingly admitted to herself—with good reason. Maple had struggled after Bill's death. She had a tendency to lose herself in projects—first regular dollhouses, and, more recently, murder investigations. When that happened, she didn't always remember to do things like eat, seek out the company of fellow humans, or check in with Charlotte to let her know she was OK.

 This was the first time Maple would be using the key Charlotte had given her, and she knew her friend would be pleased that she was finally the one initiating a visit. She opened the door and was greeted by the smell of bacon and the sound of a man singing, "Let it snow, let it snow, let it snow" along with the radio. She shrugged off her coat and hung it on a hook by the door and then made her way through the empty dining room and peeked into the kitchen, where she saw her best friend's husband cheerfully flipping pancakes.

 "Morning, Hank," Maple said. "Bacon? Mmm, my mouth's watering!"

 The breakfast meat was still in short supply, having been rationed all throughout the war.

"Maple!" He stopped midcroon to grin at her. "Good morning! Yep, we got lucky this week. We're about to eat. Join us!" He indicated a table next to the kitchen. "I put on water for tea. Charlotte will be down with the boys any minute."

"Thanks." Maple poured a mug of tea and situated herself at the table he had indicated. Within seconds, footsteps thundered above her and the twins, Michael and Matthew, exploded out the door that led to the family's apartment above the diner.

"Hi, Auntie Maple!" they shouted as they dashed through the kitchen, grabbed a slice of bacon each straight off the frying pan, and then ran out the front door.

Maple laughed. "Do those boys ever stay still?"

"No," answered Charlotte, emerging from the stairwell holding the baby, Tommy.

"Never," Hank agreed as he placed the plate of bacon onto the table.

"This is a nice surprise." Charlotte fastened Tommy into his high chair and smiled at Maple, who got up and poured tea for her friend.

"I just wanted to see you," she said.

Charlotte cocked her head and studied Maple. "You didn't sleep last night."

She phrased it as a statement, not a question. Hank returned with another plate, this one piled high with golden pancakes.

"No," Maple agreed. "I didn't."

She told her friends about the events of the previous evening. After she was done, she realized she was famished and helped herself to the pancakes and bacon.

"Oh, poor Daniel," Charlotte said softly. "We actually met him last month. Remember there was that fire in the alley?"

Maple had forgotten about that. It had been a small blaze that the firefighters had extinguished before there was any damage to property or people, but it had happened just across the street from the diner.

"That's right." Hank looked up from cutting Tommy's pancake into tiny pieces. "I remember him. Nice kid. He even showed Matthew and Michael how the fire truck worked and let them try on his hat."

Maple thought that sounded like something Kenny would do, too, and her heart lurched.

"Was it an accident? The fire at the cabin?" Charlotte asked.

Maple shrugged. "It looks that way on first appearance, but we can't really make any assumptions yet. We have to be open to all possibilities and follow the evidence wherever it takes us. Dr. Strong is performing an autopsy, we're conducting some interviews today . . ."

"I haven't met Dr. Strong yet. Is he nice?" Charlotte asked.

Maple glanced at her. "Why is *that* the question you asked about him?"

Charlotte blinked. "Well, he'll be our doctor, won't he? I want the doctor I take my children to to be nice."

"I prefer my doctors to be competent," Maple said.

Charlotte raised an eyebrow. "Can't they be both?"

It was a ridiculous conversation, and Maple wasn't sure why she couldn't have just answered Charlotte's perfectly reasonable question with a simple *yes*. She felt a headache begin to form.

"Of course they can," she conceded. "Bill certainly was. Dr. Strong has a daughter, so I'm sure that will help him relate to children."

Charlotte studied Maple. "Are you all right?"

"I'm great. The dollhouse business is booming, and I have a new case to work on. Not that I'm happy someone died," Maple added in a rush. "But it's nice to feel needed."

It was the right thing to say, but Maple felt hollow as she said it, and she was troubled by that feeling. The tea she had poured for Charlotte was fully steeped now, and she busied herself fixing Charlotte's tea just the way her friend liked it—a little sugar, a lot of milk—and handed it to her. Then, she poured maple syrup on her pancakes, marveling at the fact that the sweet liquid gold was once again readily available; for several years, it had been hard to come by and fetched a premium price because of war rations.

They ate in companionable silence broken only by the baby's happy squeals; more pancakes were getting smeared on his cheeks and thrown on the floor than into his mouth, but he was certainly enjoying himself. Maple was, too—Hank's pancakes were fluffy and delicious.

Exhaustion began to prick at the back of Maple's eyes, but she remembered the other thing she wanted to ask Hank and Charlotte about. Unlike Maple, who had moved to Elderberry relatively recently, her two friends had grown up in the town and seemed to know everything about everyone.

"By the way, do either of you know anything about a Mr. Patterson who used to live up on the mountain? He died last summer."

Hank nodded. "Quiet guy. Kept to himself. His wife died when their daughter was young, and then the daughter moved to California and didn't get back to visit very often. He never remarried."

Hank and Charlotte exchanged a significant glance.

Maple sighed. "What?"

"Well . . . are we done talking about the Pattersons?" Charlotte asked.

"Sure," said Maple, with a weary feeling that she knew what was coming.

Charlotte wasted no time asking her next question. "How's Ben?"

"Oh, would you look at that, the dishes are calling." Hank made a show of pushing back his chair and gathering up everyone's plates and utensils before beating a hasty retreat to the kitchen.

Maple raised an eyebrow. "Ben's fine."

Charlotte watched Maple take a sip of tea, clearly waiting for her to elaborate. When Maple didn't oblige, Charlotte exhaled impatiently.

"Mape . . . I mean, how are *you and Ben?*"

Maple echoed her friend's sigh. "We're both fine."

"You know we're not leaving this table until you tell me more than that."

Tommy squealed, and Charlotte handed him a spoon. He gazed at it for a moment and then began waving it around happily.

Begrudgingly, Maple recounted for Charlotte the events of the previous evening. When she told her friend about how Mack the cat had intimidated Frank the dachshund, Charlotte smiled. When she got to the part about the sheriff's phone call resulting in Maple sending Ben on his way earlier than planned, she frowned.

"What?" Maple said. "Do you think I should've offered to let him stay to watch by himself? I thought of that afterwards."

Charlotte pressed her lips together and gestured for Maple to continue.

"And then," Maple concluded, "when I walked him to the door, he nearly fell over."

Charlotte cocked her head. "What?"

"He was on the stoop, and I was just inside the door on the other side of the threshold, and the next thing I knew, he was falling toward me. I didn't want to embarrass him—it's not his fault his legs are bad—so I just said nothing."

"What happened next?"

"I took his arm and steadied him, he frowned a little, and then he left. Sam picked me up a few minutes later."

Tommy hurled the spoon to the ground, where—to his delight—it made a great clattering sound in the otherwise empty diner.

Charlotte took a deep breath. "Is it possible he didn't fall?"

Maple frowned. "What do you mean? I saw it happen. He turned toward me and staggered a little and—"

Something dawned on Maple. Charlotte bent to retrieve the spoon. When she re-emerged, Maple detected a smirk on her friend's face.

"You think . . ."

"He was actually trying to kiss you goodnight? Yep, I think that's likely based on the evidence you've presented me with."

Maple didn't appreciate her friend's smug smile or the dig at her own occupation. She stood abruptly.

"I should go. Thanks so much for breakfast."

Maple patted Tommy on the head. Whining, he reached for the spoon his mother had placed on the table out of his reach. Maple turned and headed for the door.

"Get some rest!" Charlotte called after her.

Maple waved over her shoulder, acknowledging the advice, but doubting she'd be able to rest anytime soon. Her brain was too busy.

Chapter 5

When Maple got home, Mack was waiting on the porch, sitting as still as a statue with his tail wrapped tightly around his back legs. She regarded him with a mixture of fondness and exasperation.

"You know," she said as she pulled out her key, "you could be nicer to poor Frank. He's no threat to you; he's essentially a marshmallow with legs."

Mack flicked his tail once and followed her inside.

To her surprise, Maple was able to follow Charlotte's advice and managed to take a nap. When her alarm rang at eleven, yanking her out of sleep, her subconscious clung to a dream in which her hands disintegrated into dust as she watched, powerless to stop it.

Trying to shake her disconcerted feeling, Maple fed Mack and made herself a strong cup of tea and a cheese sandwich. Nonetheless, the unease stayed with her as she bathed and dressed. She drove to the sheriff's office. To her irritation she caught herself clenching and unclenching her fists several times as if trying to reassure herself that her hands were still there.

Ridiculous.

She was annoyed when her thoughts turned to her interaction with Dr. Strong from that morning. Maple wasn't proud of her own predisposition to dislike the man, but she could understand it; after all, he was replacing her dead husband and her former mentor, so a certain amount of grief and resentment on her part was only natural. But she had a squirming feeling that blurting out her opinion about his daughter's presence at the scene may have been a step too far. She wondered what Charlotte would have said if Maple had told her about it that morning; would her friend, as a mother, have shared Maple's distaste at the idea of exposing a child to such a scene? Or would she have frowned and told Maple for the hundredth time that she was being *too honest*?

And what about Kenny? The sheriff was right; he was too close to this investigation, which could compromise their strategies and findings—but based on his reaction at the scene, there was no way he'd voluntarily quit working the case. However, the fact that he'd known Daniel so well might come in handy, as Maple had said to him back at the scene: he might spot inconsistencies or troubling details she and the sheriff would miss.

Putting aside the investigation, though, Maple also wondered how best to support her friend through a traumatic loss. And what would happen if supporting her friend and protecting the investigation became incompatible with each other?

Maple pushed these thoughts aside as she arrived at the parking lot and saw that both Kenny's and the sheriff's cars were already there. For a moment, she marveled at the fact that she even had a choice about whether to walk or drive today; for years, due to gas and tire rations, the car Bill had been so proud to buy had languished in their garage; it was only recently that Maple had been able to resume driving.

She walked into the building and saw that the secretary, Mrs. Langley, had the day off. Poinsettia plants, gold tinsel garlands, and a decorated tree were trying their best to cheer up the lobby, but there wasn't much they could do to mask the fact that a large portion of this building consisted of the harsh iron and cement of jail cells.

Just then, a low moan came from the other end of the hall where the cells were. Maple was startled, but then realized the probable source of the moan was Willy, a local itinerant man; she'd been surprised to learn back in October that he simply came in and lay down when he needed to sleep off a particularly bad binge.

She proceeded in the opposite direction down the hall to Sheriff Scott's office. There, she found the sheriff seated behind his desk and Kenny perched in one of three chairs facing it. They both sipped from cups of coffee.

"Willy had a bad night?" she asked. "I heard moaning."

Both men sighed and nodded.

"He thinks he saw a ghost," the sheriff said.

"A ghost?"

"That's what he told me." The sheriff shrugged. "Who knows if he'll even remember that."

Kenny indicated a third mug on the edge of the sheriff's desk. "I poured you some tea."

Just as she had when the sheriff had included her in the investigation last night, Maple felt a pleasant jolt of belonging.

She picked up the mug, took the empty seat that had been set out for her, and thanked him. Then, she examined his appearance.

He wore a fresh uniform. His eyes were alert, but there were dark circles under them; his cheeks looked hollowed out.

"Did you sleep? How are you?" she asked.

A fierce look came over his face; he ignored the first question but answered the second. "Ready to get to work."

"Well, we're agreed on that," said the sheriff, leaning forward. "Peter will be in soon. In the meantime, let's make a plan." He pulled out a fresh legal pad and uncapped a pen. "Next of kin notifications. Kenny, do you know where Daniel's parents are?"

Kenny frowned. "His father's been dead a while—heart attack. Last I knew, his mother was still in Boston. He doesn't talk about her much."

"OK." The sheriff made a note on his pad. "Daniel wasn't married, so no spouse to inform."

Kenny nodded.

"Any siblings?" Maple asked.

Kenny and the sheriff both shook their heads.

The sheriff nodded and scribbled something else. "Well, maybe Phillip can help us locate his sister-in-law. Obviously, we need to track him down. He's on a long-haul trip, but we don't know where he is or when he'll be back."

Kenny raised his hand. "I'll do that. I know what company he works for. I can call them and find out his route and schedule."

Maple watched the sheriff to gauge his reaction.

"Good."

Apparently, he'd decided to let Kenny help work the case—for now, anyway. He probably didn't feel energized, exactly, but at least there was a look of grim determination on his face. At the end of all this, they would either have answers or they wouldn't, but either way Kenny would know he had done everything in his power for his friend.

Maple thought of her brother, Jamie, and had a sudden pang of guilt. His death loomed large over Maple's life, as did those of her mother and Bill. Jamie was different, though—Maple remained unsettled about the circumstances in which her brother had met his end. Could she say the same as Kenny—that she had done everything in her power for her brother?

The sheriff spoke, yanking Maple back to the present. "While he's doing that, you and I can go visit that house up on the mountain."

Maple nodded. "I found out a little bit more about Mr. Patterson this morning." She filled them in on what Hank had told her about the man's daughter. "Maybe she's the one staying at the house now."

The sheriff frowned. "You'd think she'd have come into town."

Maple barely suppressed a sigh. She still wasn't accustomed to the lack of anonymity in Elderberry. The sheriff's assumption that if someone from out of town was here they would probably know about it was not incorrect, but the implication that the rest of the town was somehow entitled to such knowledge left Maple unsettled and a little annoyed.

She kept this thought to herself; she'd learned that Elderberry residents didn't take kindly to criticisms of the way they did things—and Maple, though an Elderberry resident herself, had come to terms with the fact that she, having been born and raised in Boston, would never achieve equal status in the eyes of those who had called Elderberry home for their entire lives.

"I suppose we'll find out when we go up."

They spent the next several minutes making a list of all Daniel's local friends and associates and discussing plans for interviewing them over the next day or two.

"What about the autopsy?" Maple asked. "Do we know when we might have answers from Dr. Strong?"

"He's working on it today," the sheriff said. "He took the body to the county morgue."

"He won't find drugs." Kenny's tone brooked no disagreement. "Or alcohol."

Peter appeared in the doorway. "Kenny's right. Dan quit all that stuff."

Maple and the sheriff exchanged a glance. Maple imagined his thoughts were along the same lines as hers: how likely was it that the victim's two best friends could be impartial about this?

"Thanks for joining us, Peter. Let's start there," the sheriff said, keeping his expression neutral. "After all, you knew him since childhood. I did, too, but obviously not as well as you two did." He flipped to a fresh page in his notebook. "Start at the beginning and take us all the way up through yesterday."

Peter dropped into the remaining chair. He had dark circles under his eyes. Kenny handed him the remaining mug, and the firefighter took it gratefully and gestured to indicate Kenny could begin.

Kenny closed his eyes, took a deep breath, and began.

"We met on the first day of elementary school—me, Peter, and Daniel—and we just knew we were best friends. You notice how that happens with little kids sometimes? We didn't even know each other's names yet; we just saw each other and we *knew*."

The sheriff nodded, probably thinking about his own experience or those of his now-grown children—or maybe he even remembered Kenny coming home from school with these fast friends. Maple, who lacked personal experience with this particular childhood phenomenon, listened with fascination and a twinge of envy.

"Anyway, we just did normal boy things all through our childhood. We were outside as much as possible. There were neighborhood stickball games, epic rounds of hide and seek that spanned the entire town." A ghost of a smile appeared on his face. "One time Peter hid so well that it got dark and no one could find him. His parents had to call you. Remember?"

The sheriff grunted. "Oh, I remember. We finally found him up in a tree behind the elementary school."

Peter shrugged. "It was a good spot. After that, you and our parents gave us a code phrase to say if we couldn't find the hider, and the rule was if they heard it, they had to come out."

"None of us wanted to spend an entire night looking for a kid again," the sheriff grumbled.

"What was the code phrase?" Maple asked, amused.

"Banana pecan apple pie," Kenny, Peter, and the sheriff recited together.

Kenny shot a surprised look at his uncle. "You remember that?"

The sheriff made a dismissive hand motion. "Of course. It's not every day you investigate your nephew's best friend's disappearance."

Kenny swallowed hard. The sheriff cleared his throat.

After several beats of silence, Kenny gathered himself. "Those were each of our favorite pies," he explained to Maple.

"I thought it was too cute." The sheriff glowered. "I had a different suggestion, but your mother didn't want to be yelling that particular word all over town."

Kenny smirked, and for a moment Maple caught a glimpse of how he must have been at the age of seven—bright-eyed, full of energy, a little mischievous.

"Anyway," the sheriff said, "continue."

Kenny's expression grew serious again, and Peter picked up the thread. "Well, if you remember, Sheriff, there were three of us playing hide-and-seek that day, but only two sets of parents who were panicking and searching for me—mine and Kenny's. Daniel's parents couldn't have cared less where he was at any given time."

"Why not?" Maple asked.

"Because they were bad people," Kenny's eyes flashed. "Lazy drifters who committed petty crimes and mooched off other people instead of doing an honest day's work. They only ended up here in Elderberry because of Daniel's uncle. He was trying to help out his brother, set him on the right path. He got him a job at his trucking company. It went OK for almost a year. They were staying with Phillip in that cabin until they got their feet under them, but then Daniel's dad got fired. They lingered in Elderberry another few years after that. His parents both worked odd jobs here and there, but they couldn't hold down anything steady."

"I arrested the father a few times," recalled the sheriff. "Drunk and disorderly. Petty theft."

Kenny nodded. "Finally, they took Daniel and drifted down to Boston. We were all devastated—me, Peter, Daniel. His uncle, too. Phillip even tried to convince his brother to leave Daniel with him. My parents and Peter's family offered to watch Daniel when Phillip had to go on hauls. But they wouldn't agree. Never could figure out why. It's not like they were interested in being parents." Kenny gazed at the wall over Maple's head, lost in the memory. "After that, we only saw him in the summers when he came to visit."

"But you stayed close friends?" Maple asked.

"Yes, but as we got into middle school it was clear that he was on a . . . different path than Peter and I were. He started to get wild. He was in trouble all the time at school, and by the time we all entered ninth grade, he'd decided to drop out. He still came for visits, but less often. His uncle, Peter, and I all tried to convince him to stay in school." Kenny shook his head, looking pained, and placed his coffee mug on the edge of the desk. "He wouldn't. Then, once the war started, he stopped coming altogether. He and Peter both enlisted."

"*You* didn't, though," Maple said.

Kenny looked defensive. "I wanted to. My mother insisted I go to college. It's what she always wanted for me."

Maple cocked her head. "I wasn't being critical. I was just stating a fact."

"I know." Kenny sighed. "It didn't last, anyhow. I wasn't cut out for full-time studying. I wanted to be . . . I don't know, *doing* something."

Maple, who had wanted nothing more than to study and had clawed her way from poverty to become the first female graduate of the law school at Boston City College, felt a surge of defensiveness herself.

Perhaps the sheriff sensed it, because he was the one who spoke next.

"So, you went off to school and those boys went off to war, and then what?"

"Then, we all came home," Kenny said simply. "Peter became a civilian firefighter—that's what he'd done in the navy during the war—and I became your deputy, as you know."

Peter chimed in, "And then, out of the blue a couple of months ago, Daniel showed up. He moved in with Phillip again, said he wanted a fresh start, and joined me as a trainee. He was a level behind because he'd been infantry during the war, so he didn't have the same amount of firefighting experience I did coming in."

"Is that why your pin is different?" Maple asked.

A dark cloud crossed Peter's expression as he fingered the bugle on his lapel. "Yes. I earned this last month. It's a symbol from back when firefighters used to be summoned to fires by bugles instead of sirens. It shows that we're ready and willing to answer the call whenever it comes—to come to the rescue."

Kenny clapped him on the shoulder, and they were all silent for a moment.

"Did Daniel say why he'd decided to come back to Elderberry when he did?" Maple asked.

Kenny nodded. "Being overseas shook him up and helped him get his priorities straight. The military gave him the discipline he'd been lacking his whole life, and so when he got back to Boston, he took a look around and decided he didn't want to fall back into the same old habits. He didn't want to follow in his parents' footsteps." Here, a distinct note of pride crept into Kenny's voice. "He wanted to become his own man."

Just as Kenny had wanted to do, Maple reflected as she studied her friend. He'd gone to college to appease his mother but had come back to Elderberry to forge his own path in law enforcement.

The war, she realized, had interrupted the lives of Kenny, Peter, and Daniel at a critical juncture; when it started, they weren't children anymore, but they weren't men yet, either. War had a way of making people grow up fast, whether they were ready to or not. In many ways, that was a bad thing: innocence was lost too early, soldiers returned jaded or shell-shocked or both.

But maybe—just maybe—for Daniel Perkins, it had actually been a good thing, startling him into a life of purpose and direction. Maybe his life had been yanked away just as he was on the cusp of "becoming his own man," as Kenny put it.

"Peter," the sheriff said, "Do you remember anything more about last night? Any detail, something we forgot to ask you about—anything at all?"

Peter shook his head.

"All right. Thanks for coming in." The sheriff spoke gruffly, but Maple detected a slight wobble in his voice. "We know the plan for our next steps. Kenny, make the calls. Find Philip."

He stood up, shrugged on his coat, and grabbed his keys off the desk. "Maple, let's pay a visit to that house on the hill."

Maple looked at Peter and Kenny. "Banana pie, huh? I've never heard of it before."

Peter half-smiled. "Yeah, my mom used to make it. I was . . . well, bananas about bananas, I guess, so that was my favorite."

Kenny chimed in, "Mine is—"

"—apple," Maple finished for him.

Kenny's forehead crinkled. "How'd you know?"

She shrugged. "I just do."

"Well, what's *your* favorite pie?" he asked, amused.

The sheriff exhaled impatiently. "I like blackberry. Can we get on with investigating a death now, or are you two going to put on some aprons and start baking?"

Maple ignored the sheriff and grinned at Kenny. "Mine's maple cream. Obviously."

Chapter 6

Maple and the sheriff didn't speak for most of the journey up the mountain, each lost in their own thoughts. Maple was thinking of Kenny, alone—now that Peter had also left—back at the station except for the marginally conscious Willy, placing a series of long-distance calls to locate his dead friend's uncle. She had a feeling the sheriff was thinking of the same thing.

When he turned the car onto an overgrown path that Maple would barely classify as a road, she perked up. She had passed by this path many times on her regular walks up the mountain but had never taken it. In fact, if you weren't looking for it, you'd be hard pressed to even realize it was there. The sheriff swore as branches scraped the doors and windows.

"This makes the path to the Perkins' cabin seem downright spacious," Maple observed.

"My car's having a rough week," he grumbled.

"Someone's definitely been up here in a car recently, though." Maple pointed ahead of them at tire tracks that had dug up the dirt. "And by the looks of it, they were struggling to keep the car on the path."

"I'm starting to understand why she didn't come into town more often."

"Well, what about Mr. Patterson? Before he died, that is."

"Curt Orson actually organized a monthly trip up there to bring him supplies. Just one of the many things our local firefighters do besides put out fires." There was a note of obvious pride in his voice. "But since he died, I'm not sure anyone's really been up here, so the vegetation's had all summer and all fall to do as it pleases."

After several more minutes of bumping and jostling, they came to the clearing where Mr. Patterson's house stood. It was a sturdy, sprawling log cabin with smoke curling out from the chimney. After the white-knuckle drive up the mountain, Maple felt an immediate sense of relief as they parked next to a black Ford Deluxe.

"Let's scope out the view." The sheriff indicated that they should walk around the house before announcing their arrival.

Maple followed him. They made their way past the front door, which sported a cheerful evergreen wreath with a big red bow, and walked around the side of the house, where there was a stone fire pit surrounded by three Adirondack chairs.

"Oh." Maple couldn't help the gasp that escaped her mouth. The view was simply astonishing—evergreen trees dotted the sides of gently rolling mountains as far as the eye could see.

"There it is." Maple's eyes followed where the sheriff pointed, and she saw what remained of the Perkins' cabin.

"Perfect view," she said.

From this angle—unlike when they'd been on the ground—it was impossible not to see the fire-ravaged part at the same time as the undamaged section. Maple remembered how she had wanted to put off seeing the fire damage last night, focusing first on the part of the house untouched by the flames. Being forced to see it all at once from up here made her feelings from the night before seem ridiculous. Childish.

She scanned the valley below and noticed an area in the middle of the woods where the grass was charcoal-colored instead of verdant green.

"Looks like there was a forest fire," she said, pointing it out to the sheriff.

"Huh," he said. "Seems odd timing for one. It's been cold and damp."

He suddenly pointed to another spot, and Maple saw that it, too, had been burned.

Something caught Maple's eye and she pointed to a bird flying low over a nearby valley. "Is that a bald eagle?"

"I call him George," came a voice from behind them. "As in George Washington."

Maple and the sheriff whipped around. A tall, broad woman stood there. She wore tailored trousers, a cashmere shawl, and a bemused expression. Maple felt her face flush; from beside her, she sensed the sheriff's similar embarrassment that this civilian had managed to sneak up on them while they were gawking at the scenery.

"Ma'am," he said, recovering his composure quickly, "I'm Sheriff Sam Scott, and this is my colleague, Maple Bishop."

"I'm Eliza Patterson," the woman said, holding out a hand and shaking each of theirs in turn. Maple noted her firm grip. "This was my father's house. I grew up here."

The sheriff nodded once. "I remember you. We're sorry to intrude, but we're investigating a death and need to ask you a few questions."

"The fire last night." She said it as a statement, not a question, her sharp ice-blue eyes fixing first on Maple and then on the sheriff.

"I'm afraid so," the sheriff said.

"Well, come in," she said, gesturing to the house. "I believe some hot cocoa is in order after the journey you endured up the side of this godforsaken hill my father loved so much."

Maple felt a prick of defensiveness. (For what? The hill? She wasn't sure). She glanced at the sheriff, but he was already following Eliza, whose long legs carried her quickly across the lawn. Maple stole one more glance at the eagle, which hovered above the trees, wings spread wide, before she, too, made her way to the house.

Eliza led them through the small mudroom in which a small mountain of boxes was piled. They followed her down a hall and into the kitchen, which looked out on the other side of the mountain. Eliza unwrapped the muted purple shawl from her shoulders and tossed it over the back of a chair. Maple was surprised at the casualness with which Eliza handled what was clearly a very expensive piece of clothing.

"Sit," Eliza said, indicating the other chairs. The sheriff did so, but Maple remained standing.

She watched the other woman move with ease through the kitchen, exuding elegance even as she carried out as mundane a task as making hot cocoa. Maple guessed Eliza was in her late forties or early fifties; her blond hair was shot through with silver and pulled into a loose bun. There was no wedding band on her left ring finger. In fact, the only jewelry she wore was a pair of large pearl stud earrings. Simple. Classy.

As her eyes roamed over the kitchen, Maple thought that she'd also use those words to describe the room itself. From the sturdy, polished furniture to the exposed wooden beams in the ceiling, the house exuded a calm elegance just like the woman who had grown up in it.

Maple's eyes moved to the window over the sink, which—situated as it was on the opposite side of the house—offered a view of the town. Though they were too far away to make out many details, Maple recognized Main Street immediately. Her eyes were drawn to Ben's hardware store, and she felt a prick of . . . something. Guilt? Awkwardness? At the same moment, though, a rush of affection for the kind shop owner filled her.

"Tell me about the person who was killed in that fire," Eliza said, pulling Maple away from her thoughts and back into the kitchen.

Maple turned to look at their host, who heated milk in a saucepan, her body turned sideways so she could simultaneously monitor the milk and interact with her guests. Her tone of voice made it clear that people rarely, if ever, disobeyed a direction from Eliza Patterson.

Maple sat next to the sheriff, who cleared his throat. "Well, unfortunately, it was a young local firefighter who actually lived in that cabin with his uncle."

"Oh, my," Eliza said as she stirred powdered cocoa into the milk.

The resulting smell was heavenly. Maple wondered when she'd last had hot cocoa. Her mouth watered in anticipation as Eliza placed mugs in front of her and the sheriff before taking one for herself and joining them at the table.

"Did you happen to see anything last night?"

Eliza shook her head. "I was working on sorting my father's things down in the basement all day. I had a quick dinner and then fell asleep." She blew on her cocoa to cool it. "I saw the damage when I woke up this morning, though. Actually, I smelled it before I even got out of bed; the wind carried some of the smoke all the way up here."

"How long have you been here for?" the sheriff asked.

"We arrived three days ago," she said. "My father passed in the summer, as you probably know, but I haven't been able to get here to go through his things until now. I was too upset right after his death to do it, and I live all the way out in California."

Maple and the sheriff murmured their condolences at the loss of her father. All three of them sipped from their mugs. Maple almost groaned with pleasure; the cocoa tasted as delicious as it smelled.

Before Maple could ask Eliza who "we" was, the sheriff jumped in.

"How'd a native Vermonter like you end up out there on the West Coast?"

"Hollywood drew me in." Eliza smiled. "What a cliche, right? Only I'm not an actress. I'm a producer now, but I started as a screenwriter."

"You're not a cliche, darling. You're an absolute marvel."

Maple and the sheriff looked up in surprise as another woman swept into the room. Her loose golden-copper curls framed a delicate heart-shaped face, and her slim frame was wrapped in a silk robe—beautiful, but impractical in the January cold. She seemed utterly untroubled by the presence of two strangers in the kitchen, bestowing a relaxed, dazzling smile on both visitors.

"CeCe, you're up!" CeCe planted a peck on Eliza's cheek, and Eliza grinned.

The sheriff choked on his cocoa and slammed his mug down. Maple thumped him on the back.

He gaped at Eliza's friend. "But you're—"

"Cecelia Randall. Pleased to meet you."

Maple and the sheriff were in the presence of a bona fide movie star. Cecelia Randall had starred in several feature films over the past five years or so, becoming famous for her doe eyes and sultry pout.

Cecelia reached out a delicate, manicured hand to Maple, who shook it, and then to the sheriff, who made a strangled sort of sound as he clasped her small hand in his large, meaty one.

"Do you want cocoa?" Eliza asked Cecelia.

"No, no, darling. Thank you, but I must have coffee! Don't get up; I'll make it myself."

She bustled over to the counter. Maple leaned over to the sheriff and muttered, "Careful, or you'll catch flies." He shut his mouth.

"CeCe, these are the police. They're investigating the death of a young man—a firefighter—in that cabin below. It burned last night."

CeCe turned to face them, a mug in her hand. "How ghastly!" She turned again and peered out the window.

"Not there, darling," Eliza said. "The other side."

CeCe disappeared into the hallway, and a moment later they heard the front door open, followed by an exclamation of surprise. Then, the actress dashed back into the kitchen, a hand over her mouth and tears shining in her eyes.

"Imagine! While we were right here, Lizzie!"

"She's a sensitive soul," Eliza said, unnecessarily. She rose and steered CeCe into the chair nearest the fire. Then, she picked up where CeCe had left off making the coffee.

The sheriff cleared his throat. "Uh, yes, ma'am. Did you happen to notice anything last night?"

"Not a thing."

"What about yesterday during the day?" Maple asked. "Did either of you notice anything out of the ordinary?"

Eliza frowned. "Do you think the fire was set on purpose?"

"We're exploring all possibilities," the sheriff explained. "Gathering as much information as we can. You have a bird's eye view of the property from up here, so you may have seen something no one else did."

"Anything can help," Maple added. "Even the smallest detail that might seem insignificant to you."

"I can't say I've noticed much down there, but then again, I haven't been trying to." With one hand still wrapped around her mug, Eliza gazed out the kitchen window and frowned, apparently deep in thought. "I have been spending some time out at the fire pit, though, which—as you saw—offers an excellent view of that property. My father built it, along with the chairs around it. Sitting there was one of his favorite things, so I've been out there in spite of the cold." She shivered involuntarily. "Not CeCe, though. She's lived out west her whole life, so Vermont winter weather doesn't agree with her."

CeCe nodded vigorously. "I don't know how you stand it," she said fervently.

"I've seen three trucks on the property," Eliza continued. "That black one seems to be there all the time, parked in the same spot. I remember seeing a green one my first day here, but I haven't seen it since."

Maple figured that must be the one belonging to the uncle. A quick glance at the sheriff, who nodded once, confirmed this suspicion. Maple wondered whether Kenny was having any luck tracking Phillip down.

"What does the third one look like?" the sheriff asked.

"Blue. It comes and goes."

He turned to Maple. "That'll be Peter's."

"What else have you seen down there?" Maple pressed.

Eliza scrunched her mouth to one side and squinted her eyes. "Well . . . chickens. They're always running around loose down there, and I was worried George or some of his colleagues might pick them off."

Maple sensed, rather than saw, the confused look the sheriff shot her. "George is the bald eagle," she reminded him, keeping her eyes on Eliza, who sipped again from her mug before gazing out the kitchen window.

"And yesterday I was surprised because I saw a man I hadn't seen before," Eliza continued. "He drove a black car."

"What did the man look like?" Maple asked.

"Oh, it's hard to say from up here." Eliza shrugged. "Except that he wore a black coat and hat, and it seemed like there was something wrong with one of his arms."

"How do you mean?"

"He maneuvered somewhat awkwardly and only used his right hand. It seemed like the other one might've been in a sling. The young man—Daniel, I suppose—walked the visitor out the front door and watched him drive away."

Sheriff Scott's eyebrows pulled together in surprise. "What time was this?"

Eliza slid her gaze up to the ceiling as she contemplated the question. "It must've been late morning. CeCe, you were still asleep." She looked at Maple again. "After breakfast, I'd brought some things up from the basement and took a quick break. You probably noticed all the boxes in the mudroom."

"Oh, there's not much she doesn't notice," the sheriff chimed in. Maple was pleased and amused that he had regained his faculties in the presence of the movie star.

Eliza gave him a funny look. Maple smiled and said, "It's why he hired me."

Eliza arched an eyebrow, clearly realizing this was some sort of inside joke.

CeCe sighed happily. "A woman police officer! It's just so *dashing*, isn't it, Liz?"

"I'm actually a consultant, not an officer."

"She specializes in crime scene analysis," the sheriff added, his cheeks going pink as he glanced at CeCe.

The actress placed her elbows on the table and rested her chin in her hands. "Marvelous," she said, a dreamy look on her face. "Eliza, darling, you should make a film about a woman police officer!"

Eliza looked thoughtful. "It's an interesting idea. Would you be the star?"

CeCe trilled, "I'd be simply *honored*, darling! I'm sick to death of playing all these damsels in distress. Let's get David and Ronnie involved. All the bigwigs!"

Maple and the sheriff exchanged a glance, wondering who David and Ronnie were.

"Anyway," Eliza continued, "I'm getting ready to donate a bunch of Dad's old things to charity, but I took a break in the late morning to sit out by the fire pit. That's when I saw the man."

Maple and the sheriff made eye contact. She was sure he was thinking along the same lines she was: Who was this mysterious man in black? What had he been doing at the Perkins property hours before a deadly fire? By unspoken agreement, they kept these comments to themselves while in the presence of the California women.

They thanked her for her hospitality and for answering their questions and stood to go. CeCe spilled her newly-poured coffee in her haste to clasp their hands again. Maple thought the sheriff might just float away.

"Is it alright if we take in the view once more before we leave?" Maple asked.

"Of course," Eliza said, making an expansive gesture. "Please, enjoy. It won't be mine for much longer. I'll be selling this place once I finish clearing out Dad's things. My life is on the opposite coast now."

She glanced back at CeCe, who was ineptly attempting to clean up her spill.

They thanked her, and Eliza went back into the house as they walked back over toward the spot where they had been standing when she first spoke to them. They again stood staring down at the cabin.

"Cecelia Randall," the sheriff said. "How about that?"

"Yes, well, she's not much help as a witness, is she? Eliza saw more than she did."

Sheriff Scott nodded, conceding the point. "Wait until I tell my wife I met a movie star!" His voice was full of awe.

Maple shot him a bemused look. "I hadn't pegged you as the starstruck type."

Her own instinct told her that the actress and the producer were more than friends, and she wondered whether the sheriff had picked up on that, too. Looking at his dreamy expression, though, she guessed not. She wondered whether she ought to clue him in, but quickly decided it wasn't her place.

They gazed in silence for another minute. "I'm no fire expert," Maple said finally, "but I suppose the rate of burn depends on several variables."

"Material, accelerant, weather conditions . . ." the sheriff ticked off on his fingers. "To name a few."

"But it can't have been burning long at all," Maple mused, "because of how relatively little damage there was."

"And if someone set the fire, how'd they get out without running across Peter on his way in?" the sheriff added.

They glanced at each other, and Maple knew they were both thinking about the man in black Eliza had just described.

"We need to find out who that man was and why he was there."

The sheriff looked tired. Maple's mind was busy again.

"I need to stop at the scene on the way back," she said after several moments.

"I wouldn't call it 'on the way,'" Sheriff Scott said, rubbing his chin.

"Don't split hairs, Sheriff. I need to gather some materials."

"Materials," he repeated doubtfully. "What are you planning? Another one of your nutshells?"

"Oh, no. This time, I'm going to build more than one."

He studied her for a moment, and then nodded. "You're testing different possible accelerants."

"Got it in one."

He nodded his approval. "We already know the weather conditions. If we know *what* was used to start the fire . . ."

". . . it might help us figure out *who* started it."

The sheriff squinted across the landscape. "It could've been the candle."

"It could've," she agreed. "That's one scenario I'm going to include in my test."

"It can't hurt to try."

He turned and started for the car, but Maple craned her neck and swept her eyes one more time across the vast landscape that unfolded before them, wondering where the bald eagle had gone. It occurred to her that his bird's eye view was, in some ways, the opposite of her own typical perspective. She focused on up-close, nuanced details when she made her dollhouses—and when she'd made her nutshell of Elijah Wallace's death several months ago. It wasn't unusual, for example, for Maple to spend hours painting a tiny, intricate pattern on a miniscule teacup. Birds, on the other hand, took in everything all at once.

Maple wondered if that was why eagles and owls often seemed so wise. It almost made her second guess what she was planning to do next.

"What are you looking for?" Sheriff Scott called from the car.

"George," she answered, keeping her eyes on the distant horizon. "But I don't see him."

Chapter 7

The cabin looked sad and desolate in the late afternoon light.

". . . and you're absolutely sure Phillip Perkins won't mind if I take some wood from the undamaged section?" Maple asked. "And the pieces of bedspread and curtains?"

She had already posed this same question on the ride down.

The sheriff shook his head. "No, I'm sure he'll want a thorough investigation. And, besides, a few pieces of wood won't amount to much. He's going to have a lot of rebuilding to do."

Maple had a feeling the sheriff was talking about more than the house. She set about collecting the necessary materials.

"Do you know where they've kept Daniel's clothes?" she called to the sheriff, who was still standing where they had started. "I'll need those, too—well, at least some pieces from his pants. I imagine those are the only clothing item that survived the fire even vaguely intact."

The sheriff blew out his breath. "I'll check with John about the clothes.

"When do you think you'll be able to do that?"

"Probably later today." The sheriff took half the pile from her and they headed toward the car. "And when we do see him—be nice," said the sheriff without looking at her.

"Why is everyone so concerned with being 'nice' when it comes to this doctor?" she demanded, thinking of Charlotte.

"Oh, I don't know. Maybe because we live in a civil society?" He looked bemused as they continued walking.

"Wait just a minute," she huffed, hurrying in his wake. "*You're* a fine one to lecture *me* about being nice!"

He looked over his shoulder and cocked an eyebrow at her. "What? I'm nice."

She gaped at him. "You threw me out of your office when I showed you my first nutshell!"

He stopped so she could catch up. "You burst into my office without an appointment and started lecturing me on how to do my job."

"Well, I was right, wasn't I? All you could talk about is how you couldn't wait to retire! You weren't giving the case the scrutiny it deserved."

A cloud passed over the sheriff's face.

"What?" she said. "What's wrong?"

He averted his eyes. "You're right. You're right now, and you were right then."

He started to walk again. Maple, who had become accustomed to good, long verbal sparring sessions with the sheriff, found herself feeling almost disappointed that he had given in so quickly—and she wondered why he'd done so. Disconcerted, she joined him at the car, where they deposited the wood in the backseat.

Then, she paused and looked up at the Patterson house. She wondered whether Eliza was at the fire pit looking down on them, but she couldn't tell from this angle; up there, you could watch over the whole valley and yet not be seen yourself.

When they pulled into the parking lot at the station ten minutes later, Kenny was there, but he wasn't alone; he was locked in a passionate embrace with a small blond woman. Maple and the sheriff got out of the car. The couple in front of the station didn't react to the slamming of both car doors.

"Ahem," said the sheriff.

Kenny and the woman pulled apart. He blinked at them, a flush creeping up his neck and staining his ears a bright red. Maple thought wryly that they now matched his lips, which were smeared with lipstick.

"Hello, Ella," Maple said, smiling at the young reporter.

Ella, whose cheeks turned pink, grinned at her nervously. "Hi, Mrs. Bishop."

"Maple," she corrected her.

"Maple," Ella agreed, wiping her mouth with the back of her hand.

"We were just . . ." Kenny gestured vaguely.

"Actually, Sheriff," Ella said, straightening her coat and stepping away from Kenny, "I'm writing a story about Daniel's death and the fire at the cabin. What can you tell me?"

She whipped a small notebook and pen out of her skirt pocket. Kenny took several steps back, looking a little dazed, while Ella interviewed his uncle. She wrote furiously and nodded as he relayed what they knew so far.

Maple avoided eye contact with Kenny and tried to hide her smile. She had grown very fond of Ella, whom she'd met during the investigation of her last case—so fond, in fact, that she'd sent a big scoop Ella's way when she'd had the opportunity. It didn't hurt that by doing so, she'd also denied the scoop to Harry Needles, *The County Tribune*'s abrasive senior reporter.

Several minutes later, Ella closed her notebook. Ella, Maple, and the sheriff exchanged pleasantries while Kenny traced circles on the pavement with the toe of his shoe. Ella mentioned that Harry had gone down to Boston to cover a story.

"It was a heist," she said, her eyes lighting up with excitement. "A big one. A group of thieves targeted the Perry's Armored Car headquarters. They wore rubber Halloween masks and tied up the four employees who were putting away the last haul of the night. No one knows yet how they got in or how much they stole, but it was a lot. Harry heard they left behind thousands of dollars that got scattered around the floor. He said it was like a carpet of cash. Can you imagine?"

She looked wistful, and Maple was sure she wished it was her and not Harry who had gotten to cover the exciting story.

"Anyway," Ella said, "thanks for the information, Sheriff. And good luck finding out what happened to Daniel." She shook hands with him and then gave Maple a friendly elbow squeeze. She smiled at Kenny, her gaze lingering on the young officer for a few extra seconds before she set off on foot back toward town.

Maple turned and grinned at Kenny; now *he* was the one who studiously avoided meeting *her* eyes.

"What?" he said, his tone bordering on cranky.

Maple spread out her arms, palms up. "Nothing. I'm just happy for you."

He ran a hand through his hair, trying unsuccessfully to hide his own smile.

"All right. Let's get down to business," the sheriff said.

Kenny straightened up immediately, his smile vanishing.

"I wasn't able to speak to Phillip, but I got hold of a dispatcher at his company and found out where he is on the route. He's passing through Pennsylvania right now and slated to be back in Vermont tomorrow."

Kenny looked exhausted. The sheriff quickly filled him in on what he and Maple had learned from Eliza Patterson. Maple explained her intention to construct multiple identical nutshells and use them to test different theories about how the fire started.

Kenny offered to help her move the wood and other materials from the sheriff's vehicle into her own car. The sheriff said his goodbyes and headed into the station.

"It's nice to see you happy," Maple said as they took the wood out of the sheriff's car.

A dark cloud passed over Kenny's face. "I have no business being happy when my friend is dead."

They deposited the wood in the backseat of Maple's car. Maple brushed some small pieces from her hands and shut the door, then looked over the roof at Kenny standing on the passenger side, his eyes downcast and his hands jammed into his pockets.

"Well," she said, "If the last few months have taught me anything, it's that we should seize happiness wherever—and whenever—we find it."

He looked up and flashed her a quick half-smile that didn't quite reach his eyes.

Then he turned and walked back into the station.

Chapter 8

First thing the next morning, Maple went into the garage, where she and Kenny's father, Ken Quirk Sr., had set up their workshop. Ken was already there, lining up pieces for today's first project. Maple was grateful that Ken had lit the woodstove already, which had upgraded the temperature from frigid to merely chilly.

They greeted each other and settled immediately into their usual companionable silence.

When the dollhouse business had started to take off and orders were coming in faster than she could process them, Maple had hired Ken. Before the war, he'd been a carpenter; he had even built the house where he, his wife, and their only son still lived. He had returned from overseas with tremors and nightmares that left him unable to continue his previous career.

Working with Maple to build custom dollhouses was a good fit for both of them. Ken appreciated the independence, the flexible work hours, and the chance to build with his hands again (albeit on a smaller scale). Maple appreciated his work ethic and precision; because he focused on constructing the houses, she was free to focus on the finer details—wallpaper, furniture, decorations, and the dolls themselves.

And, now, the nutshells.

She breathed in the smell of fresh wood and took a moment to run her hand over the roof of their newest house, which was nearly complete and ready for interior work. They had a waiting list of a dozen more people from around the county. At the moment, they were actually *too* busy, and when Maple felt stress about this situation, she reminded herself that the stress of having too much work was far preferable to the stress of having not enough work, which was the position she'd been in mere months before.

The wood she had collected from the Perkins' cabin contrasted sharply with the smooth, pristine boards Ken had laid out for their next customers. The cabin's wood was weathered. Dark. Maple placed her hand on a piece of it and breathed in, the faint smell of smoke now mingling with the fresh sawdust in the garage. She had taken it from the intact section of the cabin as far from the source of the fire as she could get, but still there was no escaping the smoky smell that had penetrated every inch of the cabin.

Maple had consulted briefly with Chief Orson over the phone about the most likely ways the fire might've started. Obviously, there was the candle. Daniel had been a smoker, so one other possibility was that he had dropped a cigarette while smoking in bed. If it was arson, the chief's money was on gasoline or diesel. Therefore, Maple planned to build four nutshells to test all these theories.

When Maple had built the model of Elijah Wallace's death scene, she had done it in a hurry, determined to show the sheriff—in a nutshell, so to speak—all the areas in which his investigation had fallen short. This time, it was different. She had attended this scene not because she accidentally discovered the body, but because the sheriff had invited her. This time around, she had time to think. To plan. And she needed it. She wasn't at all confident that this idea would yield any insights about Daniel Perkins's death, but there was a chance.

She considered the workspace and materials before her. Almost immediately, she realized she would need a bigger area. Deciding the glue had dried enough, she made short work of moving the completed dollhouse inside to her living room, where Mack greeted her by enthusiastically winding himself around her ankles as she walked—as though he hadn't just seen her five minutes ago and also spent the night curled up at the foot of her bed. He followed her back out to the garage, where he perched up high on a nearby shelf to observe her.

She began to sort the sections taken from the cabin into four piles, her mind churning over the different ways she might approach this project: building four identical structures wasn't something she had ever tried before. Should she build one entire cabin and then the second and the third and the fourth? Or possibly she should do it in steps and build the same section for all four before moving on to the next part. Maple wasn't concerned about remembering the steps if she chose the first option; her photographic memory and excellent hand-eye coordination made her confident she could follow any number of complicated directions over and over again. For her, it came down to which was the most efficient approach.

"Ken, can I have your opinion?"

He stopped hammering and joined her at her workbench. She explained the task at hand.

"A damn shame," Ken said, shaking his head. "The boy was only Kenny's age. It's a real damn shame."

Maple looked at him, surprised. It was the most words she had ever heard him utter in a row, and the first time she'd ever heard him repeat himself. The right corner of his mouth drooped even more than usual.

She cleared her throat. "How do you think I should go about it? Build each house in its entirety, one at a time, or do them in sections?"

"Sections."

With that, he moved back over to his workstation.

That was good enough for Maple; Ken was a man of few words, but the ones he did say were always worth listening to. She began building the base for the lower section of the first cabin.

It was midafternoon when the telephone rang. She was halfway through constructing the second wall of the second house, and she dropped the section of wood she was measuring. Mack leapt deftly off his shelf and trotted to the door. She followed, rushing into the kitchen to answer the phone.

"Hello?"

"Phillip's back," said the sheriff without preamble. "We've got him in the station now."

Her heart thudded. "I'm on my way."

In the lot, she parked next to Kenny's police car. As she climbed out and hurried into the building, she had a vivid memory of the first time she'd ridden in that car, when Kenny had driven her home after she found Elijah Wallace's dead body. She remembered Kenny's puppy-like eagerness that day—he'd been so determined to be helpful and to do things by the book—and wondered what the experience of investigating his friend's death would do to him. Would it make him jaded? Or would he feel satisfied knowing he'd personally seen to it that every angle had been thoroughly investigated?

She didn't have to wait long to meet Phillip Perkins. As soon as she stepped into the station, she saw a man sitting in a folding chair, bent over and cradling his head in his hands. Kenny crouched in front of him, his hands resting on the man's forearms as he spoke softly to him. The sheriff, who was standing somewhat awkwardly to their side, shot Maple a sad smile. Maple quickly greeted Mrs. Langley, who once again sat at the reception desk, and joined the sheriff.

"Kenny waited for him at the end of the driveway so he could be the one to break the news. Didn't want him to see the cabin alone," the sheriff told her in a low, gruff voice. "Sat out there for hours."

". . . and you'll stay with us as long as you like. My mother won't hear otherwise. She's already set up the bed for you in the guest room," Kenny was saying to the top of Mr. Perkins's head.

"Who'll repair the cabin?" Maple asked the sheriff quietly.

"Peter and some other guys who knew Daniel from back in elementary school.

"It's good that they have something they can do to help." She recalled Peter Johannsen's devastation at the scene of the fire. "It's important to feel you're being useful when a friend is suffering."

Maple felt a surge of affection for Charlotte, who had gotten her through the period immediately following Bill's death. If not for the meals and company her friend had provided, Maple wasn't sure if or how she would've emerged from that dark time. Charlotte had told Maple she'd been crawling out of her own skin, so desperate had she been to help her friend. Maple hoped Peter and the others felt at least some satisfaction in rebuilding the cabin for Mr. Perkins.

Maple also realized that this meant her nutshells would be the only remaining record of the state of the cabin in the fire's immediate aftermath, which reinforced her determination to recreate the scene in exacting detail.

She regarded the devastated man in front of her and wondered whether he would even want to return to the cabin. For her, Bill's absence was sometimes so overpowering that she almost couldn't stand being in her house.

Phillip Perkins lifted his head and ran his hands through a thick shock of salt-and-pepper hair. Despite his anguished expression, Maple could see a certain crinkling around his eyes that told her Phillip was a man who was generally quick to smile. She guessed he was in his early sixties.

"Thank you," he said thickly, grasping Kenny's hands in his own.

"Phillip," the sheriff said tentatively as Kenny rose to his feet. "I hate to do this, but we really need to ask you some questions. Could we . . . ?" He gestured down the hall.

"Of course." Phillip stood, wiped his sleeve across his face, and noticed Maple. "Oh, hello."

"Mr. Perkins, this is Maple Bishop. She's our colleague," Kenny said.

Recognition dawned on Perkins's face. "Oh, yes, the dollhouses—and you helped sort out that nasty business with Elijah Wallace in the fall."

His voice was smooth and his tone formal; Maple found herself surprised and then wondered why. Had she assumed a long-haul trucker would be more gruff? Rougher around the edges? She supposed so, and she was annoyed at her own underlying— and incorrect —assumption.

"That's me." She tried to ignore the heat rising in her cheeks. "I'm very sorry about your nephew's death."

"Thank you," he said, and they followed the sheriff down the hall to his office.

Once they settled into chairs, the sheriff looked Phillip in the eye and said, "We don't know yet how this fire started, but we're doing our damnedest to find out. Did Daniel have a candle in his room?"

Phillip blinked several times and then nodded, as if physically psyching himself up to do his best answering the sheriff's questions.

"Yes. He kept one on a small table near the head of his bed."

"And did he often light it before going to sleep?"

"No. He was very careful about fire. He prided himself on that, given his career path."

"So it would've been out of character if he'd lit the candle and then lain down on his bed to sleep, even if it was just for a nap?"

"That's correct. I cannot imagine a scenario in which he'd do that."

"I understand he was a smoker."

"Yes. He started with cigarettes overseas. Nasty habit, if you ask me. I never could abide the smell." Perkins frowned. "But he never smoked in the house. Only outside. And he was very careful to extinguish the butts fully."

The sheriff made a note on his pad. "Phillip, I'm going to have to ask you some questions now that might be difficult to hear and think about, but I need you to do your best to give me honest answers. All right?"

Perkins swallowed hard and nodded. "Go ahead, Sam."

"Thank you." He cleared his throat. "To your knowledge, was Daniel drinking or using drugs?"

"He was not." The response was out of Perkins's mouth before the sheriff had even finished asking his question. "His mother was a heavy drinker, and, while he experimented in his teens, Dan had decided to give that stuff up entirely. Never touched it anymore. He had no desire to follow in her footst— oh, God," he looked at the sheriff, his eyes a little wild. "Does Laurie know?"

"We were hoping you could help us find her."

He gave a short, humorless laugh. "Last I heard, she was in South."

"What do you mean?" Kenny's brow furrowed. "She moved down south?"

"No." There was a sinking feeling in Maple's chest. "He means the asylum in Boston."

Kenny's eyebrows lifted at the word *asylum*. Perkins's eyes met Maple's, and a flash of understanding passed between them.

"South Asylum is in the neighborhood where I grew up," she explained.

"I got a letter last month," Perkins said, his voice becoming thick. "It was her handwriting. Very shaky-looking. She'd had an 'episode.'" He mimed quotation marks with his fingers in the air. "The police picked her up and brought her to South."

"An episode?" the sheriff repeated, cocking an eyebrow.

Perkins sighed. "Sometimes, she'd just . . . I don't know how to describe it. Dan used to say *Mom lost her mind again* when he was telling me about it. Sometimes, she'd go all quiet and her eyes would get vacant, and she wouldn't react to anything. It was like she was there, but not there." He pressed his lips together. "Then other times she'd start screaming and thrashing around. She'd tear out her own hair, big chunks of it. She'd scratch her own skin. One time when Dan tried to stop her from hurting herself, she attacked him."

"Oh, my." Kenny looked gobsmacked. Apparently, Daniel hadn't told him any of this.

"Dan didn't like to talk about it," Perkins said. "After his father died, he tried to help her. Reason with her. Take care of her." He pressed his lips together. "Then he went off to war, and she broke down completely. Got herself kicked out of their apartment. She was living on the streets when he got back. When he decided to move to Elderberry, he tried to get her to come, too, but she refused."

Kenny's face had drained of all its color. "I had no idea things were that bad."

"He didn't want you to know." Perkins rubbed his eyes. "He didn't want anyone here to know."

"But why not?" Kenny sounded on the verge of tears. "I could've helped. *We* could've helped." He gestured vaguely, and Maple thought he was referring to the town in general.

Apparently, Perkins did, too. "She wore out her welcome here, son," he said quietly. "Her and Thaddeus. They used people. Stole from them. It happened everywhere they went. I stuck my neck out for my brother and got him a job driving for my company. Know how he repaid me?" He barked out a humorless laugh. "He started using his routes to launder money."

The only one in the room who didn't look surprised was the sheriff.

"But—" Kenny spluttered.

"Mind you, I didn't have any proof I could bring to law enforcement, but I knew all the same. I told him to quit or else I'd turn him in. He was risking my reputation; I'd vouched for him."

"So that's why they went back to Boston?" Kenny looked dazed.

Perkins nodded. "And I wish I could tell you that Thaddeus found a way to the straight and narrow, but that's not what happened. It turned out the money laundering had been for the Irish mob, and after they moved back to the city, Thad rose in the ranks."

Kenny pursed his lips. "Next, you're going to tell me he didn't really die of a heart attack, aren't you?"

"Is that what Dan told you? No, Thaddeus was shot in an attempted bank robbery. Bled out at the scene."

Kenny closed his eyes. Maple shot a glance at the sheriff; she could tell the same question had occurred to him.

"Mr. Perkins," she said, "was Daniel involved with the mob, too?"

Perkins looked at her, and Maple knew what the answer was before he gave it.

"Yes. He'd started doing low-level stuff for them before the war—he was just a boy, for crying out loud—but after his father's death, he wanted out. And then the war came, and that was like a clean break for him. Or so he thought. As soon as he got home and went to see his mother, though, those bastards started right off trying to get their claws into him. He realized he couldn't help his mother, and he knew he couldn't let the mob suck him back in, so he came here."

The sheriff took something out of a box on his desk. "Phillip, this was Daniel's pin. Dr. Strong removed it at the scene."

A sob escaped from somewhere deep inside Phillip Perkins as he closed his hand around the Maltese cross pin. Kenny stood, walked over to Mr. Perkins and put a hand on his shoulder. Perkins looked up at Kenny and held his hand out.

"Here," he said. "I want you to have this, Kenny. Let it remind you and inspire you as you try to find out what happened to my boy."

Kenny closed his own fist around the pin, a look of steely determination fighting with the hurt and bewilderment that had taken up residence on his face.

"Why didn't he come back to Elderberry sooner?" Kenny whispered.

"I tried to get him to, son," Perkins said thickly. "I loved that boy like he was my own. I'd have taken him in and raised him in a heartbeat. I offered to do just that many times, but he always kept going back to them. But then, after the war, he finally got away."

Maple and the sheriff locked eyes, and Maple knew, for the second time in as many minutes, that they were sharing the same thought: What if Daniel hadn't gotten away?

Chapter 9

Several minutes later, Kenny ushered Phillip Perkins out into the lobby and then popped back into the sheriff's office and closed the door behind him. He stayed standing and kept one hand on the knob; he was about to drive Phillip home and clearly didn't want to leave the man alone for long.

"I can leave first thing tomorrow. I'll be in Boston by late morning."

The sheriff waved dismissively at Kenny. "We'll discuss details when you get back."

Kenny nodded once and disappeared out into the hallway again. Sheriff Scott looked at Maple, his lips pressed into a grim line.

"You want me to go with him."

She said it as a statement, not a question.

He nodded once. "As I've told you, I'm worried he's too close to this. Plus, you know the area. Are you willing to do it?"

Maple considered this. She had known, on some level, that things were headed this way since the moment Perkins had brought up South Asylum. She thought about the sheriff's question; *was* she willing? After all, she was under no obligation.

The scope of her freelance work for the sheriff's office was to observe and analyze potential crime scenes. There was nothing in their agreement about out-of-state travel to track down wayward family members and possibly become entangled with the mob.

And then there was her business to consider. Maple's Miniatures was thriving, and who knew how long this trip to Boston would take? It wouldn't be fair to leave Ken alone to work on the dollhouses. The work would pile up quickly if she missed many days, and she was already behind today because she'd started the nutshells.

Plus, there were a lot of memories in Boston—a lot of ghosts. It was where she'd met Bill and where she'd earned her undergraduate and law degrees. Her mother and Jamie had both died there, one in squalor and one in scandal.

It was where she'd escaped from.

Someone knocked at the door, pulling her from her ruminations.

"Come in," said the sheriff.

Dr. Strong stepped into the office but remained standing.

"John. How are you settling in? Is the new house all right?" the sheriff asked

Strong gave a tight smile. "It's very nice."

Maple was itching to hear the doctor's report; based on his facial expression, it seemed he was just as eager to deliver it. She thought of the sheriff's directive in the parking lot and gritted her teeth.

"Where are you living?" Maple inquired politely, shooting a not-so-subtle glance in the sheriff's direction with the subtext: *see how nice I'm being*?

The sheriff, though, avoided her eyes as he responded for the doctor. "They're, uh, living in the Murphys' old place."

Patrick Murphy had been Maple's mentor in college and was the reason she and Bill had moved to Elderberry from Boston. Bill had taken over the practice from Patrick, who briefly came out of retirement after Bill's death. Maple's heart lurched.

"It's the only house in town besides yours that has a fully-equipped doctor's office." The sheriff's voice was gentle.

She felt a little stupid for not realizing that he would be living there. It was only logical.

"Yes," Maple said woodenly. "That makes sense." She offered Dr. Strong a weak smile. "I hope you'll be happy there."

The doctor nodded, clearly uncomfortable with the small talk and eager to get on with the business of death. Maple noticed that the doctor was tapping his fingertips repeatedly against the thumb on his left hand, which was down at his side—*pointer, middle, ring, pinky, pointer, middle, ring, pinky*. He seemed to catch her noticing this and stopped abruptly.

"A few updates," he said. "One, there was evidence of smoke in his lungs."

"He was a smoker, Doc," the sheriff said. "Could it be from the cigarettes?"

Dr. Strong shook his head. "This is different. There are thermal burns and scarring in the esophagus. Those didn't come from cigarettes."

So, he had breathed in smoke before he died. He was alive when the fire started. Maple noted her own feeling of surprise at this news.

"I'm still having trouble accepting the idea he just lay down and went to sleep when he knew Peter was going to be picking him up for his shift." Maple turned to the doctor. "Is there any way to determine whether he suffered an injury? A blow to the head, perhaps?"

Dr. Strong shook his head. "There's not enough left of his skull to determine that. But one thing I can tell you is that the body is definitely that of Daniel Perkins. I was able to match his dental records."

"Good thinking," said the sheriff.

"The first thing I like to do is make sure I know for sure whose body is on my table." Strong raised an eyebrow. "If there's any doubt at all—and in this case, the entire top half of the body was unrecognizable—dental records are a way to remove that doubt."

Maple nodded. "Teeth don't burn in the same way bones do."

Strong inclined his head toward her in agreement. "Luckily, Daniel had to have a tooth extracted recently—well, luckily for us, not him, I suppose. I persuaded Dr. Olson to allow me access to Daniel's files, where I learned a few more specifics about his dental history, and then the two of us were able to make the match. I did a course in forensic dentistry as part of my medical training. Fascinating stuff."

Maple was impressed with Strong's methodical thoroughness.

"Anything else, John?" asked the sheriff, rubbing his eyes. Maple wondered whether he had been able to take his own advice and get any sleep before coming back in.

"As we discussed, I collected samples to test for alcohol and drugs in his system."

"How long until you get results on that?"

"Well, that's the thing—if I send it off to the regional lab, it could take weeks."

Maple and the sheriff exchanged a look. Kenny's insistence about his friend's sobriety aside, the question of whether Daniel had been impaired by substances was still very much a crucial piece of the puzzle in terms of figuring out how he died—whether he had voluntarily taken something himself and inadvertently caused the fire, or whether someone might have drugged him to subdue him before committing arson.

"But," Strong continued, "I have a contact in a lab in Boston. If we can deliver the sample to him in person, he can get it done much sooner—days rather than weeks."

Maple felt the sheriff's gaze on her. She blew out a breath. There were now two compelling reasons to travel to Boston. She had some thinking to do.

Back at her house an hour later, she found one thing she expected and one thing she did not. Unsurprisingly, the sound of hammering from the garage told her that Ken Quirk was still hard at work on the upcoming dollhouse orders. More surprisingly, Ben sat on her front stoop. Frank the dachshund was perched on one side of him; his tail wagging picked up several notches as soon as he saw Maple. On Ben's other side was Mack, sitting serenely as Ben stroked his back.

Ben smiled as she climbed out of the car. "Look—they're making progress."

Maple took in the scene of canine/feline harmony before her and smiled, too; it was certainly very different from the last time these two had been in each other's proximity. Ben scooted over to make room for her on the stoop, and she slid in between him and Mack, who promptly climbed onto her lap and settled there.

"Hi," she said.

"Hi," he said.

They smiled at each other. Their hips were touching. It could've been a perfect moment for a couple to exchange a kiss, but neither of them made a move to do that. Maple was a little disappointed, but mostly relieved. They settled into companionable silence, and Maple reflected that this was one of her favorite things about Ben—he didn't feel the need to fill every quiet moment with chatter.

"So," he finally said, "how's the investigation coming along?"

She filled him in on the basic facts of the case.

"Oh, gosh. Poor Kenny. I mean, poor Daniel, too, obviously."

Maple nodded her agreement. "It's tricky to nail down a cause of death, for obvious reasons. We know he breathed in smoke before he died, but there are so many possibilities for how the fire started."

She explained her plan to build multiple nutshells and test out different accelerants on each one.

"How can I help?" he said when she finished. "I want to carry on the tradition of assisting your mystery-solving endeavors. Last time, I built you that hinged carrying case. What do you need this time?"

Maple looked down at Mack purring in her lap and made a decision. "It looks like I have to go to Boston for a few days, so what I honestly need at the moment is someone to take care of Mack while I'm gone."

Ben didn't blink an eye at this request. Instead, he reached over and scratched Mack behind the ears. Mack nipped Ben's wrist, and Ben pulled his hand back.

"Of course I'll take care of your cat, Maple," he said, shaking out his hand.

Mack jumped off Maple's lap and sauntered away across the front yard.

"Mack," Maple called after him, "haven't you ever heard the expression 'don't bite the hand that feeds you?' Well, that's the hand that's going to be feeding you." She turned to Ben. "I'm so sorry. Did he break the skin?"

"No. He was just asserting his boundaries. I respect that."

He gave her a long look. Her stomach did a few somersaults. She broke eye contact first and thought about getting up. There was work to do, and her fingers itched to resume crafting the nutshells.

Instead, she rested her head on Ben's shoulder and they sat there together, accompanied by the thwapping of Frank's ever-wagging tail, and watched Mack streak across the yard, pursuing prey only he could see.

Part II

Chapter 10

Kenny drove in silence for the first leg of the trip while Maple stared out the window, watching the thick forests of Vermont thin gradually as they made their way closer to the city. Her thoughts were a jumbled mishmash: Bill, Jamie, and her mother all made appearances. Every so often, an image of Daniel's dead body flooded her brain.

Maple felt adrift, as though she were on a rickety little boat in the middle of an ocean, and her complicated emotions were unpredictable waves tossing her to and fro. Had Daniel's mob ties followed him to Elderberry? Had the police at the time investigated Jamie's death thoroughly? Would being back in Boston raise every emotion known to man?

Maple didn't like it. She much preferred straightforward emotions, and she much preferred them one at a time.

"I suppose you think Daniel was a criminal who got what he deserved."

Kenny's tone was belligerent. It took Maple's brain a few seconds to swim through her own complicated sea of emotions and comprehend what her companion was saying. When she did, a laugh escaped her.

"Oh, now you're laughing about it?" he demanded.

Maple looked at her friend, whose eyes remained pointed straight ahead. His jaw was set and his nostrils flared. She gathered herself before she spoke.

"Kenny, that's a ridiculous assertion, and you know it. I'm sorry Daniel died. It's a tragedy to have any life cut short, and you know perfectly well that I know that better than most people. I'm offended at the notion that I could possibly celebrate anyone's brutal death."

Kenny blinked rapidly.

"And on a professional level, I've already proven myself to be utterly devoted to the pursuit of truth and justice. Elijah Wallace was extremely unlikeable, and I went to great lengths—and put myself in danger—to ensure justice was served for him."

Kenny swallowed hard. Maple smoothed her skirt.

"And so, I am forced to conclude that what you said just now—*I suppose you think Daniel was a criminal who got what he deserved*—was not, in fact, directed at me, but was actually mirroring your own complicated emotions about your friend's death. I'm acutely aware that we're currently transporting liquid that used to be inside his body, and I'm sure that's very hard for you to deal with. I'm willing to help you work through these feelings, but I'd appreciate it if you could simply discuss them with me rather than flinging unfounded accusations like a petulant toddler."

Stony silence hung in the car for several moments, and then Kenny began to cry noisily. Maple gazed out her passenger window again, giving him as much space and privacy as she could within the confines of the car. After a minute passed with no abatement of his crying, she told him to pull over, and he did.

There wasn't much traffic on this bleak January day; in fact, no other cars passed them as they sat on the shoulder of the road. Kenny's sobs slowed. Maple dug a handkerchief out of her pocketbook and passed it to him wordlessly.

He blew his nose. "I'm sorry."

"I know."

"I feel like I failed him."

Maple nodded. "I understand."

Kenny looked at her through eyes that were still thick with tears. "Do you think I failed him?"

"No. I think he was a person who made his own choices. You were there for him, just like his uncle was. You gave him options. It was up to him what to do with those options."

"But he tried to get out! This is all his parents' fault! They set him up for this."

"For what? Are you assuming the mob killed him?"

Kenny threw his hands up. "Yes! Aren't you?"

"No." Maple gestured to the backseat, where the nutshells in progress sat next to the box containing Daniel's samples. "I'm actively considering all the evidence and possibilities. That's what good investigators do."

He pounded a fist on the steering wheel. "How can you be so . . . so *calm* about this?"

The tone of his voice made it sound like an accusation rather than a genuine question.

She placed a hand on Kenny's forearm. "Let's get back on the road. While you drive, I'll tell you about my brother."

"So they found him unconscious outside the bar, but he didn't actually die until he was in the jail cell?"

"Correct." Maple could clearly recall the sneer on the face of the officer who had come to their shabby home in a rough neighborhood to tell them the news. "He died overnight in the jail cell."

"You think they covered something up? Or they were just plain sloppy?"

Kenny's eyes were bright and focused again. The only trace of his outburst was a slight redness around his eyes.

"I don't know," she said honestly, "but I've always wondered whether there was more to his death than there seemed on the surface. It's certainly within the realm of possibility that the police saw a dead drunk, wrote off his death as a clumsy accident, and moved on with their day."

She felt a surge of anger and resentment as she remembered this, partly on behalf of her dead brother and partly because that was exactly what Sheriff Scott had initially tried to do when faced with Elijah Wallace's death back in October—at least, until Maple and Kenny had finally persuaded him there was more to it.

"They discovered a head wound when they took off his cap, so it's likely he'd been bleeding internally. He was always getting into fights."

Maple could see the gears turning inside Kenny's head. "Did someone assault him that night? Did the head wound appear before or after they found him lying on the sidewalk? Before or after they brought him to the jail, even?"

"My questions exactly," Maple agreed.

He glanced sideways at her. "It's interesting how there are parallels."

Maple knew what he meant—these were similar questions to those they'd been asking about Daniel.

"Well, at least now we know Daniel breathed in smoke before he died. I'm still in the dark about the order in which things happened to my brother."

As the words were coming out of her mouth, Maple wondered whether they sounded harsh. As Charlotte often reminded her, she had a tendency to be too honest about her feelings.

But Kenny didn't seem put off. In fact, Maple could almost see him shedding the despair that had consumed him minutes earlier as he considered this new case before him. "I wonder—"

". . . whether I might be able to investigate Jamie's death while we're in Boston?"

He frowned. "Actually, I was going to say 'whether *we* might be able to investigate Jamie's death.' There's a big difference."

A lump rose in her throat. She was touched that he would even think of helping her when he was so devastated, and they already had so much to do in Boston.

"You're right. Big difference."

They passed several more minutes in silence.

"Well," Kenny said, "we'll see what we see when we get there, huh?"

Maple wasn't sure why, but her stomach lurched when he said that.

"I don't like all these unknowns," she blurted.

"Me, neither. But isn't that why we do what we do?"

Maple furrowed her brow. "What do you mean?"

"Isn't that why we're in law enforcement? To right wrongs? Or, at the very least, to try and restore some order to the chaos?"

His words hung in the air as Maple considered them. Yesterday, Cecelia Randall had called her a police officer. Just now, Kenny had said *we're in law enforcement*. Somehow, this identity—and her inclusion in this profession—had snuck up on Maple. She had spent the last few years trying and failing to get hired as a lawyer, but instead had made her way into the legal field in an accidental, unexpected way.

She should've felt proud about Cecelia's casual assumption and about Kenny's deliberate statement, both of which welcomed her wholeheartedly into a professional role. After all, hadn't she been striving for just that ever since she finished college and entered law school? She had been positively hungry for it—to be included, to be taken seriously, to be a real professional.

Then why, now, did she feel so . . . unsettled?

She decided to do what she often did with annoying emotions: tamp them down.

"Yes," she said, just as they caught their first glimpse of Boston out the windshield. "Let's go restore some order."

Wordlessly, and without taking his eyes off the road, Kenny held out his right hand. She shook it.

CHAPTER 11

The moment they set foot in the South precinct, it was apparent that order was definitely in need of restoration. Frantic secretaries scurried to and fro, uniformed cops strode grimly in and out of the main hall, and men in rumpled suits shouted into telephone receivers.

Kenny and Maple watched in fascination, then turned to each other with identical expressions of surprise and confusion. Maple compared the scene before her with the sheriff's office in Elderberry, where Mrs. Langley, the receptionist, was generally the sole occupant of the main area and where the loudest sound on an average day was Willy snoring as he slept off his most recent bender in "his" cell.

"Do you think this is what it's always like here?" Kenny asked in an awed undertone.

Out of the cacophonous jumble of noise, Maple caught several words and phrases: *Perry's, money, disguise.*

Her eyes widened. "Kenny, they're talking about the robbery Ella was telling us about!"

She watched the realization dawn on his face.

"C'mon."

She stepped up to the reception desk, where a harried-looking secretary sifted through an enormous stack of papers. The woman glanced up at them through giant round glasses.

"Yes?" she said, the annoyance clear in her tone.

"Maple Bishop and Kenny Quirk from Vermont," Maple said. "Our sheriff called ahead to arrange a meeting so we can drop off some samples to be processed." She held up the box. "We're investigating a recent death in our town that seems to have ties to this area."

The secretary sighed and rubbed her temples. Then, she shoved aside one of the stacks to look at an appointment calendar underneath. She ran her finger down one of the squares, muttering to herself. Then, she shot them the briefest of glances and pointed down a hallway.

"Detective Francis. Fourth door on your left."

The phone on her desk jangled, pulling her attention away from the visitors.

"Thank you," Kenny said, even though the woman definitely didn't hear him.

He and Maple exchanged another glance and then headed in the direction the receptionist had indicated. When they got to the fourth door on the left and saw the nameplate Det. Francis on the wall, they saw the door was ajar.

Maple leaned in and knocked on the edge of the door, and a booming voice called, "Come in!"

She pushed it the rest of the way open and immediately felt calmer. Classical music played from a radio on a small table. The detective, who was sitting behind a metal desk, placed his pencil down and rose from his chair to greet them. He was trim, medium height, and dark-skinned. His smile was warm and genuine.

"Detective David Francis," he said, shaking each of their hands in turn. Maple and Kenny introduced themselves.

Detective Francis's tiny office was an oasis. Maple's eyes swept the room, picking up on the details. There were stacks of paper and files in here, but—unlike the ones they had seen out in the reception area—these were neatly organized. Sharpened pencils had been placed in a mug on the desk, where three photographs also sat. One showed Detective Francis and three people Maple assumed to be his wife and children—two little boys—posed in front of a Christmas tree. The other showed Francis as a younger man. He wore a crisp police dress uniform and stood between a tall Black man in a suit and tie and a petite white woman in a dress, both of whom beamed with obvious pride. The third showed about ten Black uniformed officers lined up in two rows, looking formal and serious.

"That's a picture of my task force," Francis said with obvious pride. "The first all-Black one in the department's history. I started it about a year ago, and we've made great strides connecting with the community and reducing crime in certain neighborhoods where white officers hadn't historically had much success."

"Congratulations," she said, and Kenny nodded in agreement. "That's quite an accomplishment."

As she turned, Maple's eye caught a note scribbled in pencil that was pinned to the wall near the desk. It read: DET. FRANCIS—YOU MAY HAVE PUT ME IN HERE, BUT YOU'RE STILL ONE HECK OF A GUY! An illegible signature was scrawled at the bottom. Maple speculated that it had been written by someone Detective Francis had arrested; she supposed that if someone had written her a letter like that, she might've hung it on her wall, too.

"Please, sit," the detective said, indicating two wooden chairs in front of his desk. "I hope your trip to Boston went smoothly."

He pronounced it BAH-stin, which showed Maple that he was from the area. She felt heat rise in her cheeks as she considered how she had worked diligently to lose her own regional accent, but she wasn't sure why that thought brought up feelings of embarrassment for her.

"Thanks for making the time to meet with us," Kenny said. "You folks are clearly busy today!" He gestured toward the chaos down the hall.

Francis nodded. "We're working a big case with all hands on deck."

"We heard a little about it. A reporter from our local paper is down here covering it," Maple explained.

Francis nodded grimly. "They're estimating the crooks made off with over a million dollars in cash and likely much more in checks and securities."

Maple and Kenny both gasped. This was an almost unfathomable amount of money. Francis nodded and frowned.

"The FBI's even getting involved now, which we just found out this morning. However, none of that means other cases should fall by the wayside. I'm happy to meet with you folks today."

Maple liked the detective's attitude. Based on the way Kenny sat up straighter and nodded, so did he.

"Now, I pulled what we had on your victim, Daniel Perkins." He flipped open one of the files in front of him. "He's got a record going back to his teens—petty theft and relatively minor fights, mostly—but the interesting thing to me was his father." He opened another, much thicker, file. "Thaddeus Perkins was in with the

Irish mob." He listed off the elder Perkins's crimes, holding up a finger each time he listed a new one: "Money laundering, illegal weapons charges, attempted bank robbery. He even got popped peeling a few petes."

Maple and Kenny exchanged a confused look. Detective Francis chuckled. "Sorry, 'peeling petes' is street slang for safe-cracking. That's probably not as common where you're from."

"I'm actually from here, originally," Maple said, and immediately wondered why she'd shared that piece of information. "But I still haven't heard that expression before."

"Well, welcome back," said Francis with a warm smile. "I'm sorry it's not under better circumstances."

"We know Thad Perkins was killed in a bank robbery," Maple continued, hoping to save Kenny from hearing the detective rattle off details of his friend's father's death.

Francis nodded. "That's right. Ugly scene."

Kenny cleared his throat. "What about Daniel's mother? Any record on her?"

Francis shook his head, pulling out a third file. "Laurie Perkins has no criminal history, but I understand you're trying to track her down so you can notify her of her son's death, so I dug into it a little this morning. Seems like she's moved around a lot in the last few years, staying with different people. She's had a few apartments of her own but couldn't make rent consistently and got kicked out. Most recently, she's been a patient at South Boston Hospital. It's a mental institution."

Maple nodded, acknowledging the confirmation of what Phillip had told them. "And that's her last known address?"

"It's the most recent one we have for her. I'd start there if I were you. Want me to come along?"

"That's not necessary, Detective, but thanks for the offer," Maple said. "I know the way."

"I hope it's helpful. Do you have a sense yet about whether this was arson or accident?"

Kenny shook his head. "We're still exploring all possibilities at this point, Detective. We'll keep you updated. Thanks again for pulling all of this together for us."

He then shot Maple a significant look. She knew he was waiting for her to ask about Jamie, but a rock had settled in her stomach. For whatever reason, she decided now wasn't the moment.

"I'll keep these files handy just in case we need them again," Francis said. "All right, then. Let's get your samples down to the lab. Follow me."

He rose and went to the door, Kenny and Maple following in his wake. Maple studiously avoided Kenny's eyes, which made her feel like a coward. She shoved that feeling down as best she could for now. As Francis led them through a maze of hallways, Maple noticed that the detective moved with an easy confidence; he clearly had the respect of his colleagues. Multiple people stopped what they were doing to greet him—even in the midst of the robbery case chaos.

They arrived at the basement lab a minute later. Francis pushed open the heavy door and greeted a slim white man with gold spectacles and thinning, wispy hair the color of wheat.

"Gus, these are our Vermont visitors."

Gus smiled. "So you're the folks from John Strong's new town, eh? He and I go way back. How's he settling in?"

His words sent a pang into Maple's gut. She didn't really know how they were settling in, and she was feeling as though she should've made more of an effort to help them do just that. Kenny cleared his throat.

"He and his daughter are settling in just fine, sir. We'll let him know you were asking after him."

"Please do, please do."

Maple handed him the box. "Here are the samples."

"I'll get right on this. Should only take two days or so. What will you do in the meantime?"

"Family notifications and some backgrounding," Kenny said. "We're headed to South Hospital next to try and locate our victim's mother."

Maple noted Kenny's professional tone and manner; he seemed to be getting better at maintaining his professional distance from the case at hand.

"Oh, and will you be visiting Victoria?" Gus asked.

They shot him quizzical looks, and the lab technician seemed to realize his verbal misstep. His cheeks flushed red. "Never mind. Don't listen to me; I don't know what I'm talking about!" He gave a nervous laugh.

Francis intervened smoothly as Gus backpedaled. "Well, thanks very much, Gus. You'll let me know when you have results?"

"Yes, yes, of course!" the other man said, waving awkwardly as his visitors turned to go.

Maple and Kenny trailed Detective Francis back to the main lobby, where the frenetic energy had—if anything—increased in the half hour or so they'd been in the building.

"It was very nice to meet you," Maple said as they shook hands with the detective again. "Please let us know when you hear from the lab. Here's where we're staying."

She handed him a piece of paper with the name and address of a rooming house.

"Of course," Francis said. "You'll know as soon as I do. And good luck with your notification and your other investigations. Don't hesitate to get in touch if there's anything I can help with."

He pulled two business cards out of his pocket and handed one to each of them.

"Thank you, sir," Kenny said, taking his turn to shake Francis's hand. "And good luck with the robbery."

"I won't rest until we solve it."

There was a steeliness in his eyes that made Maple believe him.

Chapter 12

"Nice guy," Kenny said as they arrived back at the car. "Detective Francis, I mean."

"Yes, and he's very thorough," Maple agreed. "I was pleasantly surprised he'd gone to the trouble of pulling all those files for us."

She pulled a jar from the backseat and shook it.

"What's that?" Kenny asked.

"Soapy water."

She poured some over her hands and scrubbed. Kenny watched the water hit the pavement and almost instantly freeze into a tiny pond.

"You carry soapy water around in a jar?"

"Of course. Everyone should. Germs are everywhere."

Kenny shrugged and held his hands out. Maple poured some water over them, he mimicked her scrubbing motion, and she handed him a rag to dry them with.

"There. Much better," she said. She replaced the jar in the backseat and got behind the wheel.

"What do you make of Gus?" Kenny asked after settling himself in the passenger seat.

Maple made a face. "I'm not sure what to make of him. I wonder how he knows Dr. Strong. And I wonder—"

"—who Victoria is and why he thought we'd be visiting her," Kenny finished for her.

"Yes." Maple turned down side streets that were ingrained in her memory, even though it had been many years since she had traveled them. They were about to pass the hill where she and Jamie used to sled together with the other neighborhood kids, and she was lost in those memories. Her only photograph of the two of them had been taken on that hill.

As if he could read her mind, Kenny asked, "Why didn't you ask about your brother?"

Maple couldn't answer that question, because she didn't know herself. Maybe it was because she'd spent all these years assuming all Boston police officers were as callous as the one who'd made Jamie's death notification; that man had sneered as he delivered the news to her.

Detective Francis, on the other hand, couldn't have been more different. He struck her as dedicated, fair, and hardworking. Plus, it couldn't have been easy being a Black officer. Maple was sure he must've faced discrimination and more roadblocks than his white colleagues, and yet he still managed to command the seemingly universal respect of his fellow officers—and, apparently, maintained a steadfast commitment to truth and justice, even though Maple couldn't imagine society had consistently treated him justly.

All she said to Kenny, though, was, "I'm not sure."

"We'll have to tell Peter his nickname is also a slang term for safes," Kenny said. "He'll get a kick out of that."

Several minutes passed in silence as Maple drove. Kenny commented once on the haphazardness of the city's street layout. Maple barked out a laugh and said, "Welcome to Boston."

They passed the hill, but Maple didn't point it out to Kenny. With a pang, she thought of her mother and how she'd never come sledding with them. She was too busy working at the factory or too tired and wracked by coughing from her exposure to the dangerous chemicals.

"We're almost there," she said a few moments later.

Kenny leaned forward, squinting. "Is it that giant gray building?" His tone was dubious.

"Yes." She glanced over and saw distaste written all over his expression and posture. "Why the long face?"

"Well, it's not very inviting, is it? People are coming in here with real problems, trying to get themselves sorted out, and it's so . . . I don't know, so cold and institutional."

Maple guessed he was thinking about his father, who—while he'd never been institutionalized—had certainly struggled to assimilate back into civilian life after the war. It was likely that there were plenty of veterans inside who, like Ken Senior, struggled with nightmares, tremors, and other debilitating effects of war.

He flopped back in the passenger seat and sighed. "Maybe the inside is better."

Maple pulled into the parking lot and brought the car to a stop. Moments later, they walked in the front door and quickly determined the inside wasn't better. A small entryway emptied out into a long hallway. Cheap, brown carpet covered a thin strip of the scratched linoleum floor. There were several large, dark stains that Maple hoped were the result of coffee spills, but the longer she looked at them, the less sure she was.

"This makes the precinct lobby seem downright homey," Maple muttered, the hairs on the back of her neck prickling. She much preferred the chaos of the police station over whatever this was.

Kenny exhaled a half-laugh. Maple heard Kenny's stomach rumble and realized that she, too, was hungry. She had packed cheese sandwiches, but they had been too distracted to remember to eat.

The dim hallway finally culminated in a small lobby. For such a big building, the lobby was almost eerily silent. In front of them sat a metal desk with one chair behind it and a clipboard with a visitor's log. There were no decorations and only one small window. The walls were painted a drab, dirty-looking beige. A clock on the wall ticked loudly, marking each passing second with an ominous *click*. Maple was turning in a slow circle, taking in the entire room, when a door opened and a woman in a crisp white nurse's uniform came out. Her name tag said MARIA.

"May I help you?" she asked with the lilting accent of a native Spanish speaker.

"Yes, thanks." Kenny showed her his badge and introduced himself and Maple, explaining where they were from and—in vague, general terms—why they had come to Boston. "We need to speak with a patient of yours, Laurie Perkins. It's a matter of some urgency."

The nurse nodded once. "Wait a moment. And please sign in."

Maple and Kenny watched as she disappeared back into the room she had emerged from. Then, they each wrote their name on the log. Several minutes passed before she returned, this time with a sheet of paper in her hand.

"Laurie Perkins is not a patient here."

Kenny and Maple glanced at each other and then back at the nurse. "But we were told this was her last known address."

"That may be true," Maria acknowledged, "but it is no longer her address."

Maria handed Kenny the paper, and he held it between himself and Maple so they could read it together.

"She left A.M.A. on January 4th. What does that mean?" Kenny asked, his eyes scanning the document.

"Against medical advice," Maple answered, a cold feeling developing in her stomach. "The doctors didn't want her to leave, but she did it anyway."

Kenny and Maple locked eyes, and Maple knew they were thinking the same thing: why had Daniel's mother fled the mental institution two days before her son had died in a fire? Was it a coincidence, or was there a more sinister connection?

Maple looked at Maria, who stood impassively before them. "Can you give us any more information? Why did she decide to leave on that day in particular?"

"This I do not know." Maria frowned. "However, I might be able to find someone who can help."

"Please do," Kenny said. "It's extremely important that we find her."

"Wait here." She disappeared behind the door yet again.

Kenny immediately began to pace in the small area. "Why would she leave?"

"And where did she go?" Maple chimed in. "That's actually the more pertinent question at the moment. If we can answer that, we can track her down and find out the other answers."

"She was always erratic," Kenny said, shoving his hands into his pockets. "Even when we were kids. She didn't—I mean, we're trying to understand this as though it's the result of a logical chain of events and decisions, but what if it's not? What if she just . . . up and left for no particular reason?"

"That's certainly a possibility," Maple agreed. "But the timing of it is very curious. What are the odds she'd coincidentally choose to leave against her doctor's wishes right before her son died in a suspicious fire?"

Frustrated, Kenny ran his hands through his hair. Just then, the door opened again. This time, Maria was accompanied by a man in a white coat who introduced himself as Dr. Herbert.

"Maria told me you folks are looking for Mrs. Perkins," he said, adjusting his silver-rimmed spectacles.

"Yes," Kenny said. "It's extremely important that we find her. We have an ongoing investigation."

He showed the doctor his badge.

"I understand," the doctor said, "and I'd like to help. Unfortunately, there are rules about releasing confidential patient information."

Kenny looked like he wanted to punch the mild-mannered doctor, so Maple decided to intervene. She pulled Detective Francis's business card out of her pocket and handed it to Dr. Herbert. "Please call this detective. He'll vouch for us."

Herbert studied the card and nodded solemnly. "I'll be back."

Both he and Maria disappeared behind the door again.

Kenny clapped his hands together in annoyance. "How are we supposed to do our job if people stonewall us like this?"

Maple arched an eyebrow. "He's doing *his* job. He has to follow protocols, too. He took an oath."

Kenny made a face at her. Maple interpreted it to mean he knew she was right but didn't want to admit it.

"When you think about it, you should actually be feeling relieved at this turn of events."

"Why?" Exasperation tinged his voice.

"It means this doctor is more professional and caring toward his patients than the stark exterior would've led us to believe."

Kenny rolled his eyes. Several minutes ticked by noisily on the wall clock. Kenny continued to pace. Maple watched him.

"Detective Francis will vouch for us. His word will have more weight with Dr. Herbert since he's local. This isn't our jurisdiction. We just have to be patient."

Kenny looked ready to jump out of his own skin at her admonishment, but before he could respond, the door opened one more time and Dr. Herbert stood there. He beckoned to them.

"All right," he said. "I got a hold of Detective Francis and am able to talk to you—to some extent, at least—about Mrs. Perkins to help in your investigation. Please understand, though, that I take patient confidentiality very seriously. There may be questions I cannot answer. For example, I can't tell you specifics about her diagnosis or treatment."

Kenny looked disgruntled at this news, but Maple smiled and thanked the doctor. He handed the business card back to her, and she and Kenny stepped around the metal desk and followed him through the door. He led them down another brief hallway to his office, which had a nicer desk and better carpeting than the main area. A soft lamp gave off a more pleasant glow than the harsh fluorescent lighting of the lobby. The doctor gestured to a loveseat that faced his desk, and Maple and Kenny sat, the latter emanating tightly coiled energy; Maple could tell that he was barely able to force himself to sit. He wanted to move, to go, to figure things out. She could relate.

"What do you need to know about Mrs. Perkins?" the doctor asked.

"Why did she leave against medical advice?" Kenny asked.

Dr. Herbert frowned. "I can't be sure."

Before Kenny could spring across the desk and shake the doctor vigorously by his shoulders, Maple replied, "Can you tell us whether anything of note—anything unusual or out of the ordinary—happened in the time leading up to her departure? Without violating confidentiality, of course."

He nodded thoughtfully. "There was one thing. She had a visitor in the morning on the day she left. This is notable for a few reasons. For one, he was the first and only visitor she ever had here."

Maple felt a twinge of pity for the woman. The doctor picked up a paper and slid it across the desk. Maple and Kenny leaned forward and peered at it. It was a page from the visitor's log just like the one they had signed upon arrival, only this one was from January 4th. Dr. Herbert pointed to one entry in particular: *Alphonse Gabriel*.

"Do you recognize that name?" he asked.

Maple and Kenny shook their heads.

"Should we?" Maple said.

The doctor raised an eyebrow. "Al Capone's full name is Alphonse Gabriel Capone. My guess is that whoever signed in using this name was having a bit of a laugh."

"That's interesting," Maple said slowly.

Her brain churned over this new information. She wondered whether the person who had signed in with the name of the most famous gangster in the country had been doing more than having a laugh, though. Maybe he'd known that at some point police would be looking at this sheet. Maybe he was sending a message.

A threat.

And it seemed likely that he'd been visiting Laurie Perkins, a mentally ill woman whose husband and son both had ties to the mob, to deliver a threat to her in person.

"Does anyone recall seeing this visitor? Who was working the reception desk that day?" Kenny asked urgently.

Dr. Herbert went to the door and called for Maria, who joined them a moment later. He relayed Kenny's question, and she confirmed she had been on duty that day.

"I remember this man, yes," she said. "I couldn't help but notice him. He had only one arm."

Kenny and Maple exchanged a glance. Was this the same man Eliza Patterson had seen at the cabin?

"He had black hair and a cap pulled low over his forehead. He had mean eyes." She made a face that indicated she had found the man unpleasant.

"And he only stayed for twenty minutes?" Maple asked, noting the time at which "Alphonse Gabriel" had signed out on the log.

"Yes. It was a quick visit. I wasn't sorry to see him go. He was polite enough, but I could tell this was not a good man."

"How soon after his departure did Mrs. Perkins check herself out?"

The doctor checked his records. "Less than an hour later."

Kenny blew out his breath. "That can't be a coincidence," he muttered. "No way."

Maple was inclined to agree.

"What else do you want to ask us?" Dr. Herbert asked.

Maple and Kenny then asked for any information Dr. Herbert and Maria had about Mrs. Perkins's known associates, previous location, or clues to where she may have gone. This was a dead end; neither of them had any idea. Laurie Perkins hadn't been forthcoming with either of them about her previous address or her future plans for relocation.

A few more questions and several minutes later, Maple and Kenny thanked the nurse and the doctor, signed out, and left the hospital. When they walked out into the parking lot, the sun was already sinking behind the trees. Soon, it would be dark.

"So, where should we start?" Kenny asked.

"We should go get settled at the boarding house," Maple said. "We need to call your uncle and fill him in on the developments."

Kenny looked as though he might protest but then thought better of it and nodded wearily. They walked to the car.

With a lightheartedness she didn't really feel, Maple added, "We're going to need a hot meal and a good night's sleep if we're going to find Laurie Perkins and tangle with the mob tomorrow."

Chapter 13

The rooming house was about a ten-minute drive from the hospital, and Maple and Kenny spent the ride immersed in their own thoughts. When they arrived, they checked in under the reservations that Mrs. Langley, the sheriff's secretary and receptionist, had made for them.

Having missed lunch, they were both delighted to learn that dinner was being served in the dining room. Four other hotel guests were just finishing their meal as Kenny and Maple sat down and proceeded to inhale large plates of homemade meatloaf, mashed potatoes, and green beans.

Kenny went to find a telephone so he could call first Detective Francis to ask for his help tomorrow and then the sheriff to fill him in on the developments so far. Meanwhile, Maple returned to the car to fetch some of her nutshell materials.

She poured herself an extra cup of tea and then laid out her supplies on the table in the common room. She decided to focus on sewing the dolls and household linens, such as the curtains and bedspreads, for now; she didn't think the hostess or the other guests would appreciate it if she started hammering and using her saw. She worked for a while in silence, churning over the day's events.

Another guest came in and sat in the rocking chair by the fire. She looked to be slightly older than Maple, perhaps in her mid-to-late forties, and had a friendly face that reminded Maple of Charlotte. She and Maple introduced themselves—her name was Miranda—and briefly exchanged pleasantries, and the other woman pulled some yarn and a hook out of her bag and began crocheting.

"It's a blanket for my great-nephew," she explained. "He's not even a month old."

"Very nice." Maple's voice was a little curt; though she could tell the woman's craftsmanship was of high quality, she had no interest in babies and hoped to dissuade her new companion from chatting. Maple would have much preferred to be alone. She needed to think while she worked; she didn't want to exchange banal pleasantries with some stranger she'd never see again.

Miranda didn't get the message. "Are you making a doll?"

Maple gritted her teeth. "Mmm-hmm."

"Who's it for?"

Maple considered telling her the truth: that she was planning to set fire to this doll as well as the other identical ones she would make soon afterwards. She enjoyed imagining the woman's scandalized reaction; after all, who on earth would ever expect a fellow crafter to create an intricate thing of beauty with the full intention of destroying it?

Then, almost as quickly as she thought of it, she pictured Charlotte's disapproving frown and somewhat reluctantly rejected the idea. She settled on a less complicated version—a partial truth—instead.

"I'm going to keep this one myself, actually."

"'This one?'" Miranda echoed. "Do you make many dolls?"

Maple flashed her companion a brief, tight smile. "Yes. I have a small business in Vermont making and selling custom dollhouses, most of them fully furnished. This one is for a . . . special, personal project, though. I'm not selling it."

Maple groaned inwardly as the woman set down her crochet hook and came over to the table. She peered at the doll in progress.

"This is beautiful work. What materials are you using there?"

"Cotton and buckshot from my local hardware store," she said. "The buckshot gives the dolls a bit of heft and the cotton keeps them soft and a little squishy."

"Fascinating. May I?"

She indicated that she'd like to pick up the doll. Maple deftly tied off the piece of thread, snipped it, and handed the doll to the woman, who turned it over and examined it more closely. Maple was about to ask her why she found the doll so interesting; after all, right now it was bare bones—she hadn't even painted on his face or added hair or clothing yet. Those details, Maple felt, were where her craftsmanship skills really shone. At that moment, though, Kenny appeared in the door frame. Maple had never been happier to see him.

"Do you need me?" she asked.

"I have a few updates." The corners of his mouth turned up slightly as he read the room. Maple was sure her face revealed her desperation to escape her current situation.

His words were her golden ticket out of the common room.

"Sorry," she said, not meaning it at all. "But I'm going to have to go meet with my colleague now."

She swept her sewing materials back into her basket and plucked the doll out of Miranda's hands.

"Oh, all right," the woman replied, clearly bewildered by the rapid change in tone and events. "It was lovely to meet you. Do you have a—"

"Lovely to meet you, too. Goodbye."

Maple swept out of the room and steered Kenny to the dining room, where she closed the door behind them.

"I'm sorry to have intruded on your time with your new friend." His eyes sparkled with amusement.

Maple shot him a dark look, but secretly she felt happy to see him looking happy, even if it was as a result of her own discomfort.

"I detest small talk. What have you got to tell me?"

"I brought my uncle up to speed. He says we should proceed with caution." He rolled his eyes at this, suddenly looking more like a teenager than an officer of the law. "And we're going to meet Detective Francis at the precinct at eight tomorrow morning. He'll help us find Mrs. Perkins. He thinks he knows who the man with the missing arm is."

"Well, who is he?" she asked impatiently.

"Leo Matthews, a notorious mobster who's worked his way up the ranks and into a top spot."

A surge of excitement shot through Maple as she considered the prospect of participating in real police work—of being invited in instead of sneaking around like she'd done during most of the Elijah Wallace investigation. And yet, something wasn't sitting right. She had a distinct squirming sensation underneath that excitement. She couldn't pinpoint why, and that troubled her.

Kenny arched an eyebrow. "Sound good?"

"Yes," she said. "Good. Eight o'clock. Should we meet for breakfast in here by seven, then, and head over afterwards?"

"Sure." Kenny rubbed a hand over his face. "I'm beat. I'm going to hit the hay. Good night."

He headed to his room and she to hers. However, Maple couldn't sleep. Instead, she stayed up for hours sewing tiny doll versions of a dead man.

After a hearty breakfast of scrambled eggs, toast, and several fortifying cups of tea the next morning, Maple and Kenny got back into the car. When they arrived at the precinct at 7:45 AM, Kenny walked in the front door ahead of Maple, and she crashed into his back when he stopped abruptly just inside the threshold.

"Kenny, what—"

"You're not going to like this," he said.

"I'm not going to like *what*?" she asked irritably, rubbing her nose as she peered around his shoulder.

There were significantly fewer people in the precinct this morning than there had been yesterday afternoon—they'd even arrived before the receptionist—which made it easy for Maple to see what Kenny had warned her about: there, not ten yards in front of them, was Harry Needles, the head reporter from *The County Tribune* back home. He appeared to be interviewing a police officer.

Maple groaned.

Kenny turned to look at her, his eyes twinkling a little. "You're unarmed, right?"

Last year, Maple had received an official warning after aiming a shotgun at the abrasive newspaper man. At the time, he had been refusing to leave her property while aggressively questioning her about her discovery of Elijah Wallace's body.

She hadn't been in the mood for visitors.

Maple scowled. "That was a misunderstanding."

"Mmm-hmm. Sure, it was."

"You know what? I don't like your tone. You should—"

But before she could finish her sentence, Harry flipped his spiral notebook closed, stuck his pencil behind his ear, and saw Kenny.

"Harry," said Kenny as the reporter strode over. "Small world."

"Kenny Quirk!" the newspaper man said, crossing the room in a few strides and pumping Kenny's hand. "So good to see you."

Then, Maple stepped out from behind Kenny and watched Harry's expression shift from one of pleasant surprise to wariness.

"Oh. It's you," he said flatly.

Maple noticed that he didn't offer to shake her hand, which was just fine with her. She crossed her arms over her chest.

"What brings you to Boston?" Harry directed his question to Kenny, who gave a vague answer about next of kin notification in a bored tone that made it all seem very routine.

The reporter lifted an eyebrow. "It takes two to deliver a next-of-kin notification in another state?"

"Maple's originally from this neighborhood. Sheriff thought it'd make sense to bring a local along to help. The person we're trying to track down is known for not staying in one place for very long. What about you? You're covering the robbery, I imagine? Ella said something about it."

"Yes, yes. Fascinating story. I'll have another piece published in tonight's edition, but I'll give you a sneak preview: They think the haul's north of two million, all told. Biggest grab in American history."

Maple disliked the greedy glint in his eyes. The reporter seemed excited by the robbery and impressed by the massive amount of the theft.

"It was mostly payroll money, correct?" she said, already knowing the answer.

"Yeah," he said.

"Well, I certainly hope all those hard-working people whose wages were stolen will be able to put food on the table this week."

Harry waved dismissively. "Oh, Perry's is insured. Listen, you shoulda seen the masks these guys used . . ." He spoke animatedly to Kenny for several minutes more, describing details of the crime scene as Maple fumed.

Finally, Kenny interrupted him, saying that he and Maple had an appointment at eight o'clock.

"Sure, sure," Harry said, his beady eyes studying first Kenny's face and then Maple's. "Does your notification have to do with that burned cabin Ella reported on?"

"Harry," Kenny said, clapping the reporter on the shoulder, "you know I can't tell you that. But trust me when I tell you this is just some tedious police work we're here for today. Covering our bases, checking boxes, dotting our i's and crossing our t's . . . whatever platitude you like. The robbery sounds much more interesting."

The reporter shot Kenny one more suspicious glance before departing. Maple turned to Kenny, impressed with how he had downplayed their investigation so the reporter would leave them alone.

"Wow, you almost had me going there. Very impressive lying, Officer Quirk."

Kenny flushed.

Maple shot a look over her shoulder to make sure Harry was actually gone, and then she turned back to Kenny. "Do you get the sense that he's *rooting* for these robbers? It's almost as if he hopes they'll get away with it."

Her face wrinkled in a disapproving frown.

"It's Harry." Kenny shrugged. "You know as well as I do—actually, even better than I do—that there's no explaining that man."

He grinned and made a motion like he was shouldering a rifle. She swatted his arm, feigning more annoyance than she felt. It was nice to see Kenny in a teasing mood. She decided to return the favor.

"Too bad it's not Ella who's in town to cover the robbery," she said.

Kenny dropped his invisible rifle as his ears went pink. "Uh, I think we should stay focused on the task at hand."

"Sure thing, Officer." Maple led the way down the hall to Detective Francis's office. "Whatever you say."

Chapter 14

Ten minutes later, Maple and Kenny were sitting next to each other in Detective Francis's office poring over the file on Leo Matthews, the one-armed mobster. The detective himself had been called into a meeting and had asked one of the other officers to let the two into his office so they could get started while they waited for him.

"Basically," said Kenny, frowning as they flipped past Matthews's sixth arrest report, "this guy is very bad news."

It was true; his rap sheet ran the gamut from petty theft to bank robbery to assault with a deadly weapon. Back in 1940, he had robbed a liquor store and the pursuing officers had shot him in the arm. He had escaped with his life, but his fourth stint in prison, a nasty infection, and an amputation had resulted from that heist.

They put his file aside and open the one labeled with Thaddeus Perkins's name. Because her handwriting was far more legible than what she described as Kenny's "chicken scratch," Maple had a freshly sharpened pencil and a notepad on which she was recording all the known contacts and addresses they came across; these could be starting points for where they would check in their search for Laurie Perkins.

By the time David Francis appeared back in his own office half an hour later, they had moved on from Thad's file to Daniel's file and had a dozen known contacts written down. Maple had underlined one in particular that stood out to them: Annabel Hastings. Her husband, Jack, had been killed in the same attempted robbery as Thaddeus Perkins; the two men had also been arrested twice together in the five-year span prior to their violent and simultaneous deaths. These connections between the two men over the years led Maple and Kenny to think there was a deep, ongoing relationship here, making it logical that Laurie might turn to Annabel in her current time of need.

Francis gestured toward the files on the table.

"How's your search going?"

They filled him in on what they had learned and on their particular interest in Annabel Hastings. Francis agreed she was a logical place to start.

"Would it be possible to look at Jack Hastings's file?" Maple asked.

"Certainly. I'll ask Marsha to bring it in for you."

He moved toward the door, but stopped when Kenny spoke again. "Uh, there's one other file we'd like to take a gander at."

Maple shot him a quizzical look. Hastings was the only one they had spent any amount of time discussing that morning. Kenny avoided meeting her gaze.

"James Cooper."

At the sound of her brother's name, all the blood seemed to drain from Maple's head at once. She felt woozy, but if Francis noticed, he didn't show it.

"Another mob connection?"

Kenny shrugged noncommittally.

Francis nodded once. "You got it."

He poked his head out into the hallway, and they heard the low rumble of his voice as he spoke with Marsha. A moment later, he was back in the room with them.

Maple's jaw hung open. Had Kenny—earnest, law-upholding, do-gooder Kenny—just casually lied right to the face of a Boston cop?

Before she could say anything, though, the detective had stepped back into the room.

"How's the robbery case going?" Kenny asked. "Any new leads?"

Maple tried to rearrange her facial expression from astonishment to neutrality.

The detective sighed. "No, not really, but we just got word the FBI's coming in."

He said this in the same dejected tone someone might use to deliver the news that Christmas had been canceled.

"And that's bad?" Maple asked, her heart hammering at the prospect of seeing her brother's file.

"Well, it means more manpower and resources, which is good. But it also means they will seize control of the investigation and—eh, well, never mind. You folks aren't here to listen to my woes. I'm supposed to be helping you with your case. Tell me the other names on your list."

Maple cleared her throat and read off the names. Francis interjected whenever he recognized a name or a connection to the mob, filling them in on background information from his time walking the beat. Maple, who possessed a photographic memory herself, was impressed with the level of detail the man recalled with no notes in front of him.

When she said as much to him, he shrugged and said, "That was my beat. I walked that neighborhood for years as a patrolman, and in order to be effective at that job, that's what you do: develop contacts, get to know people and how they're connected and what makes them tick."

They all looked at the door when a knock came. Marsha walked in and handed two files—one much thicker than the other—to Detective Francis, who thanked her. As she left, he pulled his desk chair over to the table with them. He put aside the thinner file—Maple could see Jamie's name printed on the flap and felt her heart skip a beat. Were the answers she'd been hoping for now sitting inches from her? Her hand twitched.

Detective Francis flipped open the thicker file and slid it toward them.

"Meet Jack Hastings."

Twenty minutes later, they had added three more names and addresses to their list of possible contacts for Laurie Perkins—though all three of them agreed Annabel Hastings still seemed like their best bet. They were also developing a reasonably robust picture of the person Jack Hastings had been. In short, he was a likable scoundrel; Maple imagined him as the kind of criminal who would've sent a note praising his own arresting officer, just like the one Detective Francis had taped to the wall. Like Thaddeus Perkins, Hastings had kept violence to a minimum in his crimes—even the ones that could've easily resulted in bloodshed, like the occasional armed robbery.

"His record is a mile long, but he never inflicted physical harm on anyone," Maple mused. "Just like Thaddeus."

"Never seems to have ratted anyone out, either," Kenny added thoughtfully. "There's no record of him snitching or working with the police."

"Sometimes, there is honor among thieves, but given the crowd these two were associated with, I assure you that they were the exception and not the rule." Detective Francis glanced at his wristwatch. "OK, well, let me go check in with my task force."

"Why don't you two have a glance at this"—he tossed the file with Jamie's name on it onto the table between them—"and as soon as I get back, we'll see about finding Laurie."

He strode out the door.

They were now alone with Jamie's file. Maple was acutely aware of her own heartbeat pounding in her ears. The file in front of her might yield answers to questions she had been asking herself for years. Had Jamie's death been the result of a drunken accident, as it appeared on the surface? Or had officers simply written it off as such because he was a rabble-rousing dockworker?

And the deepest one of all: Had Maple let down her little brother?

Her eyes flicked to Kenny's face. She supposed her feelings about Jamie's death ran parallel to Kenny's feelings about Daniel's death. If there was anyone she could talk to about this, it was the friend sitting next to her.

The emotions jumbled inside her. Her words stuck in her throat.

"Want me to look?" Kenny asked, indicating the folder.

Part of Maple wanted to say yes. It might be a great relief to allow him to do this for her—to serve as a buffer between her and the contents of that file. She considered it for several seconds before she shook her head. She'd been relying on herself for far too long to yield now. Maple Bishop had never yet met a challenge she'd backed down from.

She opened the file.

The top sheet was his most recent arrest report. With Kenny standing behind her and looking over her shoulder, Maple read through it, noting the familiar details that the officer who'd come to her door had shared with her: Jamie had been found on the ground outside The Black Sheep, a seedy pub frequented by the rough dockworker crowd. He'd been intoxicated to the point that he couldn't stand. Other patrons reported he'd been in a fistfight before the patrolmen arrived on the scene, but none of them could (or would) name the other man, who'd fled the scene after Jamie had gone down "like a ton of bricks," as one of the onlookers had described it to the arresting officer.

The patrolmen had put Jamie in the paddy wagon and brought him to jail; presumably, they figured he would sleep it off just like Willy regularly did in the Elderberry sheriff's department—except Willy stumbled in of his own accord, and the Boston officers had to carry Jamie in and deposit him in the cell.

A wave of shame and pity threatened to consume Maple as she read those words. She'd known about it, but there was something about seeing it written in an official report for the first time that made it land differently for her now.

"Why didn't they bring him to the hospital?" Kenny asked.

Sometimes, his naivete still surprised her. She sighed.

"He was a dock worker who had multiple arrests for fighting and public drunkenness. He was no stranger to the local patrolmen, and they were no stranger to him." She flipped to the second and third papers, discovering (as she'd expected) the same officer's name—Robert Halpern—on both of those reports. She pointed it out to Kenny. "Besides, who was going to pay for it?"

Kenny grunted. Maple appreciated his idealism even as it simultaneously exasperated her.

"Is that cop the same one who came to notify you of his death?" Kenny pointed at their names.

This spring, it would be four years since that day, but Maple still remembered the officer's condescending tone and the name emblazoned on his badge.

"No. The one who came to my door was Edwards."

"Well, based on this report, I think Halpern did a decent job," Kenny said thoughtfully.

Maple looked at him quizzically. What was he seeing that she wasn't?

"I mean, Jamie was a well-known troublemaker. I know you've been concerned that cops just tossed him in the cell and didn't notice or care that he died there, and I know the one who gave you the notification acted like an ass."

She nodded, wondering what he was about to tell her. "So, based on what I see here, I'm not surprised it wasn't this guy who knocked on your door. This is actually a pretty thorough report. Halpern took the time to interview people at the scene, to record contextual details about what happened leading up to the moment they took your brother in. If he was just doing the bare minimum, he wouldn't have done those things."

"Huh," Maple said. "That's an interesting point."

And it was one that hadn't occurred to her.

Kenny looked thoughtful. "I'll be right back. I want to check something."

As Kenny walked out into the hall, Maple perused the remaining reports, which yielded no new information. They were cursory summaries of the places Jamie had been arrested, what he had been charged with, and who had been with him at the time. Despite her brother's many encounters with police involving excessive drinking, fighting, and the occasional act of vandalism, he had only served one stint in jail that lasted longer than a night; five years ago, he had cooled his heels behind bars for a month. Maple remembered how difficult that had been on her mother.

She flipped back to the first report and gazed at it again. She found herself wondering about the man who'd been in the fight with Jamie just before the police arrived. Who was he? Had Jamie known him prior to that night? What had they fought about? She scanned the names of the witnesses Robert Halpern had interviewed, committing them to memory and committing herself to tracking them down.

She looked up at the sound of someone entering the office. Kenny wore a triumphant smile and waved a small piece of notepaper in the air.

"Bob Halpern's still on the force. He's a sergeant now in a different precinct and we're meeting him tomorrow morning."

Before Maple could react, Detective Francis appeared behind Kenny. He rubbed his hands together. "Let's go find Laurie Perkins, shall we?"

Chapter 15

Jack and Annabel Hastings's last known address was in a row house in South Boston. From the station, the street was in the opposite direction—away from the docks—from the area where Maple had grown up. A headache had settled in around her temples after she read Jamie's file, and as the detective drove them through the familiar streets, she was relieved to be thinking about someone else's family troubles for a while.

One glance at Kenny, though, and she felt immediately guilty; the stress of trying to find his friend's mother so he could notify her of Daniel's death made him drawn and haggard. The revelation of Daniel's mob ties—and the very real possibility that was what had gotten him killed—had aged her young friend. Maple made a silent vow to finish the nutshells as soon as possible so that they might offer some insight or clue that could give them some answers.

"Have either of you ever made a death notification?" Francis asked.

"I've only ever been on the receiving end," Maple said before she could think better of it.

She felt the detective's gaze slide to her in the rearview mirror.

"I've accompanied the sheriff on a few," Kenny said.

"OK, well, assuming we find her, I can take the lead if you like," Francis offered. "Unfortunately, I've had to do this a number of times."

"No, sir," Kenny said. "Thank you, but I'd like to be the one to do it."

His jaw was set and his eyes fixed straight ahead.

"I respect that," Francis said. "One suggestion? Let's try to get a little information from her first if we can. Once we hit her with the fact that her son's dead, that will likely—and understandably—render her less useful when it comes to telling us any background or context we might want to know."

Kenny nodded. "You can do that part."

Detective Francis nodded. Then, he slowed down and squinted at the front of a few houses. "There it is! Number 148," he finally said, pointing to a nondescript building in the middle of a row of houses.

Maple took in the peeling paint and scraggly shrubs. "It's more modest than I was expecting for a mobster."

"Neighborhood is important to these guys, even the ones who make it big." Francis pulled to the curb and parked the car. "They tend to be very loyal to the place where they grew up."

"Did Hastings make it big?" Kenny asked.

"Nah. He was midlevel at best. And as far as I know, the mob doesn't offer pensions for widows, so I doubt Annabel had much choice except to stay put here, anyway."

All three of them climbed out of the car. Maple hadn't seen a single person, but that could partially be attributed to the weather, which was biting cold. Still, it was eerie to see an urban neighborhood looking so empty. Growing up, there had always been people out and about in her own neighborhood. She pulled her coat tighter around herself and shoved her hands in the pockets.

"We'll follow your lead," Kenny said, falling into step with Maple behind Detective Francis.

The Boston officer nodded and headed up the path. "Watch your step; it's a little icy."

They made it to the front door and Francis knocked three times. A full minute stretched on with no response, but then Maple heard a shuffling sound on the other side of the door.

"Mrs. Hastings, I can hear you in there. It's the police. Open up."

There was a pause, and then a woman's voice, heavy with suspicion, replied, "How do I know you're a cop?"

Francis furrowed his brow. "Sounds like she *wants* me to be a cop. Unusual for this neighborhood," he muttered as he held his badge up. "You can see my badge if you look out your window, ma'am."

The curtain in the window next to the door twitched. Francis positioned his badge so whoever was behind it had a better view. After a pause, the front door opened cautiously, and a woman's head emerged. She had wavy red hair that was fading into gray and wore a wary expression.

"Shouldn't you be over in Roxbury?"

From behind him, Maple saw Francis's shoulders tense ever so slightly. Maple knew that Roxbury was a neighborhood with a high concentration of dark-skinned residents. When he spoke, though, his voice remained even. "This is my precinct, ma'am. I'm Detective David Francis. Are you Mrs. Hastings?"

"Francis," she said. "I've heard that name before."

"May we come in, ma'am? We're looking for a friend of yours. We think she might be in danger."

Her eyes lit with recognition as she eyed the detective. "You arrested Jack once! He talked about you! 'Annie,' he said, 'you'll never believe who arrested me last night: a Black cop!'"

There was awe and a little bit of surprise in her voice. Maple's stomach squirmed as the woman stared in open fascination at the detective.

"He said you were a real class act, not like some of the bums they've got patrolling the streets now."

"Happy to be of service." Francis's voice was tinged with amusement, but Maple detected a weary undertone.

"I suppose you better come in." Annabel Hastings closed the door for a moment, and they heard her sliding the chain out of the locked position. Then, she opened it wider and stepped aside, allowing her three visitors to come into a small entryway with faded linoleum and wallpaper that was beginning to peel at the edges. A strong smell of cigarette smoke permeated the air, and Maple wrinkled her nose.

Detective Francis introduced Maple and Kenny as his associates. Annabel shook their hands but didn't extend the same courtesy to Detective Francis. She seemed intrigued by him, but at the same time was clearly keeping several feet of distance between him and herself.

Francis carried on as if he didn't notice. "Ma'am, we're looking for a friend of yours. Laurie Perkins. It's very important that we speak with her. Have you seen her?"

Annabel eyed him cagily. "Maybe I have. Maybe I haven't."

"I assure you that she's in no trouble with the law, but we are afraid she might be in danger, and we'd like to help. We have important information for her."

A door down the hall creaked open. Both Detective Francis and Kenny tensed, but then they all recognized Laurie Perkins as she walked haltingly toward them.

"Laur—" Annabel started in a warning tone.

"It's OK, Annie." Though her gait was wobbly, Laurie Perkins's voice was clear and strong as she interrupted her friend. "I'm tired of hiding. I want to hear what they have to say."

She came to a stop next to her friend, who put an arm around her shoulder. Mrs. Perkins began to rub her left elbow with her right hand repetitively.

"Mrs. Perkins, I'm Detective Francis with the Boston PD. This is Officer Quirk and his associate, Mrs. Bishop, from Ver—"

"Kenny!" The woman stopped rubbing her elbow and gaped; it was as though she'd seen a ghost.

"Yes, it's me, Mrs. Perkins."

She glanced at Annabel and explained, "Kenny was friends with my Daniel when they were kids." She looked back at Kenny, fear in her eyes. "Something's happened to him."

Maple noticed that she phrased it as a statement and not a question. She recognized the other woman's sense of sudden, horrible certainty; she herself had felt it a moment before the officer had informed her of Jamie's death.

"Mrs. Perkins, when did you last see your son?" Detective Francis asked.

"No," she said softly, appearing not to have heard the question. "No, no, no."

Kenny glanced at Francis, silently seeking his permission to move ahead with the notification, and the detective gave him a small nod. It was clear they wouldn't be getting any useful information from her now that she'd clocked the purpose of their visit. Kenny looked down at his feet and took a deep breath.

"Mrs. Perkins, I'm very sorry to have to tell you this, but there was a fire. Daniel's body was found in his uncle's cabin on January 6th."

Annabel pulled her friend in closer and put her other hand on Laurie's forearm, steadying her just as Laurie's knees began to buckle. A moan unlike any sound Maple had ever heard came from Laurie. Had it not been for Annabel's arms around her, the woman would have melted onto the floor like a puddle. Maple found herself thinking of the officer and the chaplain who had come to her door to tell her Bill had been killed. No one had been there in that moment to keep Maple upright.

A wave of nausea hit her as she watched Laurie react to the news of her son's death, and she swayed a little. As Kenny stepped forward toward Mrs. Perkins, Maple felt a steadying hand on her own shoulder and shot a glance at Detective Francis, who smiled sympathetically at her. She was embarrassed that he had seen her moment of weakness but grateful for his support. She took a deep breath, steadied herself, and focused on the scene in front of her rather than on her memories. He removed his hand from her shoulder but stayed next to her.

Kenny explained to Laurie what they knew about the circumstances of Daniel's death. Her eyes shining with tears, she shook her head rapidly from side to side and then clapped her hands over her ears. The gesture was childlike, reminding Maple of how Charlotte's twins used to sometimes behave when their mother disciplined them.

Laurie was clearly devastated by the news of her son's death. Maple observed that the woman did not, however, seem surprised.

"Is there a chair where she could sit down?" Detective Francis asked.

Annabel nodded and gestured with her chin toward the kitchen. Eager to have something to do, Maple grabbed a kitchen chair and brought it back to the entryway. She placed it behind Mrs. Perkins. Annabel guided her friend into the seat, continuing to hold her and as she crouched next to her. Kenny stood there, as white as a ghost.

"Mrs. Perkins," Detective Francis asked in a gentle voice, "is there anyone else you'd like for us to contact?"

She looked up at him with a tear-stained face and took a deep, shuddering breath.

"Does his uncle know?"

"Yes, ma'am," said Kenny.

"Then, no. There's no one else."

Kenny crouched on the other side of the chair so that he and Annabel flanked her like living gargoyles. "Mrs. Perkins, I'm sorry, but we still need some information from you. I hate to do it, but we're trying to get to the bottom of what happened, and—"

"Oh, I can tell you what happened," she interrupted, wiping a hand across her nose. "Leo Matthews, that's what happened."

"Laurie, stop. Think about what you're saying," Annabel pleaded. "You know what he's capable of."

Laurie Perkins resumed rubbing her elbow, but even faster. She didn't make eye contact with Annabel, and when she spoke, her voice was shrill.

"I don't care anymore, Annie. What've I got left to lose? Huh? What?"

"Was it Matthews who visited you in the hospital?" Francis asked.

Maple had the sense he was speaking quickly before Annabel could protest further; he didn't want to risk her persuading Laurie to clam up.

"Yes, it was."

She jutted her chin. There was a note of defiance in her voice, as though she were daring her friend to challenge her decision to speak to the cops. Annabel shook her head and muttered something under her breath. Maple thought it sounded like she might have said, *It was nice knowing you.* A chill shot down Maple's spine.

"Can you tell us what he said?" Francis asked.

"He said Danny was helping him with a job. I told him no way; Danny was out of the life. He laughed. He said it was too late, that Danny'd never be 'out of the life.' He made little air quotes with his fingers when he said that part, like he was making fun of me." Her expression darkened. "Then, he said he'd told Danny that if he didn't help him, *I'd* pay the price."

Her eyes pooled with tears again. "And then he stood there, chewing his cinnamon gum like he always does and just smiled at me—this slow, creepy smile."

"Any idea what job he needed help with?"

Laurie threw her hands up. "How should I know? Matthews cut Annie and me out a long time ago. You know, in our husbands' line of work, there's a code: family first. You're supposed to live and die by it." Laurie gestured from herself to Annabel and back again. "Jack and Thad did. But Matthews? Nah. He's always been out for himself. The code means nothing to him. It's despicable."

"What do you mean by 'family first?'" Maple asked, though she thought she had an idea.

"The gang's your family. You take care of each other. Look out for one another. You don't snitch, and you never leave a man behind. And if a guy gets killed, you look out for his family." Her voice wobbled and she held up a hand, indicating she needed a moment.

Annabel rubbed Laurie's back as her friend sank her head into her lap and cried. "Leo was at the robbery when Thad and Jack got killed," she said in a low voice. "He was the getaway driver. He took off when he saw the cops. Left our men in the dust. They died like dogs in the street while he went on to become the new head honcho. And if you think he took care of us widows afterwards, well . . ." She let out an ironic, humorless laugh.

So much for honor among thieves, Maple thought.

"If he's the head honcho, why's he doing his own dirty work? Wouldn't he send a lower-level guy to do stuff like visit people in public places to threaten them?" Francis asked.

Annabel and Laurie let out simultaneous, ironic laughs.

"You clearly don't know Leo Matthews." Annabel crossed her arms over her chest but didn't elaborate.

Francis frowned but didn't press the point. "And you decided to leave the hospital after that?"

Laurie picked up her head. "You're darn right I did. I was a sitting duck there, and, anyway, those doctors treated me like I'm crazy." Her expression darkened. "I'm not."

Her gaze flashed to each of their faces in succession. It was clearly important to her that they know this.

"Mrs. Perkins, when was the last time you spoke with or saw Dan?" Kenny asked, returning to Detective Francis's question from earlier.

She looked down at her hands, which she began rubbing together in a twisting, circular motion.

"It's been a while," she whispered. "Months. July, maybe? My Danny, he . . . needed some space." Then she looked up, a pleading expression on her face. "He's a good boy. It's not his fault. It's me. I can be . . ." she looked up at Annabel, searching for the words. She finally settled on, "I can be difficult."

"So," Detective Francis mused, "why do you think Matthews bothered to come see you in person to threaten your son—and you—when you hadn't been in regular touch with him?"

Laurie's hands stopped moving. She looked Francis in the eye with the steadiest, surest gaze they had seen from her yet. When she spoke, her voice was deadly calm and clear.

"Because he's a sadistic monster."

Chapter 16

After watching Detective Francis offer Mrs. Perkins police protection—which she promptly refused—the three of them thanked the two women for their help and walked back to the car. As cold as it was, Maple was relieved to be back out in the fresh air; the stale cigarette smoke inside the house had been almost more than she could stand. She breathed in, reveling in how the cold pierced her lungs. She thought of Daniel Perkins and all the smoke in his lungs. What must his last breaths have felt like?

"That's it, then." Kenny slapped his palms onto his knees as soon as the three of them were back in the detective's car.

"What's what, when?" Francis arched an eyebrow.

"The mob killed Dan because he refused to help with the job." He said it as though it were the most obvious thing in the world. "We need to find Leo Matthews and arrest him."

Maple's heart sank. Kenny was so desperate to cling to a positive view of his friend that he was twisting the facts of the case to fit his own preconceived notions. He'd done it with the drug test and now he was doing it again. She sensed, rather than saw, that Detective Francis's misgivings more or less matched her own.

"We don't know what the job was," Maple pointed out, "let alone whether Daniel accepted or not."

"We don't have any evidence he killed Daniel," Francis added. "All we have is the word of a witness who I'd describe as shaky, at best."

"A very reliable eyewitness can put Matthews at the scene of the crime in Elderberry!" Kenny's tone was frustrated.

"What crime?" Francis countered. "I repeat, we have no evidence there even was a crime."

Kenny exhaled loudly. "Fine. Let me rephrase. A very reliable eyewitness can put Matthews at the scene of the *fire*."

"Technically," Maple said, "the eyewitness saw a man who was only using one arm at the cabin on the day of the fire, and keep in mind she was halfway up a mountain at the time."

"Oh, come on." Kenny threw his hands up. "Are you going to tell me there's coincidentally *another* man with one arm involved here? It was Matthews. It had to be."

"I'm not telling you anything of the sort," Maple said. "I'm just using precise, accurate language and giving Detective Francis context. Leo Matthews is an angle worth investigating, but, Kenny, you've got to keep an open mind."

"I agree," Francis said. "It *is* worth talking to him, and you *do* need to keep an open mind."

"Well, then, let's go. What are we waiting for? We know his address."

"Not so fast," the detective said as he started the engine. "We're going back to the precinct first."

"Why?" Kenny's voice brimmed with frustration.

"Because, Officer Quirk, you don't just roll up at the house of a mob boss. I want to talk to the guys on the mob task force and get the latest on Matthews. We're going to assess the situation and decide on our approach."

He pulled away from the curb and swung the car in the direction of the precinct. From the backseat, Maple could practically see the annoyance emanating from Kenny's body. She remembered the sheriff's misgivings about allowing his nephew to continue investigating the case and wondered whether he would come to regret his decision to send Kenny to Boston.

She changed the subject. "Detective, do you suppose there's any chance those lab tests are done?"

"I doubt it, but we can certainly check in when we're there. Gus said it'd take two days."

Maple half-expected Kenny to offer petulant insistence that the toxicology tests would come back negative, but her friend remained silent—all three of them did, in fact, for the remainder of the drive.

When they arrived back at the precinct, their first hint that something was amiss came when they tried to park but found dozens of sleek, black cars filling the precinct's lot. Francis swore under his breath and swung his vehicle around, looking for a spot on the street. He finally found one several blocks away and parallel parked. Maple and Kenny exchanged a glance as they got out of the car and began to follow the detective on foot back to the building. He moved at such a quick pace that Maple and Kenny practically had to jog to keep up.

By the time they arrived at the entrance, Maple's heart was beating fast from both exertion and anticipation. As they walked inside, they were greeted by a level of pandemonium that made yesterday's frenetic chaos look downright calm. In addition to the police officers and secretaries rushing around, today there were dozens of stone-faced men in black suits as well. The secretary who was working the front reception desk appeared on the verge of tears. All the uniformed Boston cops looked as though thunderclouds had settled over their faces; they strode around the lobby with stiff gaits and tense shoulders.

"I guess the FBI has arrived," Kenny said.

"Indeed they have." Maple watched as Detective Francis disappeared into the fray.

They pressed themselves against a wall and watched the activity unfolding before them with fascination.

"I'm sure Harry Needles is around here somewhere," Kenny said.

Maple wrinkled her nose. "Wonderful. Just who I was hoping to see twice in one day."

Several minutes passed before Kenny asked, "Do you think Detective Francis forgot about us?"

Maple considered this. "No. I think he's triaging."

"Triaging?" Kenny cocked an eyebrow. "What does that mean?"

"Prioritizing," Maple said. "It's a medical term used in wartime to sort wounded soldiers into categories based on who they have a possibility of saving." She sighed, thinking of her husband but then smiled. "Bill and I were terrible gardeners. We tried, but somehow a third of whatever we planted never seemed to make it. He used to joke about triaging our plants. We'd walk around the backyard together, and he'd point at them and classify them as minimally wounded, seriously wounded, or mortally wounded."

One side of Kenny's mouth lifted in a half-smile at her reminiscence.

Five minutes later, Francis reappeared and came over to them. "I'm sorry, but I need to focus on this for now." He gestured vaguely to the activity behind him. "I'll look into the Leo Matthews angle and get back to you later today. In the meantime, do not, under any circumstances, seek him out on your own."

He locked eyes with Kenny and held his gaze for several long seconds.

"Understood," Kenny finally replied. "We've got a few other things to do this afternoon."

Detective Francis hurriedly shook both of their hands. Maple found herself thinking about how Annabel Hastings had avoided making physical contact with Detective Francis. As he hurried away and disappeared down a hallway amid a sea of overwhelmingly white faces, she wondered how often things like that happened to him. With a sinking feeling, she acknowledged to herself that it was probably a lot.

After fighting their way through the crowd down to the lab only to learn from Gus that the samples were not ready yet, Maple and Kenny made their way out to the parking lot. A stray cat streaked by. Maple recognized its posture—low to the ground and tail standing straight up—as the same one Mack adopted when hunting; this fellow was probably hot on the trail of some unfortunate mouse. She wondered how Ben was doing and hoped (at the very least) that Mack hadn't bitten him again.

Back in their car, Maple and Kenny discussed what their next move should be.

"I know our appointment with him isn't until tomorrow morning," Kenny said, "But I say we go visit Sargeant Halpern. See what we can dig up about Jamie."

Maple's gut twisted as she thought about the cop who had known her brother. Then, though, another thought occurred to her.

"Wait a minute. Why are you so agreeable to the idea of just pausing the fire investigation?"

"What do you mean?" Kenny spread his hands, palms up, and shrugged. "Detective Francis is our host. Why would I disobey him?"

She arched an eyebrow. "Half an hour ago, you were ready to roll up to Leo Matthews's house, guns blazing, and confront him."

"Detective Francis told us to wait."

Kenny was saying all the right things, but there was a glint in his eye that made Maple nervous.

"Kenny, this isn't like when you and I investigated Elijah Wallace's death behind your uncle's back. We're in a whole different league now. You know that, right?"

"Why are you so worried about this?"

"That was an evasive maneuver, not an answer."

They stared at each other for several long seconds. Maple broke eye contact first. She started the car's engine.

"You know how to get there?" she asked.

"I sure do. A nice secretary was happy to oblige me with directions."

He pulled a piece of folded paper out of his pocket and read off the first few steps in the process of getting themselves to Sergeant Halpern. Maple followed the steps, but she did so with uneasiness forming deep in her gut. She wasn't sure what was contributing more to this feeling: the fact that they were possibly getting closer to the truth about her brother, or the fact that Kenny was almost certainly hiding his true intentions from her.

For now, though, she just drove.

Chapter 17

Along the way, Maple and Kenny stopped at a diner for a quick lunch. Maple thought of Charlotte as she chewed her rubbery grilled cheese sandwich; Hank's cooking was far superior to this. She choked down the entire first half just to get a little nourishment into her body but couldn't bring herself to eat the second piece. She felt a pang of homesickness.

Interesting.

She had been desperate to leave Boston, where her brains and ambition had made her an oddity in the neighborhood where she'd grown up, but ever since she and Bill had moved to Elderberry, she had struggled to think of the little town as "home." She'd always felt like an outsider, never fitting into the gossipy sewing circles other ladies belonged to, but also never being able to land a job as a lawyer. Until the events around Elijah Wallace's death, she'd lived a kind of half-life in Elderberry, connected to the town because of her husband's job, but never feeling like part of the fabric of the community. Bill's death had left her unmoored.

Now, with her flourishing dollhouse business, her consultant position with the sheriff, and a growing circle of people she called her friends, was she beginning to find her own way in small-town life after all?

"Hello?" Kenny, looking bemused, was waving a hand in her face. She shook her head to clear it; how long he'd been trying to get her attention?

"What?"

"I asked if you're going to eat that." He pointed at the untouched half of her sandwich. She noticed his own plate was empty; he must've inhaled his burger.

"Oh. No. Help yourself." She waved at her plate.

Kenny grabbed the sandwich and devoured it in two bites. Maple marveled at his appetite and his ability to quickly quench it. She also reflected that, ever since they'd left Annabel Hastings's house, he'd been much, much quieter than usual.

She wondered, again, what he was keeping from her.

"Ready?" he asked, wiping his mouth with the back of his hand.

She nodded. They paid the bill and continued on their way.

The precinct where Sergeant Halpern worked was much smaller than the one they'd left that morning and—as far as Maple could tell—there were no FBI agents swarming around. There were only a few police vehicles parked in the lot, which was tucked into a relatively quiet corner of the neighborhood.

A smiling receptionist greeted them as they entered. Behind her was an open area where a few officers spoke on phones or flipped through files. Overall, the atmosphere smacked of the routine of an ordinary day, yet Maple's heart was in her throat. Kenny swiftly made introductions and explained that they had an appointment for the following morning but had found themselves in the area with some time to kill and wondered whether Sergeant Halpern might have a few minutes to spare.

She said she would check and disappeared around a corner. Moments later, she popped her head back around the corner and beckoned them to follow her. A moment after that, Maple found herself shaking the hand of the man who had arrested her brother on the last night of his life while Kenny made introductions again.

Robert Halpern was a cheerful, beefy man. His ruddy cheeks and short, reddish hair hinted at some Irish heritage; he had a professional air, but she also detected a certain boyish charm. As she released his hand, Maple noticed his fingernails were cut short and neat, and the backs of his hands were peppered with freckles.

"What can I help you folks with today?" He gave them a polite but quizzical look.

"Well," Kenny started, "we're here from Vermont investigating a case with ties to the area, and we—"

"It's my brother," Maple said.

Kenny's exasperation was written all over his face, but she ignored him. She knew what he'd been about to do: imply that they'd stumbled upon Jamie's case in connection to Daniel's. She couldn't let him do it. She was angry with herself for failing to speak up earlier.

This time, though, she was ready.

"James Cooper. You arrested him on—"

She stopped when a wistful expression came over the Sergeant's face. She'd been prepared for a lot of different reactions—anger, irritation, defensiveness, even the possibility that Halpern had no memory of Jamie at all—but she hadn't expected this.

"You remember him?"

"I do," Halpern said. "I like to think I knew Jamie pretty well. And, first, I'd like to say how sorry I am for your loss."

His words, and the kindness with which he spoke them, rendered her momentarily speechless. She'd spent the years since Jamie's death imagining that he'd been treated with callous disregard; Halpern's demeanor turned that notion on its head.

Kenny jumped in. "How did you know him?"

Halpern sat back in his chair with a laugh. "I arrested him many times. I used to work the beat down by the docks back when I was on foot patrol. Jamie had a penchant for drinking too much and getting rowdy, so he and I crossed paths often."

"I'm sorry," Maple whispered, tears pricking at the backs of her eyelids.

"There's nothing to be sorry for, ma'am. Your brother might've gotten himself into trouble, but he was a nice kid. Never mean or malicious. We had some good conversations, he and I, on our way to lockup." He shook his head and smiled. "It's strange, I know, but I almost considered him a friend. When he did his stint, I'd go visit him every so often. He didn't hold it against me that I arrested him, and I didn't hold it against him that he'd broken the law." He leaned forward, suddenly serious. "Don't get me wrong, he deserved the consequences he got: 'do the crime, do the time' and all of that."

The lump in Maple's throat grew, so she simply nodded.

"We understand," Kenny said. "Can you tell us anything more about the night he died? Your report was very thorough, but are there any more details you could share? Maple's always wondered about it."

Halpern leaned back again. "Now, that was a damn shame, the way he died. I was the one who found him dead. I was distraught and going off shift, so my sergeant sent another officer to do the notification." He locked eyes with Maple. "I've always regretted that I didn't insist on doing it myself. I want you to know that."

Something inside Maple's chest unmoored itself and went crashing into the pit of her stomach.

Halpern sighed. "Let me back up. The Black Sheep was a notorious source of trouble, and it was part of my normal beat. I'd check in there at least twice during an average shift. I got to the bar that night and found the aftermath of the fight. Jamie was already out cold. No one would tell me who he'd been fighting with, but I had a good idea who it was: Noah O'Hare."

Kenny flipped open a notepad and began scribbling furiously.

"Now, Jamie and Noah were great friends, normally; it was strange to find one without the other. The fact that"—here, he held up one finger—"all the regulars were acting extra squirrelly when I questioned them and"—here, he held up a second finger—"that Noah wasn't there when I arrived put the idea in my head that maybe the two of them had gotten into an argument and Noah'd fled the scene."

"Were you ever able to track him down?"

Halpern shook his head. "I never saw him again. For several months afterwards, I kept my eye out for him around the docks, the Black Sheep, all his regular haunts. He quit showing up for work—never resigned, mind you, just stopped coming. I went to the house where he'd lived with his mother and sister. No sign of him. They claimed they didn't know where he was. It's like he vanished after that night."

"Did you think that was strange?" Kenny asked.

"Sure did. But soon after that, I got transferred off that beat. Noah's family never reported him missing. It made me think he'd done a runner. Maybe when he realized his buddy was dead, he was afraid he'd get charged with manslaughter, so he took off."

Kenny asked a few more follow-up questions about known associates.

Finally, Maple spoke up. "After you put him in the cell, did anyone check on him?"

"I did," Halpern said. "Several times. The last time I checked—well, the second to last, I guess, but the last time I saw him alive—he was moaning a little bit and mumbling. I figured he was starting to come out of it." He cleared his throat. "I've gone over that night in my head so many times, wondering if I should've done anything differently. But the truth is, I'd brought him in many times in a similar state, and he'd always come out of it. I had no reason to think this time was any different."

Maple looked into his eyes and believed him. She felt strangely deflated.

They all rose to their feet. Halpern shook Kenny's hand and then Maple's.

"My prediction, for what it's worth?" Halpern said, maintaining eye contact with Maple. "If he'd lived, he'd have straightened himself out. He was a good kid, underneath it all."

"Thank you," Maple said numbly.

Chapter 18

A light snow was falling as they made their way back to the car. "I'll drive." Kenny beckoned for Maple to hand him the keys, which she did. "First snow of the season."

He used the arm of his coat to brush the dusting of snow off their windshield. Maple slid into the passenger seat, her mind spinning with everything she'd just learned. She shivered and pulled her coat tighter around herself.

Kenny hopped into the driver's seat and started the engine. He rubbed his hands together to warm them.

"Why don't you have gloves?" Maple asked.

Kenny gave her a look. "That's what you're worried about right now?"

Maple looked at her own hands, which were clenched in her lap, the embroidered maple leaves on the cuffs just visible as they peeked out from beneath her coat's sleeves. Bill had given her these gloves before he left for war. Suddenly, she missed her husband so much it hurt. Bill had known—and loved—her brother. He had comforted her after Jamie's death. How she wished he were here with her now to help her process what she'd just learned.

"Hey." Kenny's voice was soft. "You all right? That was a lot to take in."

"Yes," she answered automatically.

"Yes you're all right, or yes that was a lot?"

"Both."

He reversed the car out of the spot and edged out onto the street. "What now?"

Maple tried to think this through, but her normally sharp mind felt like it was filled with sticky mud.

Kenny cleared his throat. "Can I make a suggestion?"

Maple looked at him and nodded. She welcomed a suggestion; she needed something to cling to, something to show her which way was up.

"I think you need to work with your hands—do something useful to clear your mind." He jerked his thumb toward the backseat. "Those cabins aren't going to build themselves. I scoped out the boardinghouse yesterday and there's a big basement you can set up in. It's well-insulated, so you can hammer away down there and not bother the other boarders."

He glanced at her, presumably to gauge her reaction, and then moved his eyes back to the road. Maple thought this over and realized Kenny knew her well. While Bill was away and especially after his death, she'd thrown herself into a near-frenzy of dollhouse-making to cope. She believed that building those houses—along with visits from Charlotte—had kept her sane and helped her work through her grief. She was touched that Kenny had already thought to check on the basement situation.

"All right."

"I don't get a sense that there's a whole lot of traffic down there, though. Fair warning: you might have to swipe a few cobwebs out of your way." He paused, looking thoughtful. "That could work in your favor, though; at least that chatty lady probably won't follow you down there."

That brought a small smile to Maple's face. "True."

When they got back to the boarding house, the snow was coming down harder. It blanketed the city, softening Boston's sharp edges. Kenny helped Maple carry the supplies for the nutshells down to the basement, the stairs creaking and groaning under their weight. Next to the staircase, a haphazard stack of boxes threatened to tumble over at any moment.

Kenny hadn't been kidding about the cobwebs, which they brushed aside to create a path for themselves to a roughly constructed wooden table. Above it, a single bare lightbulb hung from a string, offering plenty of (albeit harsh) light for Maple to work by.

She placed the box she was carrying down on the table and turned to Kenny. "It's perfect."

He nodded once, a look of satisfaction on his face, put down his own box, and jogged up the steps again. Maple followed, and after one more trip, all of her supplies were laid out on the table. Her heart already felt lighter at the prospect of the period of work ahead.

"Do you want company or solitude right now?" Kenny asked.

"Solitude," she said, and he turned to go. "Kenny—thank you. I'll see you at dinner."

He waved over his shoulder as he jogged up the stairs once again. Maple thought of something and called after him.

"Don't go looking for any trouble while I'm down here!"

He paused midjog and glanced over his shoulder. "Maple, you and I don't need to go looking for trouble. Trouble always seems to find us."

He wasn't wrong, but for the second time that day, he had avoided giving Maple a straight answer. He probably wouldn't go anywhere in this snow, and, anyway, he didn't know his way around here like she did. Kenny was a little bit of a country bumpkin who was out of his depth in the big city.

She sighed and got to work. First, she unpacked the supplies she'd carefully organized in the boxes and laid out the bases and materials for the three cabins. Cabin #1 had two walls already completed, so her first task was to finish constructing the last two walls. After that, she would move on to the walls for the other cabins.

While she measured, sawed, and sanded the segments of wood taken from the real cabin, she let her normally orderly mind drift from one topic to the next, interspersing Jamie's case with Daniel's. Images of Daniel Perkins's dead body, Kenny's and Peter's backs as they watched the sun rise, and the view from Eliza Patterson's cabin flickered through her brain, interspersed with memories of the stark hospital where they had tried to find Laurie Perkins, the look on Annabel Hastings's face as she gawked at Detective Francis, and the regret in Sergeant Halpern's eyes.

Rather than try to impose any type of order onto her thinking, Maple focused her attention on the tasks she was doing with her hands: measure, saw, hammer. She allowed the seemingly random images and memories to flicker through her mind, noticing them, but not wondering too much what they meant or why they were showing up in the order they did. It was freeing. She noticed her shoulders begin to relax. Her breathing evened out and deepened.

As the cabins started to take shape, so did her thought process. From flickering images, her mind moved to questions.

Presuming Halpern was correct in his assumption, why had Noah fled the pub before Halpern had arrived on that fateful night? Did he have any answers about what had led to her brother's death? Why had Leo Matthews—the big boss himself—taken the time to go visit Laurie at the hospital, and what was the job he wanted Daniel's help with? How had the fire at the cabin started?

As she began crafting the furniture for the first cabin, Maple considered the parallels between her brother and Daniel Perkins. Both had been, by most accounts, good people who had strayed down dangerous paths. Both had died young and suddenly. Both had people who loved them and were torn apart by their loss.

She was so absorbed in her work and her ruminations that she didn't hear Kenny open the creaky door or come down the stairs. She jumped when he clapped a hand on her shoulder. With a bemused smile, he said, "Dinner time."

"Oh." She dropped the chair she'd been sanding for cabin #3. "Thanks for coming to get me."

"Well, Charlotte's not here and someone has to make sure you eat." He looked over her work. "Wow, you made a lot of progress."

It was always hard for Maple to reacclimate to social interactions after being deeply alone with her thoughts and her work for a period of time. The transition was jarring. She blinked at Kenny.

"Yes. Thanks. I did."

Now that he'd pulled her back into the real world, she became aware of how hungry she was. Dinner sounded not only necessary, but good. Maple's mouth watered as she recalled the meatloaf and mashed potatoes from the previous night. She righted the little chair and put down her sandpaper, and then she followed Kenny up the stairs.

On the way to the dining room, he filled her in on the phone call he'd had with the sheriff back in Elderberry.

"It's been quiet there, I guess. No new crimes or disturbances since we left. The only person in a cell right now is Willy, and that's because he put himself in there to sleep it off again."

They reached the top of the stairs, and he shot her a furtive look. "Sheriff says he saw Ben, and he said to tell you Mack's doing just fine."

Maple suddenly missed both Ben and Mack very much. "That's good to hear. You never know with cats. I was a little nervous Mack would try to scratch Ben or bite him."

"Well, from what I've seen, it'd take more than that to scare off Ben."

Part of Maple wanted to ask Kenny what he meant by this, and another part wanted to move on and pretend he hadn't said anything. The latter prevailed. They stepped into the dining room, and Maple rubbed her hands together in delight when she saw the spread on the table.

"Pork chops! Yum!"

The platters in the center of the table were also laden with rice, applesauce, and green beans. Maple and Kenny appeared to be the first guests to enter the dining room; all the seats were empty. A woman in an apron stood at the sideboard, her back to them, and said over her shoulder, "And save some room; I made apple pie for dessert!" She turned around holding an oversized silver lid in each hand, and Maple swallowed a groan. It was

Miranda, the woman who had been so interested in her dolls the night before.

"Oh, hello, Maple!" Her eyes lit up. "And—it's Kenny, isn't it?"

"Yes, ma'am." Kenny sat down in the closest chair and rubbed his hands together with relish.

"Please, tuck in!" She placed the lids next to the platters and then gestured to the food.

"You don't have to tell me twice." Kenny happily started heaping hearty servings of everything onto his plate before Maple had even taken her seat. "My mother says I have a hollow leg."

"You work here?" Maple said, sitting next to Kenny and waiting for her turn with the serving spoons.

"Yes, I own this rooming house." Miranda smiled. "I was hoping to tell you that and a few other things last night, but you rushed out in such a hurry."

Heat rose in Maple's cheeks. "Yes, well, duty called."

"Ah, well, not to worry; we're all here now, aren't we?"

After Maple had served herself, Miranda placed the silver lids over the platters to keep everything warm and took a seat across the table from them. Kenny began to shovel food into his mouth at an impressive and almost alarming pace.

Maple, whose appetite had suddenly diminished, put her fork down. "What else did you want to tell me?"

Miranda sat back in her chair. "I was very impressed with your dolls. Not to boast, but I have quite an eye for quality craftsmanship, and yours is top notch."

Kenny gave her a playful punch on the shoulder.

Maple glared at him. "I'm not your baseball teammate. I didn't just hit a home run to win the game in the bottom of the ninth. You don't have to give me an *atta-boy*."

He shrugged. "Sorry," he said through a mouth full of pork chops.

Maple rolled her eyes and turned her attention back to Miranda, who was watching the interaction with a bemused smile.

"Anyway," their host said, "in addition to running this rooming house, I organize craft fairs twice a year—December and June. We just had the last one a few weeks ago. For a whole week, I close the rooming house to the public and the couple who own the place across the street do, too. I invite talented crafters from across New England to stay either here or over there, and we spend the week creating art together, and then it culminates with a big sale that's open to the public."

"Oh," Maple said, unsure what to make of this.

"It's all women artists, and it's invitation only. We support each other, teach each other, and learn from each other—and we usually turn a pretty tidy profit at the sale, too! I keep it limited to people who are at the top of their game in their specialty, and I'd like to invite you to join us at the next one in June."

"Oh," Maple said. "Wow. Thank you."

She had to recalibrate her thought process from death investigations to plain old dollhouses, and her brain seemed to have a sticky gear. The houses she and Ken Sr. created for eager children seemed miles away from the nutshells that were currently occupying her.

"Think about it," Miranda said, rising to greet three more guests who had just entered from the hallway. "Let me know."

Kenny looked at Maple, eyebrows raised. "I didn't know you were a baseball fan."

"What?" Her mind was on miniatures.

He gestured vaguely. "Before. When I went like this—" he mimed the shoulder punch "—and you made the baseball analogy."

"Oh," Maple said. "Well, I am. I grew up in the shadow of Fenway Park playing stickball with Jamie and the other neighborhood kids."

He raised his hand as though to slug her on the shoulder again.

"Don't even think about it," she said, rolling her eyes.

She pushed back her chair, pulled the napkin off her lap, and tossed it onto her half-finished dinner plate. She thanked Miranda for a lovely meal and headed into the hallway. If she went right back down to the basement, she might be able to finish all the furniture before turning in for the night.

Kenny followed right on her heels. "I'm going to call you 'Slugger' from now on!"

She stopped and turned so quickly that he crashed into her.

"No, you're not," she said as he straightened up.

The twinkle in his eyes lifted her heart, and her mouth twitched into a smile. They'd had so much despair baked into their day that this moment felt all the more special—and necessary. A person could only handle so much gloom and doom at a time.

"You like it." He pointed at her, grinning.

"No, I don't." But she couldn't help herself; a giggle escaped, and she clamped a hand over her mouth as she opened the basement door with her other hand. "You're ridiculous. I'm going downstairs now."

"G'night, Slugger!" Kenny called as she closed the door.

Maple stood at the top of the stairs for a moment, relishing the feeling of lightness that flowed through her body. It was amazing what wonders laughter with a friend could produce. However, that didn't change the fact that there was still a mystery to solve.

And with that in mind, she descended once more into the gloomy basement.

Chapter 19

Several hours later, Maple had finished making the rest of the furniture. She wasn't sure exactly how much time had passed since dinner, but it had to be several hours, at least. She needed a break and a glass of water, and she had half a mind to check whether there was any apple pie left over from dinner.

Exhaustion had begun to settle in, and she rubbed her eyes as she ascended the basement stairs. When she opened the door and stepped into the hall, though, she became alert immediately; a man was skulking down the hall away from her toward the front door.

She recognized that silhouette.

"Kenny?"

He looked over his shoulder at her, but instead of the mischief that had twinkled there when he had teased her a few hours ago, his expression now was defiant.

"What are you doing?" she hissed, hurrying to catch up to him.

She saw he had his left hand clenched around something. He opened his palm and showed her the Maltese cross Phillip had given him: Daniel's pin.

"I'm going to find the mobster who killed my friend."

Maple glanced from him to the grandfather clock in the hallway.

"At ten at night? In a city you aren't familiar with? Against the orders of Detective Francis?"

"Yes, yes, and yes. I can't just sit around anymore." He moved to open the door.

"Can we please talk about this?" Maple said. "This is a very bad idea."

"I've made up my mind."

"Wait," Maple said, her desperation growing. "How are you even going to find him? You don't know where he is."

"I'm going to go back to Annabel Hastings's house and ask her and Mrs. Perkins. They'll know."

"You're just planning to knock on their door this late at night?" she asked incredulously.

"Desperate times call for desperate measures. I'm pretty sure Mrs. Perkins will forgive me for bothering her in the middle of the night if it means I can catch the guy who killed her son."

"Kenny," she said, trying to keep her voice calm. "Try to slow down and hear yourself for a minute. This is a very, very bad idea."

"Easy for you to say." He gestured toward the basement door. "You have something productive you can do. Building those nutshells might actually help us crack this case. I've got nothing. I've been pacing in my room since dinner ended, and I've had it with waiting."

"Come help me, then," Maple said, a little desperately. "I'm not making as much progress as I'd like. Two sets of hands would speed things up."

She had been thinking of retiring for the night, actually, but now that she was trying to convince Kenny to stay, she'd gotten a second wind.

"Maple," he said, "try to understand. I have to find Leo Matthews. I can't *not* go after him."

Maple threw up her hands. "I'm not saying you shouldn't go after him. I'm saying not to go after him alone in the middle of the night."

They locked eyes for several long seconds, the word *alone* seeming to hang in the air between them. Maple could read Kenny's decision on his face even before he turned and continued toward the door.

She swore and made a split-second decision. "I'm coming with you."

Tense silence permeated the car as they wound their way through Boston's nonsensical street designs back to Annabel Hastings's house. The snow that had fallen earlier had stopped but left a light layer of white on the ground. There were very few other cars on the road at this time of night. The rock that had taken up residence in Maple's stomach seemed to grow little by little the closer they got, and they made it back to the Hastings house in what seemed to her like no time at all.

Kenny parked the car near where Detective Francis had parked mere hours ago.

"Isn't it a little strange that there are no lights on in any of the houses?" she asked.

Ten-thirty was late, certainly, but not so late that literally no one in the neighborhood would have a single light on.

Kenny squinted up and down the street. "You're right. And look—"

He pointed at the path leading to Annabel Hastings's house. Footprints going in both directions marred the snow. Maple frowned as they opened their doors. Kenny turned on the powerful flashlight he always kept in the car, and they walked over to the path. From up close, the footprints looked chaotic; there were sets that indicated at least one person had traveled both toward the house and away from it.

"Do you think Laurie and Annabel went somewhere?" Kenny asked. "Maybe those prints are from them leaving and then coming back."

Maple shook her head. "Look at the size of them. A very large shoe made these. Annabel and Laurie are both petite. These were made by a man."

They studied the prints for a few more moments, and Maple noticed that the prints leading away from the house and toward the street seemed to have been made in more of a hurry than the ones headed toward the house; those prints had more of a partial look to them and snow was scattered behind them in a spraying pattern that made it look like they had been left by someone running.

"Kenny," Maple said, alarm bells starting to jangle inside her brain, "I don't like this."

Kenny pulled his gun from its holster. "Get back in the car."

She didn't even consider disobeying his order. She scrambled back to the car, ducking down in the passenger seat so she was just barely able to peer out the window. Kenny advanced cautiously toward the house, holding the flashlight in one hand and the gun in the other. He moved quietly, avoiding stepping on the footprints. At the front door, he paused.

"Police! Open up!"

Maple counted three long seconds before he tried the doorknob with the hand holding the flashlight. The door swung open immediately, and Kenny stepped inside, leading with his weapon out in front. She lost sight of him and clapped a hand over her mouth. She thought her heart might beat straight out of her chest.

Moments later, Kenny reappeared in the door frame, his shoulders sagging and both arms down by his sides. He retraced his steps back to the car, and Maple opened the passenger door. Before she could ask what he had found, he shook his head.

"They're dead," he said, his voice cracking. "Both of them."

Chapter 20

Maple and Kenny watched silently as members of the Boston Police department swarmed the house where Annabel Hastings and Laurie Perkins had been murdered. Detective Francis pointed at the footprints and barked at his men to steer clear of them as they entered.

Maple noticed with interest a man carting a camera with a large flashbulb, presumably to document the scene. Groups of officers fanned out and began knocking on nearby doors but seemed to be having a hard time rousing the neighbors.

"They won't talk," Kenny muttered, watching one policeman leave a business card tucked into a door frame across the street after no one answered the door. "This is Irish mob territory."

"The last thing most people in this neighborhood would want is to be seen cooperating with the police," Maple agreed.

"They're more afraid of Leo Matthews than of the cops."

Francis disappeared inside the house. An ambulance pulled up to the curb, and two men hopped out, opened the back door, and unloaded two stretchers.

Maple swallowed hard. "Apparently, with good reason."

They observed the activity for several more minutes before Francis reemerged through the front door, grim-faced. He strode over to Maple and Kenny, grabbed a notepad out of his pocket, and flipped it open.

"Later, you can explain to me what the hell you were thinking, coming over here yourselves. For right now, just tell me what happened when you arrived."

Kenny took a deep breath and summarized the evening's activities. He got up to the moment he entered the house before his face cracked from grief and shock.

"They . . . they were just lying there in the entryway, right where we were all standing together earlier today. I saw Annabel's hair first, spread out over the floor, and then I saw the gunshot in her forehead. And Mrs. Perkins was just behind her . . ."

Kenny buried his face in his hands.

"It appears to have been a hit. They were both shot execution-style," Francis said, his tone and facial expression softening as he witnessed Kenny's emotional reaction.

The detective asked a few more questions about what they saw and heard leading up to Kenny's discovery of the bodies. Maple mentioned the lack of any lights or discernible activity in neighbors' houses, and Francis frowned and shook his head.

"That's disappointing, but not surprising."

She then shared her analysis of the footprints, which indicated someone had walked toward the house and run away from it. At this, Francis nodded approvingly.

"That was a good catch on your part."

"You're going to bring Leo Matthews in for this, right?" Kenny asked, picking up his head again.

"Oh, sure. That is, if we can find him."

Kenny looked confused. "Don't you know his address?"

"The one that's printed on his driver's license? Absolutely. But he's almost never actually there. He moves around all the time, going from one safe house to another. His cronies hide him."

Kenny blew out a breath and ran a hand through his hair.

A steely look came over Detective Francis's face. "Believe me when I tell you I would love nothing more than to be the one who brings Leo Matthews down."

Maple believed him.

"All right," the detective said, shutting his notebook and stowing it in his pocket again. "I've got everything I need from you for now. Get out of here and go get a few hours' sleep." His expression softened. "Or at least try."

Maple and Kenny nodded. The adrenaline rush of finding the bodies was beginning to transition into a crushing exhaustion; incredibly, Maple thought she might actually be able to fall asleep. She glanced at Kenny and hoped he would as well.

"Come down to the station in the morning," Francis said. "I'll update you then."

After breakfast the next morning, Maple and Kenny made the now-familiar trek to the precinct. They had each managed a few hours of sleep, but Kenny looked haggard nonetheless, and Maple imagined she didn't look much better.

When they arrived, though, Detective Francis looked as alert and put-together as ever. His uniform was freshly pressed, and there were no bags under his eyes as he stood in the entrance hall speaking to one of the secretaries and sipping from a coffee mug.

"How does he *do* that?" Kenny muttered in awe. "He must've gotten even less sleep than we did, but he looks great."

Francis saw them, wrapped up his conversation, and beckoned them over. Maple noticed that he wasn't leading them to his office, but rather appeared to be preparing to talk with them right here in the lobby. With a sinking heart, she guessed that meant there wasn't much new information to share.

"There are no new leads on Leo Matthews's whereabouts," he informed them briskly. "The bad news is that most of the precinct's efforts and energy are currently going into the Perry heist. The good news is I was able to put my task force onto the Hastings and Perkins murders—for the time being, at least." A dark cloud settled over his expression.

"What do you mean, for the time being?" Maple asked.

Francis sighed. "I found out this morning that the task force is being disbanded."

"But you said their record was impeccable!"

Kenny looked shocked and offended, which was reminiscent of the wide-eyed expectation that justice would prevail that had been firmly in place when Maple had first met him back in October. Since then, some of their experiences had opened his eyes to the ways of the world, but—not for the first time—it appeared that his optimism had remained essentially intact through it all.

"It is," Francis said shortly, "but their skin's the wrong color."

Kenny looked as though the detective had smacked him. He opened his mouth, and Maple could just tell that he was going to launch into a lengthy protest about the injustice of this decision. One glance at Detective Francis's face told her that this wasn't what he needed or wanted to hear right then—at least, not from a white sheriff's deputy from out of town. She gently but firmly stepped on Kenny's foot, hoping to convey a message of *not now*. Kenny shot her a confused look, but kept quiet.

"We're sorry to hear that, Detective," Maple said instead. "What can we do?"

Francis rubbed a hand across his eyes; traces of his exhaustion were seeping through. "Not much, I'm afraid. Gus just sent up word that your lab results are ready. After you get those, I don't think there's anything else you can do here."

They were being dismissed. His words made sense, but Maple still felt hollow at hearing them.

"I'll go get the results."

Kenny jogged down the hall, resembling nothing so much as a labrador retriever.

"He has so much . . . energy," Francis said, a mixture of admiration and irritation in his voice.

"He does," Maple agreed.

She was very much able to relate to the detective's attitude about Kenny's energy, which had simultaneously inspired and exasperated her in the months she'd known him. Maple realized she was going to miss working with the detective. In just a few short days, she'd been impressed with his professionalism and dedication.

"I understand you're a lawyer," Francis said.

Maple looked at him, startled at the abrupt change in topic. "Well, not exactly. I graduated law school and passed the bar, but I've never practiced."

He studied her carefully. "I'm impressed with your work ethic and insights. You know this part of the city and its people well. I think you'd be a great fit in the local prosecutors' office."

"I—" Maple had the rare experience of being lost for words.

"Think about it," he said. "I have contacts over there, and I know they're looking to hire more people. I'd be happy to put in a good word for you, and I'd be honored to have you as a colleague."

"Um, thank you." Maple was impressed with herself for spitting out a vaguely coherent sentence when her mind was spinning.

"My pleasure."

She cleared her throat. "Before we go, I need to clear something up about one of the files you pulled for us. James Cooper was—"

"Your brother. I know."

Maple's jaw hung open in astonishment. "You know?"

He arched an eyebrow. "I'm a detective, Mrs. Bishop."

She flushed. "Yes, it's just . . ."

He waved a hand dismissively. "I know," he said simply, "and I hope you get some answers. Let's leave it at that."

"Thank you," she said, but the two words seemed entirely inadequate. "For what it's worth," she added, "I think it's a real shame about your task force being disbanded. It's shortsighted of your superiors to do away with it."

He smiled humorlessly. "I appreciate that."

Kenny came jogging back around the corner, brandishing a sheet of paper. "Negative! I knew it."

He handed the paper to Francis, who studied it and nodded. "Well, that's one more piece of the puzzle. He wasn't under the influence at the time of his death."

He gave Kenny back the paper and shook both of their hands in turn. "It's been a pleasure to work with you both this week. I'll be in touch about Leo Matthews. Don't worry; we'll find him."

Maple didn't doubt it. She and Kenny thanked the detective again and then went out to the parking lot, where he got into the driver's seat as she climbed into the passenger side. Maple wondered whether she should tell Kenny about the offer Francis had just made. Before she could decide, Kenny spoke.

"Do—do you think we got them killed?"

"Matthews obviously knew Laurie had talked to the police. I mean, why leave her alone for days and then coincidentally happen to kill her hours after our visit?"

"Well," Maple said slowly, "I guess you could look at it that way—but, Kenny, remember, she wanted to talk to us. She knew the risks. She'd spent her entire adult life being involved with Matthews and people just like him. Now that her son is dead, I don't think she felt she had anything left to lose."

"Annabelle didn't feel that way, though." Kenny nodded grimly as they both considered the price Annabelle had paid for her friend's decision. "I got the sense Laurie felt talking to us was a way to atone for her past."

"Yes," Maple agreed. "I had that same impression."

Kenny turned the car's engine on. "Well, I guess we can head home. I don't know about you, but I've had about enough of the big city, plus now we have to go tell Phillip Perkins that another one of his relatives just died." He sighed. "We'll just have to stop by the rooming house to pick up our bags and the nutshells."

"Actually," Maple said, "there's one more stop I'd like to make before we leave."

They pulled to the curb twenty minutes later in front of a nondescript row house. It looked just like every other house on the block; this neighborhood had the appearance of having been mass-produced in a hurry. The only individualism came from small things—curtains in the windows, welcome mats, planters that held dead stalks that had once been flowers.

Maple sat there for a long moment looking out her window. The door with the number 27 next to it—the one they were here to visit—had a small evergreen wreath hanging on it. A red tricycle was parked haphazardly nearby. Overall, Maple thought it had a more cheerful look about it than the other nearby doors.

"This is probably a dead end," she said.

"We won't know until we ask," Kenny pointed out.

She knew he was right, but something kept Maple pinned to her seat. She could feel Kenny watching her but didn't turn to look at him. She closed her eyes, and for some reason the image that popped into her mind just then was the view from Eliza Patterson's house. In her mind's eye, she saw the valley spreading out below the mountain, houses and barns set in small clearings among clumps of trees. She saw George, the bald eagle, wings spread, seeming to float above the town. She saw the smoldering remains of the burned cabin.

Maple opened her eyes, and then she opened her car door. Kenny followed her up the path that led to the door with the wreath. When she got there, she only hesitated for a second before knocking.

The woman who answered the door a moment later peeked out at Maple inquisitively. She was petite—a good four inches or so shorter than Maple herself—and had straw-colored hair piled on top of her head in a messy bun. Her eyes were bright and curious as she rested a hand on the inside of the door.

"Can I help you?"

Maple smiled down at her. "I'm terribly sorry to bother you, but I'm looking for information about someone who used to live here: Noah O'Hare."

The brightness in the woman's eyes dimmed, and her expression became guarded. "Noah doesn't live here. Why are you looking for him?"

"So you know him?" Maple asked, a vibration of anticipation shooting through her body.

She quickly considered what her next words should be. She didn't want to sound accusatory in case this woman's loyalties were with Noah; if so, and if she thought Maple bore any ill will toward him, she might be inclined to clam up from defensiveness. Maple was pleasantly surprised that someone at Noah O'Hare's old address, which Sergeant Halpern had diligently recorded in Jamie's file as part of his investigation log, had any knowledge of him; she wasn't about to scare the woman off now and risk losing her only tenuous connection to the man her brother had fought with on the last night of his life.

"I'm looking for him because he may have been one of the last people to see my brother alive about four years ago," she said carefully.

The woman's jaw dropped, and her hand fell from the door. "You're Jamie's sister."

The words came out in a whisper. Maple's brow wrinkled in confused surprise. "You knew Jamie?"

The sound of small feet running came from behind the woman. "Mommy!" called a small voice.

The woman turned, stooped down, and picked up a little girl whose hair was the same color as her own—but when the child's face turned toward Maple, it was a miniature version of Jamie looking back at her.

Chapter 21

The little girl promptly buried her head in her mother's shoulder. Maple looked from the girl to the woman, who had gone pale.

"Are you—is she . . . ?" Maple's tongue felt three sizes too big.

The woman stepped aside to allow room for Maple and Kenny to enter. "You better come in."

Mute, Maple followed her down a short hallway into a small, bright kitchen. She was vaguely aware of the sound of the door closing behind her, and then she and Kenny were sitting at a round table. The woman sat, too, with her daughter in her lap; the girl hadn't taken her face out of her mother's shoulder.

"I'm Margaret O'Hare. Everyone calls me Maggie, though." She laughed nervously. "Don't know why I said 'Margaret' at all. Sounds more official, I suppose. Anyway, Noah was my twin brother."

Maple clocked the use of the past tense. Tears welled in Maggie's eyes and she pressed her lips together.

"And Jamie . . . ?" Maple whispered.

"Jamie was my guy," Maggie said, the tears spilling down her cheeks as she stroked the little girl's hair. "This is Sophie. Our daughter."

Had Maple been standing, she was certain the shock would've caused her knees to buckle.

Jamie had a daughter. Maple had a niece.

Sophie picked up her head. "Jamie is my daddy's name."

She looked at her mother as she said it, and then darted a quick glance at Maple and Kenny before burying her head once again in Maggie's shoulder. Maggie rubbed her daughter's back and sniffled.

"I'm sorry," she said to Maple. "This must be such a shock to you."

"Yes."

The word came out automatically. Maple felt dazed and couldn't think of what else to say. Next to her, Kenny cleared his throat. She looked at him in surprise; she'd entirely forgotten he was there.

"Jamie talked about you all the time," Maggie said, still stroking Sophie's hair.

"I can't say the same about you," Maple said.

Kenny coughed again, this time forcefully. Maple ignored him. It might've been blunt—and possibly even hurtful—but that didn't make it less true.

But Maggie didn't seem offended. "I know. I'm sorry about that. We'd just started going steady, me and Jamie, right after your mother died. You were about to graduate law school and were engaged to a doctor and all." She sounded awed by these accomplishments. "He really wanted me to meet you, and then we found out I was pregnant."

Here, she closed her eyes for a long moment and took a deep breath. Sophie peeked out to check on her mother.

As if sensing the little girl's eyes on her, Maggie smiled and said, "I'm all right, baby." She looked back at Maple again. "But we decided to tell Noah first." She took another deep, bracing breath. "My brother didn't approve of us. He thought Jamie wasn't good enough for me." She exhaled impatiently and added, "Even though he and Jamie had the exact same job and even though I was the same age and could make my own choices."

Maggie's expression darkened, and Maple liked the stubborn determination she saw in the other woman.

"Noah was four minutes older than me, but he acted like he could boss me around. It came from a place of love, it really did, but he could drive me crazy with how overprotective he was. In Noah's mind, Jamie was good enough to be his best friend, but not good enough to be dating me—and definitely not good enough to marry me. My brother always wanted me to get out of here, make a life somewhere else, and if I stayed with Jamie he didn't think that'd happen."

Maggie pressed her lips together into a thin line. Maple was struck by the similarity between Noah and her own mother, who had urged both her and Jamie to get out of Southie.

"And you know what? He might've been right, but the thing he didn't consider was what *I* wanted."

She thumped her own chest, causing Sophie to sit up. The little girl checked on her mother and, finding her to appear satisfactorily intact, twisted around on her lap and popped a thumb in her mouth, studying Maple intently.

"And all I wanted," Maggie continued, "was Jamie. But when Jamie went out that night to The Black Sheep, he told Noah

I was pregnant and we were getting married and that was that. Noah . . . didn't take it well."

She cleared her throat and inclined her head toward her daughter. "Soph, why don't you go get your horsie to show our guests?"

"You have a horsie?" Kenny jumped out of his seat with great excitement. "Could you show me?"

He glanced at Maggie, who nodded her assent to this plan that would give her and her would-be sister-in-law a moment alone together.

Sophie studied him, weighing her answer before she gave it. Finally, she nodded solemnly, climbed out of her mother's lap, and held out her hand. Kenny took it gently in one of his, and she led him to the next room.

As soon as they were out of earshot, Maggie continued, "They got in an argument. Noah hit Jamie, and when Jamie didn't get back up, Noah took off. When he got home and told me what had happened, I was furious, of course—beside myself, really. I yelled at him to get out of my sight. That was the last time I saw my brother. I lost both Jamie and Noah that night."

"Noah died, too?" Maple asked.

"Not right away," Maggie said. "He left town that night. He knew the cops would be after him for assault, and he already had a record, so he'd be looking at jail this time." She shook her head. "Then, when we found out Jamie had died, our mother forbade Noah to come back. It was history repeating itself, you see; our father killed another man in a bar fight when Noah and I were babies. Our mother raised us herself. She'd already lost her husband to prison, and she wasn't about to lose her son, too. That's what she told me."

The sound of Sophie's laughter floated into the kitchen, and Maggie smiled upon hearing her daughter.

A complicated set of emotions swirled inside Maple. On the one hand, she was indignant at the idea that the person responsible for her brother's death had gone free. On the other, it was difficult not to feel sympathetic toward the woman across the table from her who, after all, had loved Jamie, too.

Maggie buried her face in her hands. "I was so devastated. I sank into a depression for weeks. My mother nursed me through it, and by the time she told me Noah was in hiding, it was too late to do anything about it. I threatened to go to the police, but she wouldn't tell me where he was, so what good would it have done?" She looked pleadingly at Maple. "I was pregnant, alone, and grieving. My mother was all I had."

"I could've helped," Maple whispered. "I didn't know."

"When I was able to get out of bed, I went to your house, but you'd already left. I didn't know where you'd gone or what your husband's last name was or anything. And then, we got word that Noah had been killed in an accident at work. He'd gone to Baltimore, as it turned out, and was working the docks there. A huge container box fell on him and three other men. They were all killed instantly."

"So much death." Maple said, her throat tight. "Such a waste."

They were quiet for a minute and could hear the sound of Kenny and Sophie's chatter from the next room. The girl laughed again.

"She's a great kid," Maggie said, smiling through her tears. "My mother helped me until her own death six months ago, and now a neighbor watches her for me when I go to work. I'm a waitress at an Italian restaurant down the street."

She gave Maple a hopeful look, as though seeking her approval. Kenny and Sophie galloped into the kitchen, both of them giggling. Kenny toted a wooden rocking horse, which he placed on the floor with a flourish.

"Ladies," he said with a grand sweeping gesture, "I hereby present to you the amazing horsie rider, Sophie!"

Clearly delighted at all the attention, the little girl swung one leg over the horse and settled herself on it. Grabbing the handles, she began to rock vigorously, pumping her little body to make the horse go faster and faster. She threw back her head and let out a peal of laughter. Maple watched this explosion of pure joy and felt something shift inside her, like a boulder moving aside to let in a ray of sunshine.

"I've done my best." Maggie looked down at her hands on the table. "She's the only family I've got left."

Maple reached across the table and took Maggie's hands. Maggie looked up at Maple, eyes brimming with hope.

"That's not true," Maple said, her voice wavering. "You have me, too."

Maggie's tears flowed harder, but she looked radiantly happy. As Sophie rocked on the floor beside them, she squeezed Maple's hands and gently corrected her.

"We have each other."

Part III

PART III

Chapter 22

After a quick stop at the rooming house to pick up their belongings, including the identical nutshells, the trip back to Elderberry passed quickly and quietly, with both Maple and Kenny lost in their own thoughts.

Maple could hardly believe that only three days had passed since their arrival in Boston. So much had happened—they found Laurie Perkins, and then found her dead. They'd become entangled with the Irish mob. They learned what had happened to Maple's brother, and Maple met a niece she never knew she had.

Bill had always doted on children; he would have adored this little girl. Maple had already made plans to come back to Boston to see Maggie and Sophie in a few weeks. She would stay at the rooming house again; Miranda had assured her there'd always be a place for her there and reminded her about the crafting fair invitation.

It was odd, Maple reflected, to be feeling so at home in a city she had longed to escape. Odd, but not entirely bad. Was that a sign that she ought to consider Detective Francis's offer? Could Boston be home once again?

She watched out the window as the city landscape gave way to more trees and fewer buildings. It was the reverse of the journey from Vermont to Boston they'd made so recently, and Maple was struck with a sudden thought: was her life going in reverse, too? After all, what really awaited her in Elderberry? An empty house she'd planned to share with her husband, no chance at a career in law, and an opportunity to fanny about with dollhouse reconstructions of death scenes? Maple suddenly felt embarrassed about all the hours she'd spent on the nutshells for this case. It had been one thing to create the model of Elijah Wallace's death; after all, she'd used it to try and persuade the sheriff but had ended up persuading Kenny instead. If she hadn't done that, Wallace's killers would have gotten away with it.

But was she fooling herself thinking that doing the same thing this time around would make any difference? After all, it was looking more and more likely that Leo Matthews was responsible for Daniel's death, and now the case was in the Boston PD's hands. Maple glanced at the nutshells in the backseat. Were they irrelevant? Silly, even? And what about Maple herself?

"Penny for your thoughts," Kenny said.

"What? Oh." Maple fumbled around for something to say; she didn't feel like airing her insecurities with her friend just now. "Well—I went to Boston expecting to find corruption and callousness among the police there, and instead Detective Francis and Sergeant Halpern were quite the opposite."

"... which is a breath of fresh air given what we went through in the fall back home," Kenny mused, nodding.

There it was again: the word "home." It was true, Maple mused, that back in Elderberry she, Kenny, and the sheriff had been forced to confront stunning acts of corruption and betrayal by people in professional roles—people they had considered friends and colleagues.

Was Elderberry home?

"It is refreshing to know there are dedicated, moral professionals there," Maple agreed.

"Just like in Elderberry." Kenny pointed a thumb at himself and then at her.

Maple's stomach squirmed. It was easy for him to say; Kenny's background made him fit in Elderberry like a glove. He'd been born and raised there, he was male, and he was related to the sheriff. Maple, on the other hand, was acutely aware of her own status. She was an outsider who had never fit the mold of a small-town doctor's wife; she'd rather practice law than gossip in local sewing circles, but she'd quickly discovered that she didn't really fit into either of those groups, anyway. The other ladies bored Maple and, anyway, seemed to find her off-putting, and the local law firms were glorified good old boys' clubs.

Maple marveled at the ease with which Kenny called Elderberry "home." He belonged to it and it to him. She realized she didn't really feel that way about the place she'd been born and raised or the place where she currently resided.

But that seemed like a lot to unload on him at the moment, so she turned the topic back to crime.

"Do you think four nutshells will be enough?"

"Yes. When do you think they'll be ready?"

"Hmmm. I'd say give me tomorrow to finish them up, and we can run the tests the day after."

He nodded his assent to this plan. Her thoughts returned to Boston.

"It was interesting to get an inside glimpse at the Perry's robbery investigation. I'll be checking the papers for updates—though I prefer to get my news from someone other than Harry Needles," she added darkly.

Kenny laughed, which made Maple happy, so she continued that avenue a little further. "I mean, could you believe his attitude? It's almost as though he was rooting for the criminals."

Kenny raised his eyebrows in amusement. "This from the woman he filed a complaint against for aiming a gun at him."

She waved a hand. "That was dismissed. Rawlings let me off with a warning, and he was laughing when he did; even *he* couldn't stand Harry."

But at the mention of Kenny's former colleague, his face fell. A heaviness settled over the car again. The lightheartedness had been a temporary interlude, which subsided once again to death and betrayal.

Maple supposed it had only been a matter of time.

Mack came slinking around the corner as soon as Maple stepped into her front hall. "Well, hello."

She dropped her suitcase and placed the nutshells, which were stacked on top of one another for easier transport, on the floor next to it. Then, she reached out her hand to scratch his ears, but he reared back, shot her a haughty look, and meowed reproachfully.

"Yes, I know—I missed you, too, you crotchety thing."

Apparently deciding he had punished her enough for the transgression of leaving him, Mack happily nuzzled into Maple's leg.

"Were you nice to Ben and Frank?"

As she said it, she looked up at the kitchen table and saw a small sprig of holly in a vase in the middle of the table. There was a note, too. She stood and picked up the paper.

Welcome home! Best I could do for fresh flowers this time of year. They remind me of Mack—brightly colored and sharp around the edges!

-B

(Just kidding. He was a very good boy and didn't even bite me once).

This brought a smile to her face, and in an uncharacteristically impulsive move, Maple decided to go visit the hardware store before she unpacked. She gave Mack one more good scratch and then straightened up. When she opened the door, though, she walked straight into Ben, who was standing on the stoop holding up his hand to knock. His fist caught her in the chin, but she turned her head just in time so that it was only a glancing blow.

You wouldn't know that from the look on Ben's face, though, Maple thought as she straightened herself up.

"Oh, I'm so sorry!" he said, aghast.

He took a step back and nearly fell off the step, his arms windmilling as he attempted to keep himself upright. Maple grabbed the front of his jacket and pulled him toward her, but in her haste to keep him from falling backward, she pulled harder than necessary. The next thing she knew, she was sprawled on her back in the foyer; a second later, Ben landed on top of her with an *oomph*.

Mack screeched, leapt deftly over them, and streaked out into the yard.

Maple's face was mere inches from Ben's, and for a moment they stayed frozen like that, eyeball to eyeball. Then, the absurdity of the situation hit and they both started to laugh. Ben rolled off to Maple's side, and they lay on their backs next to each other, looking up at the ceiling. Maple laughed until tears slid from her eyes. She could feel Ben watching her with amusement; after all, it was rare that Maple let loose with uncontrolled mirth. She actually couldn't remember the last time it had happened.

Finally, she wiped her eyes and turned her face toward him. "Well, that was ridiculous."

"It certainly was. I'm so sorry," he said again.

She waved a hand to dismiss his apology as unnecessary.

"Thank you," she said. "For watching Mack. And for the holly."

She liked the way his eyes crinkled at the corners when he smiled. "You're very welcome."

"You didn't bring Frank today?"

"No, I left him home. I figure it's best to ease him and Mack in."

Maple opened her mouth to reply but didn't get the chance.

"What on earth-?"

Maple and Ben looked away from each other and up at Charlotte peering down at them.

"Lottie!" Maple exclaimed.

"Everybody OK?" Charlotte arched an eyebrow. "You both are aware that it's January, and we live in Vermont, right?" She indicated the wide open front door.

Maple scrambled to her feet and then offered Ben a hand. Charlotte retrieved his cane from the stoop where it had landed and handed it to him. Maple and Ben exchanged a sheepish look, and then Maple turned to Charlotte.

"I was opening the door just as Ben went to knock on it, and then—" She gestured vaguely. "Anyway, come in. Tea all around."

After so many heavy emotions the last few days, it felt nice to laugh with friends. It felt light—even if Charlotte's expression had turned into something like a smirk as she glanced with very little subtlety from Maple to Ben and then back again.

Maple shut the door and led her guests into the kitchen, where she put on the kettle.

Charlotte held up a parcel. "Hank made zucchini bread. Well, technically he made it in August, but I pulled it out of the freezer last night. I had a feeling you'd be back today, Mape."

"I love Hank's zucchini bread!" She pulled three mugs down from the cupboard, placed them on the counter, and cocked her head at her friend. "You had a feeling, huh?"

"Well," Charlotte said, "after the sheriff came into the diner and told me you were coming back, yes, I had a feeling."

Maple slapped her playfully on the shoulder, and then grabbed a knife and three plates. All three of them sat at the table. Charlotte unwrapped the bread and cut them each a generous slice. They munched happily.

"Aaah," Ben said. "Tastes like summer."

Maple pictured summer in Elderberry, when ripe zucchini grew in her own garden, butterflies danced in the air, and the local lake sparkled invitingly.

"It does, doesn't it?" Charlotte looked at Ben approvingly.

The kettle came to a boil and Maple poured them each a cup. "How are the boys?" she asked over her shoulder.

"Same as always," Charlotte said. "The twins are turning my hair grayer by the day and the baby's a perfect angel."

Maple smiled to herself. She knew perfectly well that Charlotte loved being the mother of those three boys and wouldn't have it any other way. She carried Ben's tea to him first and then took her own mug and Charlotte's over on her next trip. She settled back into her seat and felt both Ben's and Charlotte's eyes on her. They were waiting for her to fill them in on her trip, but neither one wanted to rush her. She felt a rush of gratitude.

But how much should she tell them about her adventures in Boston? The restlessness she'd felt in the car had dissipated now that she was sitting here with them. Had she been overreacting about not feeling at home in Elderberry? Though the evening had started with her getting punched in the chin, this moment right here certainly felt downright homey.

She made a snap decision not to bring up the job offer. She'd fill them in about the Daniel Perkins investigation in a vague sort of way (she shouldn't be giving out details about an ongoing investigation to civilians, anyway, even if they were her best friends) and update them on what she'd learned about Jamie's death—and, importantly, about his life, including the fiancée and daughter she hadn't known existed.

"Well," she began. "It's a good thing you're both already sitting down . . ."

Chapter 23

Maple spent the next day finishing up the nutshells, stopping only to eat several more slices of zucchini bread with tea. Ben and Charlotte both stopped by to help for several hours, and Ken Sr. paused his work on the new dollhouses to pitch in on the nutshells, too. By the time she went to bed, close to midnight, she felt both tired and accomplished. Upon waking, she was relieved to find she had escaped the recurring dream about her disintegrating hands.

The next morning, as they were loading the nutshells into the backseat, Kenny glanced from them to her.

"Any qualms about this?" he asked. "I mean, you worked hard on these. You put in hours of careful effort, and now we're going to intentionally destroy them."

Maple did, in fact, feel a small twinge of regret. She thought of Miranda, who revered crafting, and imagined the look on her face if she found out the intended fate of these nutshells. There was no point in feeling sad or nostalgic, though. These were tools—finely crafted ones, to be sure, but tools nonetheless. Their purpose was to help solve a mystery.

"Maybe a few qualms," Maple admitted, "but the important thing is they're about to serve the purpose for which they were created. Mostly, I just hope they'll yield useful information for our investigation." She glanced at him and saw he was leaning against the passenger window, his eyes closed. "How are you feeling?"

"Just dandy," he replied without opening his eyes.

"Well, hopefully today's experiment will yield some answers. We're lucky the snow's gone so conditions today are more or less the same as they were the night Daniel died."

Once they hit the bumpy entrance road, Maple recalled how, the first time she traveled this road, she had smelled the smoke before she had seen it.

Had someone else driven this same road on January 6th with the intention of setting the cabin on fire? Was that why Daniel Perkins had lost his life? She clenched the steering wheel harder and drove on, determined to do what she could to find out.

When they arrived at the cabin in the clearing, an audience had already gathered. The sheriff, Chief Orson, and Dr. Strong were gathered at the north edge of the cabin. Peter Johannsen was there, too, pacing in front of his truck. When he saw Kenny climb slowly out of the passenger seat, Peter strode over to his old friend.

"Kenny! Welcome back."

The two young men shook hands.

Partly to give the two friends a moment alone and partly to move things along and stick to the timeline, Maple went around to the back of the car and got the nutshells. Making two trips, she brought them over to where the sheriff was standing and placed them on the ground.

"What do you think?" She gestured at the four nutshells. "Where should we put them?"

Orson studied them and then surveyed the nearby ground. "I think we should do one at a time. Let's put the first one there."

He indicated a spot about twenty feet from the edge of the cabin. Maple picked up one nutshell and placed it where he had indicated, leaving the others a safe distance away.

"I think that's good," Orson said. "That'll put it in close proximity to the actual site without threatening the structure. Peter's got the same hose he used to extinguish the fire the other day. He'll be standing ready."

As if on cue, Peter and Kenny walked over to join the group. They all looked around at each other as if waiting for someone to take the lead.

The sheriff gestured to Maple. "It's your show."

A little thrill shot through her body at those words, and she marveled at how far things had come in just a few months.

"OK," Maple said briskly. "The plan is to light the fire using four different methods: gasoline with a match, diesel with a match, a dropped cigarette, and a tipped-over candle. Everything in each nutshell is to scale—one foot to one inch—including the cigarette and the candle at the head of the bed. The hope is that, by comparing burn times, we can extrapolate out how long each of these accelerants would've taken to burn the amount of the cabin that was burned in real life and compare it to its life-sized counterpart. It might help us tentatively eliminate one or more theories and narrow down the investigation."

The men nodded. Maple felt a little rush of pride that helped tamp down any residual twangs of regret she had about torching her creations. She pointed to the bedspread in her first nutshell.

"I used little sections from Daniel's bedspread here," she said, "to emulate the material from the actual fire. The bed is constructed from wood that I took from the undamaged portion at the foot of Daniel's bed. I built the exterior with wood from the actual cabin. I recreated the scene with as much fidelity as I could."

The men took turns peering at the nutshell.

"Remarkable," Orson murmured.

"She's done it again," the sheriff said admiringly.

Kenny and Peter made noises indicating their agreement. Dr. Strong spent the longest of any of them studying her work, and then stepped backward without comment. Maple felt a flicker of irritation at him but tried her best to brush it away; after all, she knew she didn't need his praise or his approval.

Still, would it kill the man to give her a compliment?

"OK." She rubbed her hands together. "Weather conditions are similar to what they were on the sixth. Let's get started. Chief, can you call it when you think the damage has gotten to the right point?"

Orson nodded.

"Ready with the timer, Sheriff?"

The sheriff pulled the cuff of his sleeve back, revealing a large wristwatch. "Ready."

"Peter?"

He solemnly held up the hose.

"Kenny?"

Kenny held up his pencil and pad of paper, ready to record the burn times.

"We'll do the candle first."

The doll version of Daniel looked small and vulnerable. Maple's hands were shaking a little; it took a few tries to light the match. When the little flame flared, she crouched and held it to the tiny candle. As soon as the wick caught the flame, she blew out the match and tipped the little candle over sideways. With a mounting sense of dread, she watched the flame grow and spread, eating its way easily through the wood, mattress, and bedspread.

"That's it!" Orson said.

Peter hit the tiny cabin with a quick blast from the hose, and the fire disappeared with a hiss. Maple peered at the damage. Orson had called it at exactly the right time; the nutshell had sustained the exact amount of damage as the cabin had.

"Fifty-five seconds," the sheriff announced.

After Kenny recorded the time, he stepped up next to Maple and winced at the sight of the scorched doll.

"Well, the candle probably wasn't our culprit," Orson said. "The exterior wall is still intact. There's a light wind coming from that direction." He paused and jerked a thumb behind them. "Same as there was that night. Looks like the fire from the candle would've spread down the bedspread like it did here, not behind the bed and through the wall."

Maple had come to the same conclusion. "And that means that the cigarette dropped onto the bedspread will likely have the same result."

She moved the damp, smoking wreckage of the first nutshell out of the way and retrieved the second one. Placing it in nearly the exact same spot, they repeated the experiment, only this time dropping a miniscule cigarette onto the bedspread, which ignited almost immediately. Indeed, as she had predicted, the burn pattern and timing were nearly identical to the candle, leaving the wall behind the bed unharmed.

Third, they repeated the experiment with diesel. Maple dripped a little bit on the exterior wall behind the bed. This time, Orson insisted on lighting it himself to avoid the chance of Maple burning herself on the volatile accelerant.

"One minute and one second," the sheriff announced.

They all looked at the burn pattern, which very closely resembled the one they had seen on the night of the fire, wall and all.

"That's more like it," Orson grunted.

"Unfortunately," Kenny agreed.

Finally, they lit the fourth nutshell using gasoline instead of diesel. It burned in much the same pattern as its counterpart, but more quickly; it clocked in at forty-two seconds.

After Peter extinguished it, everyone gathered in a circle.

"Well, it looks like it was likely set from outside the house using either diesel or gasoline," the sheriff said.

"My money's on diesel," Orson said. "Gives it longer to burn before Peter got here and put it out. Given the scale Maple used, we can extrapolate the burn time out to about ten minutes with the diesel. That's pretty much what I thought when we arrived at the scene."

For his part, Peter had gone pale and mute. His eyes were fixed on the tiny, singed doll in the final nutshell. Maple supposed the macabre miniature dredged up horrible memories for the young firefighter who had thought he was going to pick up his colleague and friend for work, only to arrive and find him dead.

Maple shivered as she thought of how close the time frame was. Had Peter, by sheer chance, unknowingly managed to escape death himself by mere moments?

"Either way," the sheriff said grimly, "It's looking less like an accident."

Chapter 24

They stood in silence for a long moment, each of them contemplating the implications of their experiment.

"Leo Matthews killed him," Kenny finally said. "Laurie was right. He couldn't outrun his past, no matter how hard he tried."

Kenny's face had gone pale, and he spoke in a measured, quiet voice that gave Maple the impression he had become resigned to the idea that the mobster had killed his friend. She watched as Peter put a hand on his shoulder.

"It's definitely a possibility," she agreed. She turned to the sheriff. "Can you bring the nutshells back to the office? Kenny and I can meet you there in the morning to go back over everything we know so far."

"You got it."

"I'm heading home. I've got another house to finish."

"No rest for the weary," he said, eyeing her intently.

"All in a day's work," she said airily. "Have to pay the bills somehow."

The sheriff looked at her solemnly. "Great work today."

For some reason, this compliment brought tears to her eyes. Maple was not a crier; she must have been more tired than she realized. Not trusting herself to speak, she turned and walked toward her car, giving him a little half-wave over her shoulder as she left.

On the drive back to her house, Maple contemplated the job offer in Boston—the opportunity to actually practice law, which was something that would never happen if she stayed in Elderberry with its one law office that wanted nothing to do with her. Bill was the reason they had moved to Vermont, but now he was gone and she'd discovered she actually did have family in Boston. She could help Maggie and spend time getting to know her and Sophie. She could have one steady job instead of cobbling together a living making dollhouses and consulting for the sheriff when needed. It would be a level of stability she had never yet experienced.

But here in Elderberry, she had begun building a different sort of life for herself. As she pulled into the driveway, she thought of Ken Quirk Sr., who worked so hard on building the dollhouses with her. She thought about Kenny and the sheriff, and Charlotte and Ben. Hadn't she inadvertently built a de facto family for herself right here in Elderberry?

In her kitchen, Maple found that Charlotte had left a note on her counter.

Dinner's in the fridge. EAT.

And stop thinking about death for a few minutes.

—Lottie

It was as if her friend had read her mind. Maple smiled and discovered a plate heaped with sliced turkey, rice, and roasted butternut squash. She devoured it gratefully, fed Mack, and went out to the garage to put the finishing touches on the current house.

The next morning, Kenny and Maple both arrived at the sheriff's office at 8:00 AM on the dot. Mrs. Langley greeted them and let them know that the sheriff had put the nutshells in one of the interview rooms. It turned out to be the same one in which Maple herself had been briefly questioned a few months earlier.

Oh, how times had changed.

The nutshells gave off a faintly acrid smell. Maple thought it was appropriate that they should smell the aftermath of fire in this room while they reviewed the evidence. It was a visceral reminder of what had happened and why they were there. It meant they couldn't forget their mission.

Kenny went to grab all the files they had about the case. While Maple waited in the room, she looked at the nutshells: four tiny replicas of Daniel Perkins's death. She found her attention lingering on the two models with intact exterior walls. She imagined how an arsonist must've felt, walking up to that wall and dousing it with fuel. What had the perpetrator felt as the cabin began to burn?

Kenny returned with the paperwork, and they began going through everything again. Maple found that she kept pausing her perusal of the coroner's report to look over at the nutshells.

"You want to know one thing I keep coming back to?" she finally said. "Assuming it was arson, we need to figure out a way to explain how the person got to the cabin and left again without Peter seeing him."

Kenny looked up from the death scene summary. He rubbed his eyes and nodded. "I suppose he could've come on foot, but it would've been tricky in the dark."

"It could mean we're looking for someone who's an experienced woodsman," she mused, thinking of the Boston-born-and-bred mob boss.

"I doubt that Leo Matthews is one," Kenny said, arching an eyebrow.

"I was having the same thought. I wonder if Detective Francis has found him yet."

They lapsed into pensive silence again.

"Theoretically," he said, "it's possible someone could've come in with a vehicle, set the fire really quickly, and then hustled back out just before Peter arrived."

"What would that timeline look like?"

Kenny grabbed a pencil and a blank piece of paper.

"OK," he said, flipping back several pages to the police report. "Peter got to my house at 5:05 PM. I then immediately called the chief and the sheriff—"

"—who then called me."

Kenny nodded. "And then Peter and I raced back to the cabin, arriving at 5:24. Peter said he'd gotten to the cabin to pick Dan up for work at 4:45. He knows this because he left his house at 4:35 and it takes exactly ten minutes to get from there to Dan's place."

"And we know the fire hadn't been burning for very long before he showed up; he said he started putting it out within two minutes of arriving on scene and had it more or less extinguished in about three minutes."

"Then, assuming it was diesel—which would've given the arsonist the most time to escape, based on our accelerant tests—and the fire burned for under ten minutes . . ."

". . . and it takes probably a good five minutes to get from the street all the way to the cabin or vice versa. . . ."

". . . then he must've set the fire and driven away pretty much immediately."

They looked at each other, both calculating in their heads.

"He would've had to be clear of the driveway by the time Peter was pulling in," Maple said. "Is that even possible?"

Kenny looked thoughtful. "Well, Chief Orson was able to extrapolate out the burn time of the cabin based on your models . . ."

She nodded, seeing where his train of thought was going. "We could reenact the arson—without actually setting a fire, of course—and time ourselves driving away."

"It's a good idea," he agreed. "The thing *I* keep coming back to is this: why was he in the bed and why didn't he wake up?"

That was the very question Maple had been planning to bring up next. "We've ruled out drugs and alcohol, and it would've been a weird time for him to be asleep, given that his shift was about to start."

"But we know from the autopsy that he inhaled smoke before he died."

Maple was stumped on that one for now. The two of them sat in silence for a minute.

Finally, Kenny held up his car keys. "Should we drive out to the cabin again?"

"I thought you'd never ask. Let's go."

Chapter 25

They drove out to the cabin for the second time in less than twenty-four hours, but they weren't the first to arrive. Peter Johannsen was already there when they arrived, bundled in a parka and hammering a board into place.

He nodded a greeting but didn't stop his work.

"I should be helping more," Kenny muttered, lifting a hand in greeting. "I feel bad that he's out here all by himself today."

"Don't be too hard on yourself," Maple told him. "After all, you're working on figuring out how Daniel died."

He nodded glumly. "Got the watch?"

She reached into her pocket and fished out the Elgin timer that used to belong to Bill. The army had sent it to her along with his other possessions. She liked the clean, cold feel of it in her palm, where it fit neatly; she took a moment to admire the perfect circle, which looked so simple and yet housed complex mechanisms beneath the surface that kept it ticking along, marking seconds and minutes with pristine accuracy. She squeezed it, imagining her husband holding it in a field hospital in France.

"Yes."

Remaining in the passenger seat, Maple wound the timer while Kenny jogged over to where Peter was working. Maple could see them exchange a few words. Then, Kenny turned and looked at her expectantly. She nodded. With her thumb, she pressed the little button at the top that looked like a crown. Kenny sprang into action. He mimed pouring something onto the edge of the house. Then, he pretended to strike a match and drop it. He paused for a second and then sprinted toward the car. He hopped in the driver's side, fired up the engine, and floored it. They sped down the driveway as fast as they could safely travel. Kenny made a right, drove a few feet down the road, and then pulled over. Maple stopped the watch.

"Five minutes and twelve seconds."

That was within the realm of possibility in the diesel scenario, but just barely.

Kenny nodded. "Your turn."

They got out and switched seats. Maple handed Kenny the timer and drove carefully back to the cabin. This time, Peter put down his hammer and watched them.

"Ready?" she called to Kenny, her breath puffing in the cold air.

"Aaaaaand . . . go!"

Maple went through the same motions as Kenny had. When they arrived at the same spot on the road, Kenny stopped the watch and announced, "Five minutes, thirty seconds."

That was pushing it.

"Once more?" Maple asked.

Kenny nodded. They returned to the cabin yet again.

"I have an idea," Kenny said as Maple parked and turned off the engine. He opened his door. "Hey, Pete! Want to help us with something real quick?"

Peter was packing up. He jogged over to the car, and Kenny asked if he'd be willing to run the scenario for a third time so they could have more data.

"Anything to help," the firefighter said.

"Sorry to pull you away from the work," Kenny said. "It'll just take a few minutes."

"It's OK. I was just getting ready to leave. I'm on duty in an hour."

Maple got out of the driver's side and waved at Kenny to indicate that she would wait this one out. Peter then went through the same motions Maple and Kenny had, miming starting the fire. As the men pulled away in her car, Maple walked over to the cabin, realizing this was the first time she had been alone at the site. Maple found herself drawn to the new section that Peter had just been working on. Running her fingers gently along one of the beams, she marveled at how quickly they'd been able to make so much progress with the reconstruction. Before he knew it, Phillip Perkins would have an intact house once again.

Maple thought of her own home, which—though physically intact—hadn't really felt whole since Bill died. Would Phillip Perkins live out the rest of his life in the same space where his nephew had burned to death? Could it ever feel like home to him again?

Could hers?

Maple walked away from the cabin and swept her eyes over the surrounding landscape. Her eyes were drawn to Eliza

Patterson's house up on the mountain. Smoke curled from the chimney, and Maple thought about the hot cocoa Eliza had made and how warm and comfortable she'd felt sitting in that kitchen. The sound of the car coming back into the clearing pulled her out of the memory. Peter pulled the car to a stop next to her, and Maple looked at Kenny expectantly as he stepped out from the passenger side.

"Four minutes, fifty-eight seconds," he announced. "Pete got the best time of the three of us. Really put my car through its paces."

He handed her the timer.

"So, it's theoretically possible someone slipped in, set the fire using diesel, and slipped out again just before you arrived, Peter," Maple said.

"Looks that way," the firefighter said as he came around the side of the car.

"Leo Matthews is definitely slippery enough to have done that," Kenny said darkly.

They said goodbye to Peter, who got in his truck and headed down the driveway, throwing them a salute as he did. Maple cast one last look at the house on the hill, and then she and Kenny got back into the car and left.

Halfway down the driveway, Kenny slammed his fist against the steering wheel. Maple looked over in surprise.

"It's not fair," Kenny whispered, his face scrunching up in pain. "It's just so damn unfair."

Maple, running her finger along the ridge of Bill's timer, couldn't help but agree.

Chapter 26

Back home, Maple got right to work on the backlog of dollhouses. Mack slipped into the house as soon as she opened the door. Maple continued out into the garage, where she found a completed frame ready for decoration and assorted pieces of tiny furniture that would go inside once they were sanded and stained. Ken would be in later that afternoon to continue his own work.

Maple put on a smock she kept out in the garage and chose a piece of sandpaper. For the next hour, she lost herself in the rhythmic motions as she rubbed the tiny chairs and tables smooth. When she made a dollhouse for her niece—just thinking that word gave her a small thrill—she would definitely make her a tiny rocking horse to go in it. The idea cheered her.

The work was repetitive but satisfying. She liked the feeling of taking away the sharp edges, of creating something both beautiful and useful—of turning what used to be a tree into elegant furniture. It was the act of simultaneously stripping away all the excess and of making something entirely new.

It was amazing, really, when she thought about it.

As she began to stain the furniture, Maple's thoughts turned to Laurie Perkins and Annabel Hastings, who had outlived their husbands only to fall victim to the same type of violence themselves. It was a sobering reminder that the type of life they had been involved in wasn't easy to escape from, no matter how much Laurie had wanted to.

And no matter how much her son had tried. As much as Maple had cautioned Kenny about jumping to conclusions, it certainly seemed likely that Leo Matthews had executed Daniel. What job had the mobster demanded the young man help him with? Had he refused? Was that why he'd been killed?

But something was nagging at Maple as she dipped a tiny brush into a can of stain and carefully moved it over a kitchen chair. The mobster had demonstrated an affinity with firearms and an utter lack of concern for leaving bodies in his wake. If he had killed Daniel, why change his method and set the fire instead?

She set down the brush and wiped her hands on a nearby rag. While the first coat of stain dried, she pulled out a box filled with wallpaper scraps. This customer wasn't particular about colors or styles and had given Maple free range to decorate the house as she saw fit. Maple rooted around in the box. Her hand landed on a scrap of rose-patterned wallpaper that brought back a rush of emotion. She held it up and remembered how she'd used it in the dollhouse she made back in the fall for Angela Wallace—the very dollhouse she'd been delivering when she discovered Angela's husband's body.

With a shudder, Maple tucked that scrap under all the other pieces in the box, burying it at the bottom. It was too small for any of the rooms in her current project, and she couldn't imagine using it again, anyway.

She settled on one that had a light green background with a pattern of darker green blooms that looked like the heads of chrysanthemums. This paper was rich and textured; it looked elegant enough for her vision of the living room, plus there was enough of it to cover all four walls easily. She prepared the glue and water mixture and set to work. As she covered the bare walls with the decorative paper, let it dry, and trimmed carefully around the doorframe, Maple found herself thinking of the burned cabin. That house, like this one, had once been new. Fresh. Full of possibility and hope. Now, it was burned—nearly destroyed—and one of its inhabitants had died inside it. Maple shuddered. Whether it had been murder, arson, or an accident, Daniel Perkins's death had been unnatural; no one should die swallowed up by flames like he had.

She stepped back and studied her handiwork, catching sight of a small bubble in the paper and smoothing it with a flat tool called a bone folder. She pictured the cabin's living room in her mind's eye; unlike this house, the cabin's interior walls consisted of exposed logs, which were rough-hewn and cozy at the same time. There was no elegant wallpaper there. In fact, everything about the Perkins's home was well-worn with a homey, lived-in appearance.

Everything except . . .

Something clicked into place in Maple's brain. When she had been at the cabin that morning, she'd been focused on the exterior, particularly the new beams Peter had been nailing into place. But now, she was thinking about the inside of the cabin.

She removed her smock, hung it on its hook, and hurried inside, noticing with some surprise that the sun had passed its peak in the sky and was starting on its downward journey toward evening. A glance at the clock told her it was just after 2:00 PM. Knowing Kenny had planned to spend the afternoon helping his mother, she placed the call to his house and within moments heard Kenny's voice on the other end of the line.

"Miss me already?" he asked, bemused, when he realized it was her.

"Listen, I just thought of something. It might be nothing, but I want to check it out. Can you come to the cabin with me?"

"Uh, sure," he said.

"Thanks. And one thing—has there always been a rug in the cabin's living room?

Maple could sense Kenny's shrug through the phone line as he said, "Beats me."

She sighed and tamped down a surge of impatience, reminding herself that not everyone had a photographic memory.

"Why does that matter?" he asked.

"I was thinking about it just now and it strikes me as out of place. Remember those stripes? It's downright garish."

"Are we home decoration experts now?" He sounded amused.

She glared at the telephone. "Actually, yes, I am."

"Oh. Right." Through the telephone line, she could sense the redness flushing his face and ears; he had clearly forgotten for a moment her other business—the one she had hired his own father to help with.

She rolled her eyes and continued, "Everything in that room has a certain style. It's cozy, but very spare—simple lines, understated colors. Is Phillip Perkins at your house right now?"

"Yes. Why?"

She closed her eyes and breathed through her nose a few times. When she was confident her next words wouldn't come out as an impatient bark, she spoke.

"Can you ask him about the rug?"

There was a pause, and then Kenny said, "What about it?"

She couldn't contain her irritation any longer. "Just put Phillip on the phone."

After a momentary pause in which Maple could hear shuffling and muffled conversation from the other end, Phillip Perkins's voice came on the line.

"Hello? Mrs. Bishop?"

"Hi, Mr. Perkins. Sorry to interrupt your evening, but I wanted to ask you about the rug in your living room."

"Oh, I noticed that when I walked through," he said. "Dan must've bought that while I was away."

Maple's heartbeat picked up. "All right, Mr. Perkins. Can you put Kenny back on the line?"

"Of course."

He sounded puzzled, but a moment later Kenny's voice was back. Maple wasted no time.

"I'll pick you up in five minutes. I'm leaving now."

She and Kenny climbed out of her car at the cabin, and Kenny followed as she hustled down the hill, taking the same route she had that first night. This time, though, instead of walking slowly all the way around the exterior of the house, she went right in the front door, which opened into the kitchen. She spared it barely a glance—just long enough to notice someone had straightened up the chairs and put away the plates and utensils—before hurrying into the living room, where she stopped just inside the threshold. Someone had been here with a dustpan and broom; though the room was far from clean, at least the amount of ash covering everything had been greatly reduced.

"It was covered with ash that first night, so it didn't stand out to me then," she mused.

"Can you clue me in?" Kenny's voice was the one tinged with irritation now.

She looked at him. "Why would Daniel buy a rug?"

Kenny threw up his hands in exasperation. "People buy rugs!"

"Have you ever bought a rug?"

"Well, no. I live with my parents."

"Exactly. Why would a young man in his twenties who lives with his uncle suddenly be seized with the urge to buy a rug?"

Understanding dawned on Kenny's face. "What are you thinking?"

"I'm thinking that, for starters, we need to move that rug."

Kenny grabbed one end and Maple the other. They made short work of shifting the rug over several feet. Kenny's eyes widened as he pointed to the floor that had, until seconds ago, been covered by the rug.

"Those floorboards have been cut."

He was correct. The floor in this room was constructed of long sections of board, but the area beneath the rug had been sawed (recently, it appeared) into smaller sections.

He and Maple exchanged a glance. Wordlessly, they began to pry at the loose board sections with their fingers. They pulled off one, revealing a hollow area under the floor. With increasing speed, they pried off another board, and then another until the contents of the space were clearly visible.

They were looking at the biggest pile of cash either of them had ever seen.

"Holy cow," Kenny breathed. "How much is this?"

Maple's mouth went dry. "It has to be hundreds of thousands of dollars. Maybe a million."

"What did Daniel do?" Kenny asked in horror.

"I think," Maple said slowly, "he may have helped with the Perry's robbery. I think we just found the missing loot."

Kenny's jaw dropped. Before he could say anything, though, a metallic click sounded behind them. Maple and Kenny froze.

"Actually," a man's voice said, "it's nearly two million. Now, put your hands on the back of your heads and don't move."

Chapter 27

From their kneeling position, Maple and Kenny complied with the order and placed their hands behind their heads.

"All right, we're gonna take this nice and slow. If you follow directions, nobody has to get hurt."

Maple placed his accent immediately. He was from Southie.

"Just a minute," Kenny said, his voice steady and calm. "Let's talk about this. I'm a police officer."

The man barked out a laugh. "Oh, excuse me, *Officer.*" He put a sarcastic emphasis on the last word. "Now that I realize who you are, let's call the whole thing off. We can hug each other, and I'll ride off into the sunset, give up my life of crime, and become an upstanding citizen."

"Now, listen, Mr. Matthews—" Kenny started.

Hearing the name aloud hit Maple with a jolt.

"Stay real still, the both of you. I'm going to take your gun, *Officer.* If you don't cooperate, your friend will be the one to pay the price, and I've got an itchy trigger finger."

Kenny stiffened next to her. Maple felt her own body start to shake. It had been one thing to think about Leo Matthews as a theoretical idea—as someone who hurt other people. It was quite another to be in the same room with him. Even though it wasn't touching her, Maple could feel the gun behind her. She could also feel the cold indifference of the man who was holding it.

"Let her go," Kenny said. "She's a civilian."

There was a sudden, quick movement behind Kenny. In her peripheral vision, Maple saw Matthews's hand slam the butt of his handgun into the back of Kenny's head. He went down hard, and Matthews made short work of pulling Kenny's weapon from its holster and tucking it into his own waistband.

Maple gasped. Matthews turned his attention to her.

"You're not going to try any funny business, are you?"

She shook her head, biting her lip to keep from whimpering. Kenny lay silent and motionless on the ground.

"Good. I'm going to check you for weapons now."

"I don't have any," Maple said.

"You'll have to excuse me if I don't take your word for it."

Maple's veins turned to ice as the man roughly ran his hand over her waist and then each leg. Finding nothing, he stepped back again and Maple heard a rustling sound. A second later, he tossed a large black bag that landed near Maple's feet.

"Start loading the cash into that bag."

Kenny moaned and stirred next to her. Maple sagged with relief: he was alive.

"On your knees, copper, and help the lady. Remember what I said before: try anything, and I'll shoot her first."

Those words send a river of dread down Maple's spine. The man's voice was cold and hard; she believed he would carry through with his threat. Kenny struggled to his knees as Matthews tossed another bag onto the floor next to Kenny.

The money was bundled into little packages. Silently, they began picking it up and placing it into their bags. After Maple had moved about ten of the packages from the floor space into her bag, she realized what a monumental task this was going to be; Kenny was moving at the same pace she was, and it didn't look like they had even made a dent in the enormous pile of money. She also realized why Matthews needed their help. If this was a difficult task for two people who had all their functioning limbs, it would've been nearly impossible for a one-armed man. Despite the cold, Maple began to sweat.

She wasn't sure how long they worked like that in silence. Eventually, Kenny said, in a carefully conversational tone, "So, Mr. Matthews, tell us how you pulled off this heist."

Maple noticed Kenny didn't break his pace of loading the money into the bag when he spoke.

"Just keep working, officer," the man behind them sneered.

Kenny caught her eye and glanced quickly backward and then back at her again. Then he closed his eyes and swayed a little, and she thought he was going to lose consciousness again. He swallowed hard and remained upright. She looked away, not wanting to give Matthews any reason to shoot her. But she gave an almost imperceptible nod to indicate her understanding of Kenny's message: *keep him talking.*

"This money isn't going to fit into these bags," Maple said.

Hers was almost half-full already, Kenny's was about the same, and they weren't even a quarter of the way through the stack in the space below them.

There was a shuffle behind her, and she flinched. The man laughed—a low, humorless rumble—and another empty bag landed on the ground next to Maple.

"Don't worry about it," he said.

"I wasn't worried," she said, continuing to move stacks of bills. "I was making an observation."

"She does that," added Kenny faintly.

"I'm aware of what you do, Maple Bishop," the man said.

Maple froze at the sound of her own name coming from this man's lips. Seconds ticked past as she processed that he knew who she was and also, apparently, what she did for a living. What else did he know? Her address?

What kind of danger had she managed to land herself in?

"Keep going," Kenny muttered.

She forced her trembling hand to continue moving stacks of bills into the bag. She fell into a rhythm—pick it up, put it down—and noticed that her breathing pattern changed to match the beat of her hands as they moved cash from a criminal's hideout to his bag. She wondered what he was going to do with the money now. Where would he take it? How many accomplices would split it? These types of thoughts seemed ridiculous as she was having them, but she supposed her brain needed something to focus on aside from the man holding a gun to her head.

"Well, if you know my name, it only seems fair that we know yours," she said. "Are you Leo Matthews?"

"Of course I am."

Kenny exhaled a burst of air. Maple, meanwhile, had to remind herself to keep breathing; the confirmation of his identity had momentarily robbed her of breath.

"You're not crying," he said to her. "I like that in a woman. Steady, you are. No hysterics."

"Thanks?" Maple said, unsure how one was supposed to respond to this type of backhanded compliment from a gun-wielding mobster.

"Laurie Perkins, on the other hand," he continued. "She was hysterical right up until the end."

Maple's stomach dropped. Kenny's shoulders tensed momentarily.

"Is that so?" His voice was calm and his shoulders back to normal when he spoke.

"Oh, yeah," Matthews replied. "She sobbed like a baby. *Why'd you hurt my Daniel? What did he ever do to you?*" He said the last part in a mocking tone. "That's how I found out he was dead: from dear old Mommy."

"You didn't kill Daniel?"

The words were out of Maple's mouth before she could stop herself. She snuck a glance at Kenny; he, too, looked astonished at this turn of events. She was tempted to turn and look at the man behind them, but she also very much didn't want to get shot. She forced herself to continue moving the money as she waited for his response.

"Why would I kill him? His death was an inconvenience to me," the man snarled. "The plan was to leave the loot here until the heat died down in Boston. But now with all these do-gooders swarming the cabin, rebuilding it and whatnot, I gotta find a new spot. We're just lucky the cash didn't burn up in the fire. That would've been a real problem."

Maple was sure that the disgust she felt at that moment was palpable—that Matthews could see it emanating off of her. But he didn't say anything. She kept loading the cash until the bag was full, her hands shaking more and more with the effort of keeping her emotions in check.

There was also the dawning realization that as soon as they were done filling these bags, Matthews would have no use for her and Kenny anymore. He had confirmed his identity and admitted to several crimes. In an instant, the two of them would go from laborers to liabilities. She moved on to the second bag and tried to focus on making an escape plan. Yes, Leo Matthews was a notoriously vicious gangster, but there were two of them and only one of him; was there any possibility that they could outsmart or overpower him?

Maple's shoulders were beginning to ache from being hunched over and doing such repetitive motions. She slowed her pace slightly, hoping Matthews wouldn't notice and that Kenny had come to the same conclusion she had: the longer they could stall, the better the chance they could postpone the moment when Matthews didn't need them anymore. She thought she felt Kenny's pace slow almost imperceptibly to match hers.

"Why'd you pick Daniel for this?" Kenny asked. "He was out of the life."

Matthews's laugh was harsh.

"Are you kidding me? It was perfect—remote cabin in the middle of nowhere. Who'd expect the money from the biggest heist in American history to be out here?"

Maple felt a surge of defensiveness about Elderberry but chose to keep her mouth shut this time. The man was building up a real head of steam now.

"Besides, his mother was an easy piece of leverage. Using her helped me to remind Danny boy that he's mine. He can't just leave the life. No, sir."

"Well, it was quite a heist," Maple said, struggling to keep her tone neutral. "I've never seen so much money in one place."

"Of course you haven't," Matthews scoffed. "It was an historic haul."

"My back's starting to hurt. May I take a short break?"

"Sure," he replied, and there was ice in his voice. "If you want me to shoot you."

Fear skittered down Maple's spine. "Never mind, then. I'll keep going."

They loaded in silence for several minutes, the only sound the soft *thwap* of bundles of money hitting the inside of the bags. They each moved on to a third bag and then a fourth. Maple's shoulders had begun to burn by the time she finally placed the last bundle in the last bag.

"OK, now you're gonna carry those out to my car," Matthews instructed. "One bag in each hand. Nice and easy. No funny business. Remember, officer, I'll shoot the lady first."

"No, you won't."

This time, the grim voice that came from behind Maple, followed by another click, was a welcome and familiar one: Sheriff Scott was here. Maple had never been so happy to hear his voice.

"Freeze, Matthews," came another familiar voice.

Incredibly, it belonged to Detective Francis. Before she could wonder why on earth the Boston police detective was here in Elderberry, though, she heard the sound of Matthews dropping his gun to the ground.

"OK, boys, you got me," the mobster said calmly.

Why was he giving up so easily? This wasn't right. Alarm bells clanged in Maple's brain just as Kenny began yelling.

"My gun! He's got my gun! Maple, *get down*!"

As she hurled herself into the hiding hole where the money had just been, Maple caught a flash of motion out of the corner of her eye as Kenny streaked toward Matthews. She curled up into a tight ball and instinctively wrapped her arms around her head. She heard a scuffle and shouting; she squeezed her eyes shut.

Then, the sound of a gunshot shook the cabin.

Chapter 28

Not again, not again. Maple had only been in close proximity to a gunshot once before—when the sheriff had been wounded while apprehending one of the people responsible for Elijah Wallace's death—and she would've been quite happy to finish off her days without doing so again. Above her, the sound reverberated. She braced herself for another shot, but none came. She began counting in her head. When she reached sixty and there had still been no further gunshots, she decided it was time to see what was going on and whether any of the officers needed her help.

Ears still ringing, she uncurled herself, shifted to a kneeling position, and peeked over the floorboards. Kenny, Francis, and Matthews were gone. The sheriff was hurrying toward Maple, apparently unhurt.

"Are you all right?" he asked as he helped her out of the hole.

He sounded as though he was speaking from the far end of a tunnel.

"Yes." She could barely hear her own response.

He pulled her up.

"Is anyone hurt?"

"Kenny's gonna have a black eye," he said. "Matthews punched him while he and Detective Francis were cuffing him. Other than that, everyone's fine." He pointed at the top of the wall. "Bullet's lodged up there."

"Oh, thank goodness. But Kenny might have a concussion, too," she said. "Matthews hit him on the head with the butt of his pistol; that's how he got his weapon off him."

The sheriff put an arm around her and they walked outside just in time to see Kenny and Francis wrestling a very angry Leo Matthews into the sheriff's car, one handcuff around his right wrist and the other fastened around his belt behind his back.

Maple was suddenly freezing cold. "How—how did you know?" she asked through chattering teeth.

"That you were here?"

She nodded, and he pointed up toward Eliza Patterson's house. "Cecelia Randall saw you and Kenny arrive and then saw Matthews follow you. She pointed him out to Eliza, who recognized him as the same man she'd seen at the property before the fire, so they called it in."

Maple's mouth hung open in disbelief.

The sheriff winked at her. "A movie star saved your life tonight. How about that?"

Later, after Leo Matthews had been locked up in one of Elderberry's two cells and the two million dollars had been locked up in the other, the four of them sat down to debrief in the sheriff's office down the hall.

Dr. Strong had been summoned to check out Kenny's injury and was examining Kenny's eyes.

"There's a very strong likelihood of a concussion," he said.

"What about my eye?" Kenny asked.

The doctor shone a light on Kenny's injury.

"Well, he got you pretty good, but I don't expect there will be any lasting damage. Keep ice on it for ten minutes at a time, several times a day, tonight and tomorrow. And rest is crucial for treating a concussion."

Kenny winced and blinked as the doctor turned off his flashlight. "OK, Doc."

"I'll be right back with your ice. Stay put."

As Dr. Strong left the office, he passed Mrs. Langley, the receptionist. She bore a tray with four mugs of steaming tea, for which Maple was incredibly grateful; she was wrapped in a blanket as well as her winter coat, but she still couldn't seem to stop shivering.

Once they had their tea and Mrs. Langley had left, Maple turned to the Boston detective.

"It's nice to see you again, Detective Francis, but what on earth are you doing here?" Maple asked, wrapping her hands around the mug.

"Soon after you left, my task force brought in one of Matthews's guys. They turned him—got him to confess his own role in the Perry's robbery and give up the other guys, too, in exchange for a lighter sentence."

The detective was clearly proud of his task force's work. Maple figured it was even more impressive given the FBI's involvement; there was probably an element of extra satisfaction when the local guys could solve a big case right under the nose of the federal government.

"But how did you find out Matthews was in Elderberry?" Kenny asked.

Dr. Strong reentered the room and handed Kenny a towel filled with ice, which the young officer promptly held against his injured eye.

"Our perp told us they'd stashed the loot with a former member who lived in rural Vermont," Francis explained. "He didn't know any more than that, but it was enough to put two and two together. I called the sheriff, got in the car, and headed straight here."

"I was waiting for him here at the office," the sheriff said, "completely unaware that you two had decided to go on a little field trip out there yourselves."

With this, he glared first at Kenny and then at Maple.

"In our defense," Maple said with as much dignity as she could muster, "we didn't know we were about to find two million dollars and an irate gangster. I just wanted to look at a rug."

The sheriff's exasperated sigh could probably be heard across town.

"Well, we solved one mystery, but another one still remains," Kenny said, his voice tinged with frustration. "Matthews told us he didn't kill Daniel. He said Dan's death was actually an inconvenience to him, and I believe him. Given what we know now about the robbery, killing him while the money was stashed there wouldn't make any sense."

"I'd been wondering why Matthews suddenly turned to arson when he's clearly quite comfortable killing people with guns." Suddenly feeling cold, Maple pulled her coat more tightly around herself. "Shooting people is more efficient. More confrontational. It seems to match Matthews's personality more so than sneakily setting a fire while someone's asleep and then running away."

"Our tests indicate it was set intentionally, though," the sheriff mused.

"Tests?" Francis repeated, frowning.

"Oh, we set four more houses on fire," Maple explained.

Francis's eyebrows just about popped off his forehead. "You . . . what?"

"Well, nutshells," Maple corrected. "They're right over there."

She led him into the room next door as Kenny slumped in his chair, continuing to press the ice against his injured eye.

The faint smell of burned wood greeted them when Maple opened the door to the interview room. She quickly explained their experiment and the resulting conclusions.

"That was some impressive work," he said. "I'll be telling the DA about this when I get back. Between that work and your help in bringing down Leo Matthews, you're all but guaranteed that job. It's yours if you want it."

Did she want it?

Maple's stomach squirmed, but she wasn't sure whether it was from pride, embarrassment, or anticipation—or possibly some other as-yet-to-be identified emotion. The detective was studying her face closely. Her mouth was suddenly very dry.

"Thank you," she managed to choke out.

He nodded once. "Let me know."

When they rejoined the others, they found Chief Orson had arrived. The sheriff was in the middle of explaining how Cecelia Randall had placed the phone call that led to Leo Matthews's arrest.

Something pinged in Maple's brain at the thought of the actress looking down on them from above. "Chief, do you know how those other fires started?"

The chief shot her a quizzical look as the sheriff slapped himself on the forehead. "I forgot to ask him!" He turned to Orson. "When Maple and I went up to the Patterson place to question them about the cabin fire, we saw that there'd been two fires in the forest. What do you know about it?"

Orson looked taken aback. "The only other fire we've had lately was the one near the diner."

A boulder of dread started to form in Maple's stomach.

"Well, we saw evidence of them." The sheriff looked quizzically at the chief. "You mean to say you didn't know about it?"

"No," said the chief, and Maple suspected a similar boulder of dread was growing inside him.

Maple and the sheriff exchanged a sideways glance.

"I think you'd better see this, Curt," the sheriff said.

The fire chief nodded.

"I'll drive," Maple said.

The chief, the sheriff, Maple, and Kenny all got to their feet. Dr. Strong pulled Kenny back down.

"Not so fast, son. You're staying right here."

As she hurried down the hall with the chief and the sheriff, Maple could hear Kenny arguing with the doctor.

Chapter 29

On her second trip up the mountain, Maple steered with confidence. Fewer branches scraped against the car; Maple wondered whether someone had trimmed them or if enough trips had been made up and down the mountain that vehicles had done the trimming in the course of their journey. She reflected that there was also something reassuring about being the one in control of the car. A glance at the sheriff, who sat beside her, reinforced this feeling; his hands were gripping the seat so hard his knuckles had turned white.

As Maple parked her car, the front door opened and Eliza Patterson emerged. When she recognized them, a relieved smile spread across her face.

"Maple!" She strode over and clasped Maple's elbows. "That was you down there, wasn't it? Are you all right?"

"Yes, thanks to Cecelia," Maple said. "Is she here? I'd like to thank her in person."

"She's taking a nap," Eliza said. "All the excitement wore her out. Was that the man who set the fire that killed the firefighter?"

"No, it doesn't look like it," Maple said. "But he did kill at least two other people and was the mastermind behind the Perry's robbery in Boston."

Eliza's jaw dropped. The sheriff shook her hand and introduced the chief, explaining that they were hoping to use the vantage point from her property to check out some new angles.

"Pleased to meet you, ma'am. I was very fond of your father. Lovely property you have here," said Orson.

She shook his hand. "Well, soon it won't be mine anymore. It'll still be lovely, though. Feel free to walk around and take in the view."

The chief and the sheriff thanked her and then walked over toward the fire pit.

Maple and Eliza stayed in the driveway, where Maple gave the other woman a quick summary of how they had accidentally solved the biggest bank heist in American history.

Eliza laughed incredulously. "But that's an incredible story!" She covered her mouth. "I'm sorry; I shouldn't laugh, but it's just so . . . zany."

She asked Maple a few follow up questions, which Maple answered. Unlike Harry Needles's intrusive, abrasive ways, Eliza's genuine curiosity and excellent listening skills made it . . . well, fun to tell her a story.

"I'm certainly glad Matthews has been caught," Maple said, "but we still have the mystery of Daniel's death to solve."

Eliza eyed Maple shrewdly for a long moment, and Maple wondered what was going through the other woman's mind. "Of course," Eliza finally said. "Good luck!"

Maple thanked her and joined the two men, who were looking at the burned section of forest.

"Whoever put them out didn't tell me about it," Orson was saying with a frown. "Burned a decent stretch of woods, too."

Maple saw the chief's eyes scan the landscape below. He pointed off in the distance. Maple and the sheriff squinted in that direction.

"What do you see, Curt?" the sheriff asked.

"Right there—that gap in the trees. That was another fire."

Maple focused hard on the spot he was pointing to. Sure enough, when she looked closely, she could see that there had indeed been a fire in that spot.

"Huh," said the sheriff. "What does—"

But the fire chief was on the move. He made a slow circle of the property, his eyes cast outward. It reminded Maple of the way she had approached looking at the cabin on New Year's Eve, except then her attention had been focused on what was right in front of her.

Maple and Sheriff Scott followed Orson. By the time they'd made a full circle, he'd pointed out two other fire sites.

"Is it unusual for there to be this many fires in the winter?" the sheriff asked.

Maple knew the firefighter's answer before he gave it, and she had a feeling the sheriff did, too.

"Yes, and it's also unusual that we'd have so many fires that weren't reported."

The sheriff gestured at the land below them. "Is there a chance these started and stopped naturally?"

Chief Orson was shaking his head before Scott was done asking the question. "Absolutely not. Someone set them and then put them out."

Maple looked from the sheriff to the fire chief, taking in both of their grim expressions. "Are you implying what I think you are?"

"There are a few possibilities," Chief Orson said, his expression darkening further "and I don't like any of them."

"Could different people have set all these fires?" Maple asked.

"That's one of the possibilities," Orson said.

"That'd be an awfully big coincidence, wouldn't it?" Maple asked skeptically.

"It would," Orson agreed.

"I don't believe in coincidences," the sheriff grumbled.

"Neither do I," said Orson.

"So, then, the more likely scenario is that the same person set them all," Maple said slowly.

Chief Orson nodded. "It looks like we have an active arsonist on our hands."

Several seconds of shocked silence followed this statement as they all absorbed what that likely meant.

"Then," Maple said, looking from the sheriff to the chief, "is that the same person who set the cabin on fire?"

"Well," Chief Orson said, looking thoughtful, "not necessarily. The modus operandi—the details about how the fires started and stopped—is different." He gestured toward the areas where there had been forest fires. "These were set in remote areas and caused no property damage or injuries; heck, even the fire chief didn't know they'd happened."

A rueful expression came across his face, as though he felt disappointed in himself for missing this.

"Well," the sheriff said, "it's not uncommon for an arsonist to escalate—you know, start with small backyard fires and then get more ambitious. They might set bigger fires, let them burn longer, set them closer to inhabited areas, things like that."

Orson nodded in agreement while his eyes swept the landscape again. He was silent for a long minute.

Finally, he said, "Sam, I think we ought to go check those scenes out. See if there's anything that connects them before we jump to any conclusions."

Just then, a wonderful and terrible idea struck Maple. It must've shown on her face, because the sheriff cocked an eyebrow inquisitively at her.

"Uh oh. You've got that look."

"What look?"

"The look that means you're about to do something that's simultaneously brilliant and a very bad idea."

"OK, fine. Yes, I have an idea, and no, you're probably not going to like it. I don't particularly like it myself."

"And that idea is . . . ?" the sheriff prompted.

"While the two of you go look at the fire scenes, I'm going to go talk to someone who might have information."

"Who?"

She sighed and said, with resignation, "Ginger Comstock."

Chapter 30

Maple arrived at Ginger's front door an hour later, armed with a small loaf of bread she had bought at the diner on her way. The two women had a complicated history that was primarily underlined by a strong sense of mutual dislike going back to Maple's first day in Elderberry. Ginger thought of herself as the town's unofficial social director; Maple thought of her as a nosy busybody. Ginger had been offended when Maple had snubbed her by declining an invitation to join her sewing circle; Maple felt she had better things to do with her time than exchange idle neighborhood gossip while pretending to sew.

Things had changed a few months earlier, when Maple, Kenny, and the sheriff had saved Ginger's life. Subsequently, it was revealed that Ginger had been involved in some unsavory business, for which she had paid in at least two ways: the official fine and her own social capital. The sewing circle kicked her out and moved to another woman's house, and most of the ladies in town now wanted nothing to do with their former queen bee.

But that didn't mean Ginger didn't still have her finger on the pulse of everything that was happening in Elderberry.

Somewhat reluctantly, Maple knocked.

The door opened, and Ginger's eyes widened immediately when she saw Maple standing there. A greedy glint flitted across them, and Maple watched the other woman bite back whatever cutting comment had been on the tip of her tongue.

She was almost disappointed when Ginger simply said, "Oh, it's you."

Maple was of the opinion that they could still engage in the verbal sparring that had been a hallmark of their relationship before the Elijah Wallace case had changed everything. Apparently, Ginger didn't feel the same way.

"It's me," Maple agreed. "May I come in?"

She didn't look happy about it, but Ginger stepped aside to allow Maple to enter. Maple thought Ginger's entire appearance had taken on a faded, droopy quality. Even her previously vivid red hair seemed duller than it used to be.

"Here." Maple handed her the bread. "It's cornmeal and molasses bread from the diner. A fine batch."

"Hank's batches always are," Ginger said. "Thank you. But why—"

"I'm here to see whether you know anything about a spate of small fires around Elderberry."

Ginger's eyes widened. "Is this related to the fire at the Perkins' place?"

Maple sighed. "You know I can't tell you that."

Ginger sat down across from Maple and gave her uninvited guest an appraising look. "Did you really catch Leo Matthews and solve the Perry's robbery?"

Maple marveled at the fact that Ginger already knew about that, but she fought to keep the surprise off her facial expression.

She shrugged. "I had help."

Ginger's mouth hung open, which gave Maple a jolt of smug satisfaction. Before she could ask a follow-up question, though, Maple spoke again.

"What about the fires? Do you know anything?"

Ginger sat back and eyed Maple unabashedly from across the table. Maple knew that, as an experienced trader in information, Ginger had to be sizing up this situation from multiple angles. Before she answering Maple's question, she would try to maximize the return on her investment—in this case, the information she could receive in exchange for the information she'd give.

Maple found this an exhausting, but potentially necessary, game to play. "Tell me what you know, and I'll tell you about Leo Matthews."

Ginger looked satisfied. "OK. Well, I knew about one fire in the woods, but I didn't know there were others."

Maple marveled at the woman's capacity for information. How had she known about this when the fire chief hadn't?

"And?" she prompted.

"And of course there was that one over near the diner," she said slowly, "but I'm sure you already know all about that one because of your buddy Charlotte."

"What do you know about the one in the woods?" Maple was starting to lose patience.

"Just that it was relatively minor." Ginger sniffed. "And there might be someone who knows more about it than I do."

"Ginger, I swear—" Maple started.

Ginger held up her hands in a calming gesture. "All right, all right."

It was all Maple could do to keep herself from rolling her eyes. "The other person who might know something more than I do is Willy."

Now it was Maple's turn to gape.

"Willy?" she asked incredulously. "You mean the Willy who—"

"—regularly goes on benders and gets blackout drunk? Yes, that Willy."

If Maple had thought Ginger looked smug before, it was nothing to how she looked now that they were discussing someone whose social status was even lower than her own. Willy had always seemed harmless to Maple; the first time she had seen him, he was stumbling into the jail to sleep it off; one of the cells was generally acknowledged to be his so that he always had a spot to stay.

But where did he live during all the times he wasn't in his cell? Did he even have a home? Maple had never thought about it before, and that realization brought with it a feeling of guilt.

"How do you know this?" she asked Ginger sharply.

"I can't reveal my sources," Ginger said smugly.

Maple threw up her hands in exasperation. "Of course you can! You're not a journalist."

They stared at each other, neither willing to blink or break eye contact at first. Finally, Ginger looked away.

"All right, fine. It was me. I'm the source."

Now, Ginger was avoiding eye contact with Maple. Her patience for Ginger's theatrics was wearing thin.

"Explain," Maple said through gritted teeth.

"When I was, um, doing things I didn't necessarily want the rest of the town to know about—"

"You mean when you were breaking the law," Maple interrupted.

Ginger tilted her chin up but didn't verbally acknowledge Maple's words. "I got to know the woods around here very well, and at one point I came across Willy. He lives in a shack out there."

She gestured vaguely.

Maple waited for her to continue, but she didn't. "And how do you know he was near the scene of the fire?" she asked with barely controlled impatience.

"I still go out there sometimes." Now, Ginger looked down at her feet. "I . . . came to like the solitude. And once, about a month ago, I was walking out there and I could smell smoke. I went toward the smell to see what was going on, and there was this smoldering patch of woods. The fire had clearly just been extinguished. The next thing I knew, I saw Willy come crashing through the woods—stumbling, you know? He didn't see me."

Maple gaped at her. "And you didn't think it might be a good idea to, I don't know, report this to the sheriff?"

Ginger shrugged. "Report what, exactly? That I saw the town drunk stumbling through the woods? And don't forget; I'm not exactly the sheriff's favorite person."

Maple hadn't forgotten.

"Besides, I have no evidence he committed any crime." Her eyes narrowed. "Was there definitely a crime? Was it arson? Did he start the fire at the cabin, too?"

Maple waved dismissively. "You know I can't talk about that."

And even if I could, I certainly wouldn't choose to tell you about it.

Ginger sat back and crossed her arms over her chest. "Quid pro quo. Your turn."

Maple sighed and recited as brief a summary as she could about her encounter with Leo Matthews. Ginger pouted when she was done.

"What?" Maple asked crossly.

"Well, all of that's basic information that will be in the paper. You haven't told me anything special."

Before she could stop herself, Maple blurted, "He smelled like cinnamon."

She felt just as surprised as Ginger looked. Had he smelled like cinnamon? She hadn't even consciously registered it in the moment, but the detail was lodged in her brain so firmly now that she supposed it had to be fact. This unsettled Maple, whose photographic memory conveniently stored everything she saw.

"Cinnamon," Ginger repeated.

It must've seemed as incongruous to Ginger as it did to Maple. After all, cinnamon was in warm and cozy baked goods. It was the round candies Charlotte's twins loved. It was the gum her mentor, Dr. Murphy, used to chew.

"I have to go," Maple said.

She stood up quickly, not pausing to push her chair back in. Ginger's house suddenly felt twenty degrees too warm. She loosened the collar of her coat as she fumbled for the front door, welcoming the burst of cold air. Images swirled in her brain: smoke, cinnamon candies, the look on Kenny's face right after he'd found Laurie Perkins' and Annabel Hastings' bodies . . . was it really possible that barely a week ago she'd been watching President Truman on the television and feeling bored and restless?

The sensation that her hands were crumbling seized her again, and it panicked her just as much as it had the first time it had happened. She flexed her fingers and then clenched and unclenched her fists several times to reassure herself they were still there.

She climbed into her car and turned it on. She took a deep, shaky breath and then put it in gear. It was time to update the sheriff on what she'd just learned.

Willy had just become a person of interest.

Chapter 31

"Nothing?" Maple asked.

"Nothing," Sheriff Scott repeated. "We visited all the sites we saw from the Patterson place and found nothing of interest to narrow down how the fires started or how they were extinguished. And I had to hike. I hate hiking."

He sat back in his desk chair and rubbed his eyes.

"We did establish they had to have been set by someone on foot," Chief Orson pointed out. "There's no way a vehicle got all the way in there. And we narrowed down the time frame. Based on the state of leaves on the ground and new growth at the perimeter, they were all set within the past three months."

"Well, I can narrow down one of them even more." Maple then filled the men in on what she'd learned from Ginger Comstock.

"Willy?" The sheriff looked as incredulous as Maple felt.

Kenny appeared in the doorway. "What about Willy?"

"Ginger saw him at the scene of one of the fires."

Kenny's eyes widened. "*One* of the fires?"

Maple realized they needed to back up to fill Kenny in on the newest developments. The sheriff provided a succinct summary.

Kenny looked dazed. "Is Willy our arsonist, then? Did he kill Dan?"

"I don't know," the sheriff said doubtfully. "Willy's . . . Willy, but he's never shown any inclination toward violence or destruction. I've known him a long time. He lives alone in a shack out in the woods—been out there ever since his wife and daughter died—and only shows up in town once in a while."

"Willy had a family? What happened to them?" Maple asked.

"Influenza swept the town about twenty years ago," the sheriff said, shaking his head. "All three of them caught it, but his wife and their little girl never recovered."

Maple's heart sank. "How awful. I had no idea."

"It was well before your time," the sheriff said. "Dr. Murphy did his best, but half the town was sick, and Willy wasn't the same afterwards. It's like part of him died when they did, and his mind hasn't been right since."

They were all silent for a moment, taking this in.

"When's the last time you saw him?" Kenny asked.

Sheriff Scott frowned. "Right after New Year's. But Willy, an arsonist? I just can't see it. Even when Willy gets so drunk in town that he can't make it back home, he just comes in here to sleep it off so as not to bother anyone. And when I give him some coffee the next morning before he goes on his way, he's always grateful."

Maple recalled the first time she'd encountered Willy, which had been the same day she'd first met Kenny. It had been right here in this office, when she'd come to speak to the sheriff, and Kenny had popped into the office, wide-eyed, to announce that a man had just walked into one of the cells and lain down. The sheriff had waved away Kenny's concern and explained that that was Willy's cell. At the time, Maple had found this odd; based on his astonished expression at the time, Kenny had, too.

But maybe, Maple thought now, looking at the tired man in front of her, neither of them had given the sheriff enough credit. He often came off as gruff and cranky. In fact, Maple had spent essentially the entire month of October actively disliking the sheriff—but for the last two decades he'd been quietly taking care of a down-on-his-luck man.

"You know where he lives?" Maple felt another pang of guilt at having never considered this herself.

"Sure," the sheriff said, rising from his seat. "I helped him build that shack years ago. Let's go pay him a visit—and we'll collect the doc along the way. This has potential to be a welfare check as much as it is an interrogation."

"Willy," the sheriff said, "it's me. Sam."

Maple and Kenny exchanged a glance. The three of them, plus Dr. Strong, stood outside the door of a small structure that Maple guessed was about twelve feet by twelve feet.

"Go away," came a muffled reply.

The sheriff turned to them and raised his eyebrows. "Willy, I just want to check on you. We haven't seen you in town in a while. I'm getting worried."

After a pause, the voice replied, and this time it was less muffled; Maple thought the man inside had moved closer to the door.

"I'm sorry, Sam, I can't open the door. They'll get me if I open the door."

"Who'll get you, Willy? There's nobody out here but me and my friends. They're your friends, too."

Maple had never heard the sheriff's voice so gentle before.

"You're wrong, Sam. They'll get me. I know they will."

This statement was followed by some incoherent mumbling.

"Willy," the sheriff said in a firm, but kind, voice, "I'm coming in now. There's nobody out here trying to get you. I promise."

With that, he pushed open the door and stepped inside. The others followed him, and Maple's eyes quickly took in the entirety of the scene. The shack consisted of a bed, a fireplace, and a small table with one chair. There appeared to be no bathroom or electricity. The sheriff gestured for her and Kenny to stay near the door while he—followed closely by John Strong—took two cautious, slow steps toward the man who was now curled into a ball and rocking on the bed. The place smelled sour, and Maple fought the urge to cover her mouth and nose.

After a minute of gentle coaxing, the sheriff persuaded Willy to uncurl himself enough to let the doctor have a look at him. While Strong performed a cursory examination, the sheriff kept up a pleasant monologue about the weather. Willy whimpered quietly.

"He's dehydrated," Dr. Strong said, placing his stethoscope back into his black medical bag. "And clearly malnourished. He has several rotting teeth that need dental attention. And I'm no psychiatrist, but . . ." he trailed off and shrugged.

"All right, Willy. We brought you some water and some dinner, OK?" He gestured to Kenny, who brought him the picnic basket Mrs. Scott had packed before they left. "I want you to drink something and eat something."

"They're coming," Willy moaned. "They'll get me." He looked wildly around at his guests. "They'll get you, too!"

"Who, Willy?" asked the sheriff.

"The ghosts!" Willy shrieked.

Several minutes of sobbing ensued, during which Willy began rocking again and pulled at his own hair. Maple and Kenny exchanged an uneasy glance again.

"Did you *see* the ghosts?" the sheriff asked when the sobs had abated.

"Mmm-hmm," Willy whimpered. "Saw them. They chased me!"

"When did they chase you?"

"First I saw the fire, then I saw the ghosts." He shuddered. "Scary ghosts with monster faces. Long noses like elephants!"

Maple's spine began to tingle. She glanced at Kenny, whose forehead was wrinkled in confusion.

"Did the ghosts talk to you?" the sheriff asked.

"No, no, no," Willy began rocking again. "They can't talk. Just glide through the smoke." He placed his hands over his eyes.

The sheriff and the doctor rejoined Kenny and Maple at the door.

"Well, I'm not sure what to make of his story, but he definitely needs some help," the sheriff said grimly.

"You think he really saw something? What could he be—"

"I have an idea. I'll be right back," Maple said, and she bolted out the door without waiting for a response.

She went straight to the back of Chief Orson's fire truck and rummaged around until she found what she was looking for. She picked it up and brought it inside, moving right past the officers and fire chief and not stopping until she got to Willy's side. She crouched next to the man and held up Chief Orson's respirator mask, the one with bug eyes and the long tube protruding from the center.

"Willy, is this what you saw?"

Willy peeked out from between his fingers. Maple saw all the color drain from his face as he looked at the mask.

"No, no, make it go away!" he begged.

"I will, I promise, but I need you to tell us if this is what the ghosts looked like." Maple's voice shook as her mind swirled with new possibilities.

Willy pointed one shaking finger at Maple. "That's the ghost! That's the ghost! I told you they'd get me if I let you—"

And then, he fainted.

Chapter 32

Dr. Strong and the sheriff worked on reviving Willy while Maple, her hands shaking, handed the respiration mask to Chief Orson.

"What does it mean?" Kenny whispered, but from the look on his face, Maple guessed he had already come to the same conclusion she had.

Chief Orson's face was pale as he studied the respiration mask in his hands. "It was them. Daniel and Peter. They were the ghosts."

"No," Kenny said, shaking his head. "No, they couldn't—they wouldn't—would they?"

He looked pleadingly at Maple, who pressed her lips into a thin line. "I think—"

Kenny held up a hand to stop her, and she complied. The sheriff came over to join them, looking somber. Maple could see that Willy was sitting up now and talking quietly with Dr. Strong. Kenny put his hands over his face. Orson looked like he might vomit.

Maple waited a moment and then spoke again. "I think we need to investigate the possibility that they might've."

"Let's take this outside." The sheriff shooed them all out the door and closed it, leaving the doctor alone with the patient.

"They wanted to become smokejumpers." Chief Orson looked dazed as he ran a hand through his hair. "You know, those guys who parachute into wildfires to put them out? That's what Peter and Daniel wanted to do, eventually."

"They didn't tell me that." Kenny's face displayed a combination of indignation, hurt, and confusion.

"I read about those guys," the sheriff said. "Program started, what, about ten years ago out west?"

Orson nodded.

"So, what were they doing? Practicing for that by setting fires here so they could put them out themselves?" Kenny looked horrified.

"Maybe," the sheriff said, his face grim.

"But that would be like me committing crimes so I could investigate them. That's . . ." Kenny trailed off, apparently at a loss to explain what, exactly, that was.

"Unfortunately," said Orson, "it wouldn't be the first time firefighters turned arsonists."

"Then . . . then, was it *Peter* who—" Kenny couldn't bring himself to finish the thought, but they all knew what he was getting at.

"But, why," Orson asked, anguished, "if they were in this together, why on earth would Peter kill Daniel?"

"Maybe Daniel wanted to stop and Peter didn't?" Maple offered.

"I just—" Kenny choked on his own words, and the sheriff clapped him on the back.

"If we think about the scene," Maple said slowly, "this could explain several things we've been wondering about. If they had a struggle, that could be when the dining room furniture got all knocked about."

"And the tight window of time for the arsonist to escape," the sheriff said, realization dawning on his face. "If Peter's the one who set the fire . . ."

". . . then the time frame is irrelevant," Maple finished.

"*But, why?*" Kenny very nearly howled the words.

Just then, Dr. Strong appeared at the door, an arm supporting Willy, who walked unsteadily beside him.

"I'd like to bring him to the office overnight for fluids and observation," he said. "At least as a starting point. He's agreed to come."

Maple gestured to Chief Orson to hide the mask behind his back, which he quickly did. They didn't need to worry Willy with the ghosts anymore.

As she watched the doctor help the confused old man into the passenger side of his car, Maple realized it was now their turn to worry, and it was about something much scarier than ghosts.

They worked out their strategy on the way to the house where Peter lived with his parents. The sheriff rode in the passenger seat while Maple and Kenny sat in the back of the fire truck. Chief Orson drove.

Maple's eyes kept landing on the respirator mask that rested on the seat between her and Kenny. How could something that saved the lives of the people tasked with saving other people's lives have become so . . . sinister?

She looked away from it and out the window, where she watched dusk settling over Elderberry. They drove down Main Street, and as they passed the hardware store, she could see Ben's silhouette through the window. She had a sudden pang and wished she could be in there with him, helping prepare the store for closing, instead of where she was: hurtling toward a confrontation that just might solve a mystery, but at the same time break Kenny's heart. She waved, even though Ben couldn't see her.

It seemed like mere moments later that they pulled to a stop by the curb in front of a modest Cape Cod-style house. It was blue with black shutters, and there was a soft glow coming from the interior; someone was home. Neatly trimmed bushes lined the area underneath the windows, through which Maple could see the outline of a Christmas tree in the living room. Maple thought of a little boy who loved banana pie. Her heart squeezed.

"Let's go," Sheriff Scott said, and they all climbed down from the truck.

Maple's legs felt like they were made of lead as she followed the men to the front door where Kenny, standing at the front of the group, rang the bell. Peter opened the door. Fear flickered across his face as he took in the somber group assembled on his front steps. Quickly, though, it was replaced with a look of resignation.

"You better come in," he said as he stepped back to allow them the space to do so.

They followed him down the hallway and into a softly lit kitchen. There were four chairs around the table. Peter sank into the one facing the doorway they had just come through and pressed his palms onto the table; Maple wondered whether he was trying to steady himself or preparing to flee. Kenny sat across from him. As they had planned, Maple hung back while the sheriff and the fire chief took the other two seats.

When Kenny spoke, his voice was calm and steady. "Peter, you know why we're here."

Peter looked down at the table and nodded.

"Tell us about the fires."

Peter clasped his hands together, interlocking his fingers, and his reply was barely audible. "I'm so sorry."

Maple watched Kenny's shoulders slump forward. A moment later, he straightened up and said, simply, "Tell me."

Peter looked up, and Maple saw tears streaming down his face. "I didn't kill him, Kenny. You gotta believe me. It was an accident."

Now, Kenny's shoulders tensed. Maple saw him give the slightest shake of his head as he repeated, "Tell me."

Peter wiped his eyes with the back of his hand. "Me and Dan, we loved fighting fires. But there just weren't that many here. After the war, it just seemed . . . boring." He closed his eyes and then opened them again. "That sounds so stupid when I say it out loud. You won't understand, Kenny, you weren't over there, but the two of us? We got used to these sudden rushes of adrenaline when an attack would happen, when we'd have to mobilize on a second's notice, when we'd get woken up from a sound sleep because the Nazis decided to bomb us . . . it was chaos, but it was exciting."

His face twisted and he took several deep breaths. Everyone else in the room stayed totally silent.

"And I guess . . . well, I guess we got used to that, you know? And when we came back, it was almost driving us nuts to not have that anymore. We had heard about the smokejumpers out west, and we really wanted to go out there and do that. We were saving money, making plans to go join them. But in the meantime, we were stuck here with barely any fires to put out, so we . . . well, we made some ourselves."

Maple saw Chief Orson squeeze his eyes closed, and Peter must've seen it, too.

"I'm sorry, Chief. You can't imagine how sorry I am. All I can say is that it seemed like a good idea at the time. The first one we set in the forest, it was such a thrill to watch the flames start up and then to put them out. It gave us the rush we were craving. We told ourselves we were practicing for smoke jumping. How were we going to prepare for that if we never put out any forest fires?"

He grabbed his hair and pulled it.

"So you did it again?" Kenny prompted.

Peter nodded. "Mostly in the woods, but one time we did it in town. Little kids came over to see us. They acted like we were heroes." He shook his head. "It sounds dumb, I know."

"What about Willy?" Kenny asked, his voice betraying no emotion.

Peter looked confused. "Willy? The town drunk? I don't know—what about him?"

So, they hadn't even seen poor Willy, who had been living in terror and isolation for the past month. Maple imagined the two faces emerging from the smoke looking like some sort of aliens, and it was hard not to sympathize with Willy.

"Now, tell me about the night Dan died," Kenny said, and for the first time since he'd sat down, Maple heard his voice crack.

Peter nodded and took a deep breath. It was time.

"We'd set a fire in the woods that afternoon. It started off like it had every other time—we'd done it about five or six times by then. Dan was on the north side and I was on the east. I saw that he'd taken off his respirator mask. He was holding it in his hand. I yelled to him to put it back on; the wind was shifting. I don't know if he didn't hear me or just didn't want to, but when I could see him again, it wasn't on his face."

Peter paused and looked at Chief Orson, who was shaking his head in disbelief.

"I tried to save him. I ran as fast as I could, but by the time I got to him, he was unconscious. I dragged him away into the woods, and I rushed to put out the fire myself. I was afraid it'd get out of control and take the whole forest. By the time I got it extinguished and went back over to him, his pulse was gone."

That, Maple realized, explained the presence of smoke in Daniel's lungs. He had inhaled the smoke somewhere else, in a different fire, before he'd ended up in his own bed. The sheriff caught her eye; he'd realized the same thing.

Peter stood abruptly and began pacing the kitchen, wringing his hands. No one else in the room said a word as they waited for the young firefighter to finish his story.

"I carried him out on my back, probably about a mile. I put him in the truck next to me, sat him up like he was still alive. I drove to his house. I don't even remember coming up with the plan; I think I just knew that was what I had to do. Then I put him in his bed, and I lit my second fire of the day."

He stopped midpace and looked right at Kenny. "I meant to burn the whole cabin, but I couldn't stand there and watch him burn any more. I put it out almost as soon as I'd started it. I hoped enough of his body had been burned to cover up what we did. What *I* did."

Kenny had started shaking his head. "Did you think you were going to get away with it?"

"I don't know what I thought."

"You lied to us right from the start," Kenny said in disgust.

"I didn't know what to do," Peter said through a fresh wave of tears. "I'm not like you, Kenny, OK? I'm not *good* like you. Neither of us was."

Kenny reared back like Peter had hit him. He stood up so quickly that his chair tipped over, crashing onto the kitchen floor. It was reminiscent of the scene in the burned cabin's kitchen.

"I can't look at you anymore," he said, his voice low with fury.

He turned and stalked out of the kitchen and down the hall. Maple heard the front door open and slam closed again.

On the other side of the table, Peter Johannsen sobbed as the sheriff pulled his arms behind his back and cuffed him.

Chapter 33

Maple knew, somehow, exactly where she would find Kenny.

After telling the men not to worry about giving her a ride home, it only took about five minutes to walk to the elementary school from Peter's house. Kenny stood at the base of a tree, gazing up into it.

"I haven't been here in a long time," he said as she approached. "It's funny; I remember this tree being bigger."

Maple stood next to him. She could easily imagine Kenny, Daniel, and Peter as little boys, giddy as they hid from each other and their parents—and then, suddenly, their giddiness turning to fear when one of them disappeared.

Kenny pulled his hand out of his pocket and uncurled his fist. Maple saw Daniel's Maltese cross pin resting in the palm of his hand.

"How did everything go so terribly wrong?"

Kenny began to turn the pin over and over in his hand.

Maple let his question hang there for a long moment before offering a response. "Well, when you're all but raised in the mob, I suppose it's hard to emerge unscathed."

Kenny looked down at the cross as he continued to methodically flip it. "It wasn't just himself he was endangering, though. *We* very nearly didn't emerge from that cabin unscathed."

Maple shivered, but it had nothing to do with the weather. "If Cecelia hadn't seen us, we probably wouldn't have emerged at all."

Kenny stopped turning the pin, leaving it face down on his palm. "And the fires. How could they?"

Maple's heart squeezed as she pictured Daniel's burned body and Willy's terrified face. She didn't have an answer for him. It was all so tragic and so . . . preventable.

He held up the pin. "This symbolizes commitment to protection and honor, and they totally violated it. I mean, why couldn't they just be happy with a normal life?" Kenny closed his fist around the pin. "I guess the war took that from them."

Just as it had taken Bill's life and Ken Sr.'s nerves. Maple had a sinking feeling they'd only glimpsed the beginning of the war's toll.

"I could've been there for them." Kenny's eyes shone with tears. "I would've, if they'd just let me."

Maple patted her friend on the back. "I know."

"Here," he said, holding out his hand to give her the pin. "You take this. I don't want it anymore."

He flipped up his jacket collar, turned, and walked off.

Maple stood there for a long moment, looking at the pin that now rested in the palm of her gloved hand. For now, she'd keep it safe for Kenny. There might come a time when he'd decide he wanted it back.

She slipped the tarnished pin into her coat pocket and began her own walk home.

Back home, Maple found herself staring into the same tiny house she had been looking at just before Ben had come over and the sheriff had called and a burned cabin had turned the world upside down. It was complete and ready for delivery. Tomorrow, Ken Sr. would load up this house and three others and make a delivery trip, dropping them off to the people who had ordered them. Maple would get back some space in her living room and some more money in her bank account; the family would get this new dollhouse to enjoy.

A melancholy settled over Maple as she looked around her living room. Her gaze landed on the television set in the corner, which hadn't been turned on since their failed attempt to watch the State of the Union. She walked over and turned it on, but then almost immediately turned it off again.

The thing was crackly. Intrusive. Annoying.

Why had she bought this contraption that she didn't even like?

She sighed and wandered through the empty rooms of her own life-sized house. Mack got up from his spot on the couch and dashed ahead of her through the hall to the kitchen. The door to Bill's old office was ajar, and Mack darted through the crack. Maple followed him, not really knowing why. She turned on the desk lamp just in time to see Mack's tail disappear under the bookshelf.

Bill had spent so much time here, seated at this desk, his bowtie askew. She missed him tremendously, but she'd stopped expecting to see him. That had been one of the worst parts of the first few months; her brain knew he was gone, but her heart kept getting its hopes up.

Now, alone in the room except for a stealthy cat, Maple remembered her husband's easy, crooked smile. She remembered how gently he talked with patients and how his whole face lit up when he treated children. It was massively unfair that he'd never get to meet his niece.

And Jamie—for all his troubles and poor choices, Jamie had a heart of gold. Maple shook her head and smiled as she imagined her brother as Sophie's father. She was certain the little girl would have had him wrapped around her pinky finger in absolutely no time.

Maple herself was the least-equipped of the three of them to build a relationship with Sophie. In general, she tried to avoid children (except Charlotte's—and, if she was being honest, she even preferred Tommy, Matthew, and Michael in small doses). Nervousness prickled at her neck; would she be able to bond with her niece? Kenny had seemed to gain her trust very quickly. He had gotten down on the floor with the little girl and shown interest in what she was interested in. Maple thought about it and decided she could probably do that, too. It might be awkward at first, but Maple could study, practice, and persevere.

After all, if she could solve murders, she could play with a toddler.

Mack still hadn't reemerged from under the bookshelf. Maple sighed and walked back to the living room, where she contemplated the television set once again. Maybe, on some level, purchasing it had been an attempt to distract herself. She chided herself for this, feeling she should've known better—Maple was not an easily distracted person.

At the moment, she couldn't distract herself from the fact that she had a big decision to make. She knew she should talk to Charlotte about the job offer in Boston, but she'd been putting that conversation off. She was similarly reluctant to discuss it with Ben, Kenny, or the sheriff. If she stayed, she'd be surrounded by friends who'd become like family—but she'd continue to piece together a living. Going to Boston offered financial stability in the career she'd trained so hard for and a chance to get to know the only actual family she had left.

Two options, both of them complicated and imperfect.

The telephone rang.

Hoping it wasn't the sheriff calling with news of another body—she was rather looking forward to her robe and slippers—Maple answered.

"Maple? Is that you?" It was Eliza Patterson's voice on the other end of the line.

"Yes, it's me! Eliza?"

"Very good! Yes, this is Eliza."

The two women exchanged brief pleasantries before Eliza got down to business.

"Now, Maple, you know about the reward money for information leading to the capture of Leo Matthews."

"Yes, I heard they're giving it to you and Cecelia. Congratulations."

"Well," Eliza said, her voice lowering dramatically, "we know how we'd like to use it, and I have a proposition for you."

Maple listened to Eliza outline her idea, and just like that, she found herself with a third option.

Chapter 34

Maple placed her overnight bag in the backseat of the Chrysler Saratoga and shut the door. There was a feeling of finality to that sound, she reflected, but also of possibility. She was heading down to Boston to visit Maggie and Sophie. She found herself looking forward to staying at the rooming house again; it would be refreshing to visit with Miranda this time and only talk about regular crafts instead of being consumed by arson, robbery, and murder.

This feeling, she supposed, was why people went on vacation.

It was also the opposite of how she had felt on January 6th when she'd been so pleased to get the sheriff's call.

And it was, indeed, a true vacation. Just the night before, Maple had called David Francis. She thanked him for the job offer but informed him she was turning it down. It had been a pleasant conversation filled with mutual respect, and Maple hoped their paths would cross again. She had a few pangs as she considered what she might be giving up. Deep down, though, she knew it was the right decision.

She got into the driver's seat and fired up the engine. Before she left the state, she had a few things to do. Her first stop was the sheriff's office. She parked beside the coroner's car and went inside, where she found a girl sitting in a chair in the reception area, her arms crossed tightly across her chest.

"Hello, Audrey. I'm Maple. I work with your dad."

The girl's expression softened a little. Maple stuck out her hand, and Audrey shook it. Close up, Maple could see a spark of intelligence and curiosity in her eyes; she felt disappointed in herself for having written Audrey off as a surly teenager the first time she'd seen her.

"Nice to meet you."

"You, too," said Audrey.

Maple continued into the sheriff's office, where Dr. Strong was waiting.

"How's Willy?" she asked.

"Good," the doctor replied. "I heard from the doctor at South yesterday, and he said he's settling in well. They're evaluating him and will be adjusting his medications over the next few weeks."

"That's great news," Maple said, and she meant it.

She studied him as he sat in the chair, one long leg crossed over the other.

"You don't have to talk about this if you don't want to," she said, "but Victoria's your wife, isn't she?"

He looked startled. "What—how-?"

"When we were dropping the blood sample off in Boston, Gus, the lab guy, asked Kenny and me if we were going to visit Victoria. We had no idea what he was talking about at the time."

He let out a deep breath. "Yes. She's my wife. Audrey's mom. She's a patient there in the long-term ward."

Maple nodded. "I hope you got to see her when you brought Willy down there."

"I did." The doctor's face softened, and Maple had a glimpse into a side of him she'd never seen. "Thanks. We moved here so Victoria could get treatment at South. They have a program I knew about, and I have some connections—including Gus—in the Boston area." His expression grew concerned again. "I'm not ashamed of her or anything like that," he said hurriedly. "It's just that the situation is tricky, and Audrey and I don't always like to—"

Maple waved a hand, indicating that he owed her no further explanation. In fact, she was too busy reconsidering her own harsh judgment of the man for bringing his daughter along on the call out to the cabin. After all, she had no idea what it must be like to be a single father in a new place

Sheriff Scott walked in holding two cups of coffee. "Maple! I would've brought you tea if I knew you were here."

"Thank you, Sheriff, but you've run out of hands—and, besides, I can't stay long. I do have a bit of good news to pass along, though: I spoke with Detective Francis last night, and he's not going to be a detective much longer: he's being promoted! And based on their work in the Perry's case, the police chief reversed his decision on the task force. It's going to stay."

The sheriff was pleased to hear this. The three of them engaged in small talk for a minute or so. Somewhat to Maple's surprise, she didn't find it all that painful. The sheriff walked her out to her car. Maple and Audrey exchanged little waves as she passed through the lobby. Maple felt, rather than saw, the sheriff raise an eyebrow, but he didn't say anything.

He was silent as they walked across the parking lot, too, and Maple wondered why he was there. At her car, she turned to ask him, and he cleared his throat.

"I wanted to thank you," the sheriff said, looking at his shoes.

"Thank me? For what?"

He looked up and met her gaze. "For reminding me why I do this. I was losing my way last year; I got bitter and complacent and jaded. I'm not proud of who I was—of how I behaved—when we first met on the Elijah Wallace case."

"Oh," Maple said, at a rare loss for words.

"Working with you on that case, and now on this one . . . it reset something inside me. You reminded me what's really important—you and Kenny both, actually." He scuffed the toe of his boot on the ground. "Anyway, I just wanted to say thanks."

"You're welcome," she said. "Thanks for helping me branch off into a new career."

He laughed. "I don't think you needed my help to do that, Maple. You're a force of nature. There was no doubt you'd find your own way."

Maple was surprised to hear him say that. After Bill died, she'd very much doubted whether she'd ever find her own way.

"Uh, thanks," was all she managed in response.

"Anyway, we'll have a chance to work together for a little while yet; I've decided to postpone my retirement." Determination blazed in his eyes. "I'm not quite finished yet."

Suddenly overcome with emotion, Maple blinked back tears. "I'm glad to hear that, sheriff. Though I hope it's awhile before we have to team up on a death investigation again. We all need a little break from that."

He clapped her on the shoulder and headed inside.

Back behind the wheel, she steered the big car down Main Street, and before she got to the diner, she saw the four people waiting for her at the side of the road. She pulled over, and Charlotte hopped into the front seat as Ben, Kenny, and Ella climbed into the back, Kenny holding Ben's cane for him while he got settled. Kenny's black eye was still prominent, but she was pleased to see him looking relatively cheerful. Maple figured Ella's presence had something to do with that; she'd seen them holding hands when she pulled up. It was also nice to see Kenny wearing blue jeans and a flannel shirt instead of his uniform; he was taking a well-deserved day off.

"Ready?" she asked.

"Ready!" her friends answered.

Charlotte took her hand and squeezed it. Maple smiled at her friend, and they set off.

The journey up the side of the mountain went smoothly, probably in part because of how much the vegetation lining the road had been trimmed back, but partly, Maple reflected, because her heart felt light as she listened to her friends chatting as she drove.

She parked next to Eliza Patterson's car, which was laden with boxes and bags; she and Cecelia were leaving for California any time now.

Eliza came out the front door and grinned broadly. "Welcome home, Maple!"

She dangled a keychain in front of her as she strode across the driveway. Maple took it, still not quite believing all that had transpired in the last few days. She introduced Eliza to her friends. Then, the front door opened again and Cecelia swept out.

"Maple! Darling!"

In a cloud of expensive perfume, the actress kissed Maple on each of her cheeks. Then, she turned to greet Maple's awestruck friends.

"I couldn't be more excited about our project," Cecelia said as she turned her attention back to Maple, taking both her hands and squeezing them. "I'm so looking forward to working with the two of you."

She included Kenny in her dazzling smile. He ducked his head and Maple saw the tips of his ears turning red.

"Me, too," said Maple, "but it still seems surreal—you and Eliza making a film inspired by us."

"And you're really going to play Maple in the film?" Charlotte asked.

"I am!" Cecelia trilled. "And I'm looking forward to such an interesting part. I'm sick of playing all these damsels in distress. I crave an interesting character—a strong, intelligent woman who stands on her own two feet."

"Well, you've found her, then. That's Maple," Ben said.

Maple felt heat rising in her cheeks.

"When they told us about the reward money, we knew immediately what we wanted to do," Eliza said. "And I'm so glad you and Kenny were willing to sell us the rights to your story. Don't worry, though—per our agreement, your names will be changed to protect your privacy. I'm going to be returning to my roots and writing the screenplay for this one myself."

The group chatted for a few more minutes, and then the Californians excused themselves to finish packing. Maple led her friends over to the fire pit, where they oohed and aahed about the view the whole time. Maple's eyes swept over the areas damaged by the fires. She reflected that within a few short months, new vegetation would begin to grow. It would take a long time, and the scars of those fires would remain, but eventually new growth would reclaim those damaged areas. She looked at Kenny and knew he'd been thinking the same thing. Their eyes met, and he nodded once, smiling sadly.

As she stood there looking down at the town, Maple felt a sense of calm settle over her.

"I could get used to this view," Charlotte sighed happily.

"Well, I expect you, Hank, and the boys to visit me often," Maple said in a mock-stern tone. "And I imagine they'll love to meet Sophie. Plenty of room for them all to run and play up here."

Charlotte, Kenny, and Ella wandered off to look at the view from the other side of the house.

"And what about a hardware store owner and the laziest dachshund in the world?" Ben asked, his tone hopeful and a little nervous. "Is there room for us to visit, too?"

She looked at him and felt a happy glow settle through her body. She took his hand in hers.

"You'd better believe it. But I'm still not sure I like watching television. I prefer watching this."

She indicated the sweeping view.

"I'm happy to watch anything with you," Ben said, squeezing her hand.

"Oh, look!" came Charlotte's awed voice from around the side of the house.

Maple looked toward her friend just in time to see a bald eagle swoop across the landscape. The majestic bird soared over

"Maple! Darling!"

In a cloud of expensive perfume, the actress kissed Maple on each of her cheeks. Then, she turned to greet Maple's awestruck friends.

"I couldn't be more excited about our project," Cecelia said as she turned her attention back to Maple, taking both her hands and squeezing them. "I'm so looking forward to working with the two of you."

She included Kenny in her dazzling smile. He ducked his head and Maple saw the tips of his ears turning red.

"Me, too," said Maple, "but it still seems surreal—you and Eliza making a film inspired by us."

"And you're really going to play Maple in the film?" Charlotte asked.

"I am!" Cecelia trilled. "And I'm looking forward to such an interesting part. I'm sick of playing all these damsels in distress. I crave an interesting character—a strong, intelligent woman who stands on her own two feet."

"Well, you've found her, then. That's Maple," Ben said.

Maple felt heat rising in her cheeks.

"When they told us about the reward money, we knew immediately what we wanted to do," Eliza said. "And I'm so glad you and Kenny were willing to sell us the rights to your story. Don't worry, though—per our agreement, your names will be changed to protect your privacy. I'm going to be returning to my roots and writing the screenplay for this one myself."

The group chatted for a few more minutes, and then the Californians excused themselves to finish packing. Maple led her friends over to the fire pit, where they oohed and aahed about the view the whole time. Maple's eyes swept over the areas damaged by the fires. She reflected that within a few short months, new vegetation would begin to grow. It would take a long time, and the scars of those fires would remain, but eventually new growth would reclaim those damaged areas. She looked at Kenny and knew he'd been thinking the same thing. Their eyes met, and he nodded once, smiling sadly.

As she stood there looking down at the town, Maple felt a sense of calm settle over her.

"I could get used to this view," Charlotte sighed happily.

"Well, I expect you, Hank, and the boys to visit me often," Maple said in a mock-stern tone. "And I imagine they'll love to meet Sophie. Plenty of room for them all to run and play up here."

Charlotte, Kenny, and Ella wandered off to look at the view from the other side of the house.

"And what about a hardware store owner and the laziest dachshund in the world?" Ben asked, his tone hopeful and a little nervous. "Is there room for us to visit, too?"

She looked at him and felt a happy glow settle through her body. She took his hand in hers.

"You'd better believe it. But I'm still not sure I like watching television. I prefer watching this."

She indicated the sweeping view.

"I'm happy to watch anything with you," Ben said, squeezing her hand.

"Oh, look!" came Charlotte's awed voice from around the side of the house.

Maple looked toward her friend just in time to see a bald eagle swoop across the landscape. The majestic bird soared over the woods and the town. Maple had the sense he was keeping watch over everything and everyone below, noting the big picture and the tiny details all at once.

She liked it.

THE END

Author's Note

Maple Bishop was inspired by Frances Glessner Lee, a woman known as the mother of forensic science. Like Maple, Lee built extremely detailed miniature recreations of death scenes; she used them to help train police investigators from around the country. Inspired by the well-known saying "Convict the guilty, clear the innocent, and find the truth in a nutshell," Lee called the models her Nutshell Studies of Unexplained Death.

Eighteen of them still exist, and two in particular helped inspire the events of this novel. The first is called "Burned Cabin." This Nutshell served as the impetus for the Perkins's home, but there's more to the story of how Maple came to investigate this particular death. Several years ago, I attended a Zoom writing workshop. One of my mentors, novelist and writing teacher Erin Celello, led us through an exercise in which she gave us prompts and a short amount of time to free write. One of them was *Walk slowly all around the outside*. Immediately, I pictured Maple circling the wreckage of the burned cabin; thanks to Corrine May Botz's excellent book *The Nutshell Studies of Unexplained Death*, I already had an image in my mind of what that particular Nutshell looked like. That writing exercise became the first scene I wrote for this novel.

The other Frances Glessner Lee Nutshell that makes an appearance in this book is "Saloon and Jail." This one depicts a man who is found unconscious outside a saloon and later dies in jail. It was actually in my mind as I drafted *Death in the Details* and Maple was wrestling with the murky circumstances around her brother's death.

I knew I wanted to take Maple back to Boston this time around and let her find some closure about her brother; this meant the book's main investigation would also need to lead to the city. In researching Boston around the time the book is set, I stumbled upon information about the infamous 1950 Brinks robbery. As I learned about the seven men who walked into the armored car company's garage one night and made off with over two million dollars in loot, I was fascinated. The character of Detective Francis is based loosely on Lt. Francis Wilson, one of the BPD officers who investigated this crime. Around the same time, I did some reading about the notorious Boston gangster James "Whitey" Bulger. Gradually, I realized how I wanted to connect Daniel Perkins's death to a fictional version of the Boston criminal underworld.

I really enjoyed diving down these historical rabbit holes and letting my imagination wonder *What if . . . ?* I hope you enjoyed reading the result!

ACKNOWLEDGEMENTS

In this story, Maple learns some truths about her family, but I have long known the truth about mine. Mom, Dad, Kelley, and Phil—thanks for your love, support, and encouragement.

A huge thank you to the entire team at Crooked Lane for bringing this book to life: editor extraordinaire Faith Black Ross, production guru Rebecca Nelson, marketing/publicity mavens Dulce Botello and Mikaela Bender, editorial whiz Thaisheemarie Fantauzzi Pérez, Director of Publishing Operations Doug White, Publisher Matt Martz, and subsidiary rights superheroes Stephanie Manova and Megan Matti.

My agent, Chelsey Emmelhainz, continues to be a source of excellent advice and good humor. I'm incredibly lucky to have her in my corner.

Dayle Bensenhaver is the kind of friend I can randomly text on a Sunday morning with questions like, *How would you handcuff a perp who only has one arm?* I'm grateful for her law enforcement insight and cheerful willingness to talk me through bizarrely specific scenarios.

Similarly, Steve Stockwell shared his firefighting knowledge and patiently answered my many questions about hypothetical burn time scenarios. Any errors in my fictional depictions of police work and firefighting/arson investigation are entirely my own.

Thanks to Delia Regan for popping into the library at just the right moment and helping me figure my way out of a sticky plot situation.

Fellow authors and "Crooked Ladies" Samantha Hastings (aka Samantha Larsen) and Jenny Adams were generous enough to read an early version of this book and give me some great advice.

Thanks to the Connecticut chapter of Sisters in Crime for the camaraderie and networking opportunities.

After the publication of my first book, *Death in the Details*, I was gobsmacked at the outpouring of enthusiasm for my little murder mystery. I'm lucky to have such a stellar community of extended family, friends, neighbors, former teachers, and colleagues. It also reinforced how awesome public libraries and local bookstores are; I felt so supported as a debut author.

And, of course, thank you to my three favorite guys: Matt, Liam, and Sean.